Celebrity lookalike escort Astrid Lepler is tired of running. When an old friend invites her to apply for a role at Rowan House, she travels to Scotland to show off her skills as a purveyor of fantasy and in-demand Mistress in hopes of securing a position.

Long time Rowan House employee Benita Azevedo would do anything for Tessa Morgan, the woman who warms her bed and fills her soul like no other, even if she has to shatter her heart to secure Tessa's happiness.

Tessa has worked hard to put her past behind her and make a place for herself at Rowan House. Respected by her peers, desired by clients, surrounded by friends with all the benefits, she has everything she has ever wanted.

It all comes crashing down when Astrid arrives at Rowan House. Faced with their undeniable attraction to each other, Tessa and Astrid rekindle their past romance. When the Widow threatens to end Astrid and Rowan House for good, it will take everything Tessa and Astrid have to save Rowan House and keep their love alive, but will it be enough?

FOLLOW SPOT

Rowan House, Book Six

Brenda Murphy

A NineStar Press Publication

Published by NineStar Press
P.O. Box 91792,
Albuquerque, New Mexico, 87199 USA.
www.ninestarpress.com

Follow Spot

First Edition
July, 2023

Print ISBN: 978-1-951057-84-8

Also available in eBook, ISBN: 978-1-951057-83-1

Warning: This book contains sexually explicit content, which may only be suitable for mature readers, graphic violence, and death. This book is part of a series but can be read as a standalone story.

To C, Always.

Chapter One

"DO YOU THINK this is too much?" Tessa tugged her MacLeod tartan bow tie into a tight knot and met Benita's gaze in the mirror.

"For what? You're picking her up from the ferry, not taking her to a ball." Benita smoothed her hands over Tessa's shoulders and pressed a quick kiss under her ear. "Besides, you look adorable. Good enough to eat." Benita waggled her eyebrows.

Tessa turned to face her. She leaned her head against Benita's brow and absorbed her confident tone and love like a sponge. "Thank you."

Benita stepped back. "Now go. Or Millie will leave your ass standing in the driveway."

"Oh hell." Tessa snatched her suit coat off the bed on her way out of the door. She stormed the steps, the clatter of her shoes echoing in the stairwell. She pushed through the kitchen door and skidded to a stop. Robin and Myfanwy turned to look at her. "Millie's gone?"

"Calm down, love, she's in the washroom." Myfanwy

crossed the room. She inclined her head toward two picnic baskets and two thermos bottles on the table. "The black thermos and small basket is for Mistress Lepler, the other is for you two. Since you missed breakfast." Myfanwy raised an eyebrow.

"Sorry." Tessa's mouth watered as the scent of warm chocolate laced with the faint tang of orange rose from the baskets. "And thank you."

Myfanwy frowned. "You all right?"

"Fine. I'm fine. Just nervous."

Myfanwy lifted her chin. "She's a Mistress—act accordingly and you'll be right."

"Aye, and she'll be an angry Mistress if we're late picking her up." Millie's voice boomed in the kitchen. She picked up the picnic baskets. "Get the flasks, Tessa." Millie kissed Myfanwy on the cheek. "I'll text if we'll be late."

"Don't be. Elaine is on a tear. She wants everything perfect for Mistress Petra's friend."

Millie strode out of the kitchen. "When is she not? You heard her, Tessa, ass in gear unless you want to explain to Elaine why we were late."

Tessa picked up the two thermos bottles and bolted out of the door after Millie.

The gravel crunched under their feet on the way to the garage. Tessa hurried to catch up to Millie's long strides.

In the garage, Tessa waited while Millie placed the smaller picnic basket on the backseat.

"Put the flask next to it and wedge it so it won't roll around." Millie shrugged out of her suit coat.

Tessa placed the black flask next to the smaller basket before opening her door. She passed Millie the other basket and flask of tea.

"Take your jacket off or you'll look the devil when we get there."

Tessa shed her suit coat before she entered the car and laid it over the seat next to Millie's. The leather seat was cool through her shirt, and she shivered. She clenched her fists to stop her hands from trembling.

"The seats will warm up quick once we're rolling." Millie turned the key, and the low rumble of the engine filled the car. "Take a breath. We're not late." Millie backed the car out of the garage and made the turn out onto the drive. "Did you sleep?"

"Some."

"You going to tell me why you're so skittish?" Millie piloted the car down the lane leading away from Rowan House.

Tessa chewed her lip. A storm of emotions squeezed her heart as a swirling montage of images blinded her to the scenery rushing past the car. She picked at the seam of her trousers. The dull ache of a headache eddied behind her eyes. This was a mistake.

"Tessa?" Millie's gentle prompt broke into Tessa's spiraling thoughts.

"I haven't been honest with the Mistresses. I worked with—I mean for Mistress Lepler. I'm an idiot for not telling them."

"I won't have you talking badly about yourself, but Tessa, why the devil didn't you say something before?"

Tessa shifted her gaze to Millie's profile. "I didn't want the Mistresses to deny my request to work with her."

Millie shot Tessa a quick glance before she returned her eyes to the road. "Were you pledged to her?"

"No." Tessa rolled the crease of her trousers between her fingers. "Nothing like that." She turned toward the window. "I worked for her for three years, before she let me go and ghosted."

Millie reached over and squeezed Tessa's knee. "Mistresses can be a capricious lot."

"I should've told the Mistresses. Elaine knew about Mistress Griffin when she asked me to apply to Rowan House, but I left previous work off my resume." Tessa rubbed the ache in her stomach. "And then I saw the photo on her application. And I should have told them everything, but I didn't." She rocked in her seat. "What if she's angry?"

"Not that Elaine needs a reason, but I can't see her being angry over this. Well, not more than usual. She's settled a bit since she and Robin convinced Petra to pledge to them."

"I meant Mistress Astrid."

"What does that matter? You're not her property. You're pledged to Rowan House. And I'll be happy to remind her of it if she forgets." Millie glanced at Tessa before turning back to the road. "She may be auditioning but she doesn't have full privileges."

Millie's firm tone soothed Tessa's nerves. She wasn't alone. Her Rowan House family would always be there. She was loved. For who she was, quirks and all. She laid her hand on Millie's forearm and squeezed gently. "Thank you. She wasn't that kind of Mistress. She was more like Mistress Lucia, quiet, but you obeyed."

"But she abandoned you without explanation? What kind of Mistress does that?" The car shifted sideways as Millie dodged a pothole.

"We didn't have a contract." Tessa shifted in the seat. "But we were—we had a—well, I don't know what you'd call it. At least I thought we had something. But not enough of something for her to keep me, I guess." Tessa hated the uncertainty in her voice. She rolled her shoulders, stiffened her spine. She wasn't a wide-eyed, giddy twenty-year old anymore. "And whatever it was, I need to talk to her outside of Rowan House. I don't want her to feel like she was tricked into something or that I'm going to sabotage her audition."

"Well, anyone who'd walk out on you is a complete idiot. Get yourself some tea and something to eat. Everything will look better on the other side of a chocolate orange muffin and Two Steps From Hell." Millie grinned and pressed a button on the steering wheel.

The rich orchestral sounds of "Tokyo Showdown Mania" boomed from the speakers as Tessa unwrapped her still warm muffin. "I swear I'd have pledged to Rowan House just for these muffins." Millie's booming laugh filled the car as Tessa settled back into her seat.

*

ASTRID LEPLER STOOD by the rail, waiting her turn to disembark. Families with small children in hand trailed by reluctant teens crowded the exit. Gulls wheeled and called overhead. She wrinkled her nose at the sharp smell of diesel fumes and the harbor. After navigating the gangplank in her pumps, she strode the length of the dock, leaving the crowd of day trippers and tourists who had been crammed on the ferry behind.

The wheels of her rolling bag clattered over the

macadam as she moved away from the busy terminal. She scanned the parking area as she walked, searching for the car that would take her to Rowan House.

"Nice coat, love. You have a light?" A burly man in dark sunglasses, dressed in dark-blue pants and a worn windbreaker, stepped in front of her. He set his feet wide, blocking her path on the narrow sidewalk. An unlit cigarette dangled from his mouth. He held out his cell phone in the other. The small hairs on the back of Astrid's neck rose. She glanced around. The crowd had dispersed, leaving the parking lot mostly empty. They were alone on the sidewalk at the back side of the building. Astrid swept her gaze over the area again. They were far away from any structure that could hide an accomplice or serve as cover if he had other intentions.

"No." Astrid held firmly to her luggage handle and slid her hand into the outside pocket of her purse. She wrapped her hand around her stainless steel pen. The knurled barrel was cool under the fingertips. Unable to see his eyes behind his dark sunglasses, she glanced down at his body searching for clues to his intent. His stance was relaxed, his feet positioned for a quick exit. Astrid removed the pen, taking care to conceal it against her coat as she took a step toward the man. "It's a filthy habit. Now, excuse me."

"What's your hurry?" The man made no move to leave. He shoved his phone into his pocket and set his feet.

"Get out of my way." Astrid glared at him, released the handle of her suitcase, and balled her fist. They stared at each other a long moment.

"Ms. Lepler? Astrid Lepler?" a deep voice called from the parking lot.

Astrid kept her attention on the man in front of her.

A slimy smile split the man's face. "Lucky bitch," he mumbled under his breath as he turned and hurried away from her. Astrid tucked her pen back in her purse and grasped the handle of her suitcase. She turned to face the direction of the voice.

"Ms. Lepler?"

A broad-shouldered ruddy-faced woman in chauffeur's livery approached her. A slightly shorter handsome woman with light-brown skin dressed in a dark-blue suit with a tartan bow tie flanked the large woman. Astrid's gaze landed on a scar that blazed from the shorter woman's hairline, narrowly missing her eye before it continued across her cheek. Stunning in its length, it added an intriguing hardness to the woman's countenance.

Astrid removed her sunglasses. "Yes?"

"I'm Millie. We exchanged emails."

"From our exchange I expected you would be here promptly."

"I apologize we were not waiting on the dock." Millie pursed her mouth and gestured to Astrid's suitcase. "Is that all you have, Ma'am?" The woman next to her fidgeted, rocking back and forth on her toes. Astrid looked away from her distracting behavior.

"Yes. I have more coming on—"

"I'll take it." The younger woman darted forward before Astrid finished speaking.

Her shoe caught a bit of loose gravel. Astrid winced as the woman's knees hit the pavement and she fell against her luggage. The large bag fell over with the woman half on top of it. She flailed a moment and landed on her side on the macadam. Astrid clutched her purse strap and stepped back.

"Tessa!" Millie clasped Tessa's arm and helped her to standing. Her bow tie was skewed. Millie held her by her shoulders and peered into her face. "You okay?" The tender concern in her voice was a sharp contrast to her burly form.

"Let go. I'm fine, Millie." Tessa twisted out of Millie's grasp and faced Astrid. Twin rips in her trousers exposed her torn skin and bleeding knees. Tessa snatched the handle of the luggage and righted the bag. A large scuff marred the suitcase. "Forgive me, Mistre— Ms. Lepler."

"You're injured." Astrid searched her handbag and found a pack of tissues. She held them out to Tessa.

"Sorry about your bag." Tessa's fingers grazed Astrid's as she took the offered tissues. Averting her gaze, she stuffed the packet into her jacket pocket.

Astrid paused, cocked her head, and studied Tessa's face. Her faint Bakersfield accent teased a memory from her mind. "Easily replaced. I'm sorry your enthusiasm ended so painfully." A sharp stroke of recognition squeezed her chest as she paired the soft twang with memories of long nights half a world away. Astrid peered into the woman's eyes, searching for signs she recognized her.

"Not the first time." Tessa's gaze flickered to Astrid's eyes briefly before she rested her chin on her chest. "I'll get this to the car." She walked away from them toward a large black town car.

Astrid frowned at the dejected set of her shoulders and near miss of using Astrid's honorific. She knew her, had known her intimately. Her face burned. Why hadn't Tessa acknowledged it? Embarrassed? And yet she was an employee of Rowan House. Astrid pursed her lips, her gaze following Tessa as she loaded her suitcase into the car.

"Ms. Lepler?" Millie's whisper cut into Astrid's thoughts. "Do you need the facilities before we leave? There're not many places to stop on our way."

"Yes. I'll only be a moment." Astrid turned toward Millie.

Millie touched her cap. "We'll be ready when you are, no need to hurry."

"Thank you. Would you take my coat?"

"My pleasure." Millie assisted her out of her heavy faux fur, draped the coat over her arm, then left Astrid alone on the sidewalk with her thoughts.

Chapter Two

TESSA'S KNEES STUNG as she stood by the car door. She glanced down at her ruined suit and swore as she calculated how much another pair of matching pants would set her back. Movement caught her eye and she turned to watch Astrid as she walked toward them.

Her blonde shoulder-length hair billowed around her face. The late-morning sun cast a golden glow over her body. She was tall, with curves in all the right places, and her gait was sure in her pumps. The staccato of her heels was a steady beat that matched the pounding of Tessa's heart.

Astrid's tailored dress moved with her, accenting her full hips and breasts. An ache pulsed in Tessa's chest. Model gorgeous, with a blazing intellect, Astrid had been, and was everything Tessa had ever dreamed of and more.

She risked eye contact. Astrid held her gaze, her face a mask of icy reserve. Tessa stumbled down the slope of adoration she had sworn she would never tread again. When Astrid arrived at the car, the faintest hint of a flush colored her creamy cheeks.

Tessa's mouth went dry as she stared into her blue eyes. The doorframe cut into her palm where she gripped the door. Astrid entered the car and settled back on the seat.

Tessa's gaze drifted over her form, her eyes lingering on Astrid's thigh where her skirt had pulled back. "There are—um, refreshments in the basket. Muffins, and your coffee." She forced her gaze back to Astrid's face.

Astrid smoothed her skirt into place. "Thank you."

The moment strung out between them as Tessa stared into Astrid's face, searching it for signs she recognized Tessa. Her fingers ached where she held tight to the door.

"Tessa, I promised Elaine we'd be back in time for Ms. Lepler to rest before tea." Millie's prompt from the front seat startled Tessa out of her trance.

"Sorry." Tessa made to close the door.

Astrid put her hand up, palm out. "No. Back here. With me."

"Nothing is permitted outside the house." Tessa took a step back from the open door.

"I will remind you, as has Tessa, that nothing is permitted outside the house proper." Millie's voice was clipped as she started the car engine.

Astrid frowned and pursed her lips. "Would that include first aid? Or must poor Tessa wait to be properly tended to? Is that a house rule too?"

Tessa's already pounding pulse spend up as Astrid's voice shifted from gracious to hard-edged Mistress.

Millie twisted in the front seat. She peered at Tessa's knees before glancing at Astrid. "I see your point, Ma'am."

"I can wait, Ma'am." Tessa met Astrid's gaze and chewed her lower lip, caught between Millie's protectiveness and Astrid's command.

"Millie, is this car equipped with a first aid kit?" Astrid lifted her eyebrow at Tessa.

"Yes, Miss."

"Give it to me, please."

Millie removed a blue and white kit from the glove box and passed it to Astrid.

"Now." Astrid waved the box at Tessa. "Get in." Her tone left no room for Tessa to refuse.

Tessa stepped into the car and settled back onto the cool leather seats. She closed the door and locked it.

"There. That wasn't so hard, was it?" Astrid lifted her chin.

"No, Ma'am." Millie pulled out of the car park.

"Since you seem worried about my character and intentions, Millie, leave the partition down."

"Sorry, Ma'am, didn't mean to offend." Millie pulled out of the parking spot.

Astrid sniffed loudly. "I don't know what kind of Mistresses you've dealt with previously, but I can assure you I play by the rules. Always."

"Aye, Ma'am." Millie piloted the car though the parking lot and out onto the road toward Rowan House. The back of her neck was red above her starched white shirt.

Tessa perched on the edge of the buttery soft seat. "You don't have to—"

"Have and want are two very different things. Sit back. Let me see your knees."

Tessa leaned back against the door and extended her legs.

Astrid reached down and lifted Tessa's legs across her lap. She sucked her teeth. "There's a bit of gravel in your skin."

She opened the kit and pulled on a pair of vinyl gloves. Tessa studied her expression as Astrid picked through the contents of the first aid box. A memory of Astrid tending to her after an encounter with a single tail that had gone further than Tessa intended squeezed her heart. The brisk scent of antiseptic filled the car as Astrid tore open a packet and poured it onto a gauze square.

"Pity about your suit. It looks lovely on you. This will sting." She gingerly applied the antiseptic to Tessa's abrasions. "You'll need a bath to soak the rest of this gravel out. You will do that as soon as you are able, understood?" Astrid lifted her chin, held Tessa's gaze a long moment.

"I will, Ma'am." Tessa reached out and risked touching the back of Astrid's hand.

Astrid paused in her work. She lifted her gaze to Tessa's face. "Is it too painful? Do you want me to stop?"

"No." Tessa dropped her voice to a whisper. Her fingertips tingled where they touched Astrid's skin. Overwhelmed by her tender care, she shoved aside her fear. "Do you remember me, Mistress Roxanne?" Tessa clamped her teeth on her lip.

"Yes," Astrid whispered. She inclined her head toward Millie. "Is it safe for you to speak freely?"

Tessa pitched her voice low. "Millie's a friend. And she knows I knew you from before, but not all of it." She knotted her fingers together in her lap.

Astrid dabbed the wet gauze over Tessa's torn flesh. "Of course I remember you. How could I not? But please, for both our sakes, keep the name you knew me as to yourself. Have you made it known to the Mistresses?"

"No. I—" Tessa squared her shoulders. "I didn't tell them."

"Why?"

Fine lines etched Astrid's forehead and her eyes narrowed. Tessa's hands ached to smooth away Astrid's worries, to draw her fingers over the tiny lines at the corners of her eyes. "I didn't want to cause—I didn't want to make trouble for you."

Astrid placed the red-stained gauze into the plastic trash container and peeled off her gloves. "I think you'll heal better if we don't cover your wounds."

Tessa nodded her agreement.

Astrid reached out and drew her fingers over the scar on Tessa's cheek. Tessa braced for the questions so many people could not help themselves from asking. Astrid held her gaze as she traced the line of thickened skin with her fingertips before her hand drifted to her lap.

Tessa looked down and away, grateful for Astrid's unspoken understanding. "Yes, Ma'am."

Tessa moved her feet from her lap and scooted to the far side of the car, and Astrid's too tempting touch. "Are you hungry, Ma'am? Myfanwy and Robin sent snacks." She opened the lid of the picnic hamper.

Astrid lifted a wrapped muffin from the basket. The crinkle of waxed paper filled the silence of the car as she unwrapped her baked treat. The scent of chocolate and orange rose, followed by Astrid's hum of pleasure. She took a large bite and chewed slowly with her eyes closed. Unable to resist, Tessa watched Astrid. A flush burned her skin. Astrid's throat worked when she swallowed.

Astrid opened her eyes and smirked. "Delicious." She

flicked her tongue over her lower lip and caught a stray crumb.

Tessa tugged at her tie in the now too-warm car. "House specialty." She pressed herself against the car door. Her fingers twitched with desire to touch her. Tessa imagined herself tracing her fingers over the delicate column of Astrid's throat, following her touch with kisses, tracing the soft swell of her cleavage with her tongue. A flood of desire wet her boy shorts, and she squirmed on the seat as she imagined Astrid's nipples hardening under her tongue.

Astrid took another bite and chewed slowly as she held eye contact with Tessa.

Tessa fell into Astrid's ice-blue gaze.

Astrid finished her muffin and wiped her mouth. "How much longer to the house?" She smoothed her hand over Tessa's thigh.

Tessa eyed the dashboard time display, then shifted her gaze back to Astrid. She dug her nails into her palms, the pain grounding her. "Another two hours at least, Ma'am."

"I can't wait to try the rest of the house's offerings"— she teased her tongue over her lower lip, before she tidied her lipstick with her pinkie—"Tessa."

Pleasure rocketed through her at the sound of her name on Astrid's lips. The teasing tone of her voice did nothing to stop the raging fire of want burning in Tessa's belly. She pressed her lips together against the torrent of words that bubbled inside. Astrid did remember. And cared enough to tend to her.

It didn't mean she still had feelings for Tessa. Not at all. Tessa was a grown woman, not the wide-eyed girl she had been. She could handle it if nothing more than sex happened between them. And that was the lie she told herself for the rest of the drive to Rowan House.

*

MILLIE STOPPED THE car exactly in the center of the circular drive in front of the house. Astrid looked up from her e-reader as the car rolled to a stop. She turned toward Tessa. Their gazes held a brief moment. Astrid inhaled sharply at the unbridled admiration reflected in Tessa's eyes. Trouble. This was trouble. She lifted her chin. "Don't forget your promise."

"I won't. And thank you." Tessa shifted her gaze to the floor of the car. "I'll tell the Mistresses about before."

"I meant your knees." Astrid tapped her shoulder to draw her attention. "Although I do think you need to tell them about..." What? What was it they had? Astrid had regretted nothing in her life more than walking away from her escort business. No. Nothing more than walking away from her burgeoning relationship with Tessa. How often had she lain awake in the months afterward wondering what might have been? "Our previous contact." Astrid squeezed Tessa's shoulder lightly.

"I will. Promise."

"Excellent." Astrid turned from Tessa and placed her e-reader into her purse.

Tessa exited the car and hurried around to open Astrid's door. She offered her hand. Astrid held loosely to Tessa's fingertips to assist her from the car.

"Tessa." Astrid leaned close to her. The soft scent of her cologne wafted to Astrid. A delicious warm spicy scent. So tempting. Astrid swallowed her desire to pull Tessa into an embrace, kiss her way along her strong jaw, and plunder her mouth.

"Yes?"

"Don't forget to take care of your knees. I can't wait to see you on them." Astrid squeezed Tessa's hand once and resigned herself to the dance of introductions before her.

She turned to face the house. Perfectly landscaped, the manor house rose up before her. Understated in appearance, it whispered of old money and secrets.

"We'll take your bag to your room, Ma'am. May I have your phone, please? And any other electronics?"

Astrid rummaged in her purse and produced her phone and an e-reader. "Make sure you get the reader back to me before bed, please." She passed the pair to Millie.

"I'll be sure to have them to you well before then. And I'm sorry about before, Ma'am. Thank you for taking care of Tessa."

"Apology accepted. I imagine it's hard for many of your guests to resist such an exquisite temptation." Astrid shifted her gaze to Tessa's perfectly displayed ass as she bent over to pull Astrid's bag from the car.

"Astrid!" Petra's shout drew Astrid's attention.

Petra rushed down the stairs and trotted toward her. "So good to see you again." Petra hugged Astrid, her embrace grounding. "Did you have a good trip? Come, meet everyone."

Astrid let Petra's enthusiasm distract her from admiring Tessa. She turned to the group of formidable Mistresses gathered on the porch. The tallest approached, her red hair falling about her shoulders like wildfire flames.

"Astrid, welcome, I'm Elaine." She placed her hand on Petra's shoulder, a not-so-subtle reminder of their relationship. Petra raised an eyebrow but said nothing as Elaine moved past her to greet Astrid.

Astrid extended her hand. "So lovely to finally meet you. Petra sings your praises."

Elaine clasped Astrid's hand, her grip firm. She squeezed once and let go. "Very pleased to meet you. I'm most anxious for your audition. When would you like to start?"

"Give the woman a moment, Elaine." A woman, nearly as tall, with black hair shot with strands of gray, strode forward. "I'm Martha, and you'll have to excuse my sister's enthusiasm." She glared at Elaine.

"What's wrong with getting to the point?" Elaine crossed her arms over her chest.

"Easy, love. We've company." Petra rested her hand in the middle of Elaine's back.

"Nothing, but whatever happened to hospitality?" Martha rested her hands on her hips. Her mouth pulled into a thin line.

"Are you suggesting I don't understand hospitality? Where were you when I was planning the menu? Making staff arrangements for this? Locked up in your study with your spreadsheets and financials. That's where. Not even giving it a second thought." Elaine's voice had risen as she spoke.

"Elaine. Martha. Enough." A low command cracked from the front steps. And with nothing more than those words and a tone that could cut glass, a shapely woman shut down the arguing sisters.

The woman walked past the stunned sisters and extended her hand. "I'm Lucia."

Astrid took her hand, entranced by her luminous green eyes and voice. Lucia was even more beguiling than Petra had spoken of.

"You'll have to forgive all of us. Come in, please. Millie and Tessa will attend to your things. Would you like coffee? Something to eat? Or would you like to rest from your trip?"

"I would love to lie down before we discuss anything." Lucia's words and calming spirit flowed over Astrid and the weariness she had pushed aside rose in her.

"Of course." Lucia placed Astrid's hand on her forearm, covered her hand with her own, and led her up the steps. Petra joined them and they left Elaine and Martha standing in the drive.

Chapter Three

BENITA SAT AT the dressing table in their room, her back to Tessa. Tessa shrugged out of her suit coat and then toed off her shoes. She untied her bow tie and tossed it on top of her coat.

"*Como foi? Boa*?" Benita called over her shoulder.

"No. Well, sort of."

Benita turned to Tessa. Her eyes went wide. "*Nossa*! What happened?" She crossed the room and wrapped her arms around her, pulling her into a hug.

"Just me being me. I fell trying to get her luggage to the car." Tessa leaned her head on Benita's shoulder.

Benita hugged her tighter and rubbed her back. "Bebê, what do you need?"

"I promised her I'd take a bath."

Benita held Tessa at arm's length. "She remembered you?"

"She did." Tessa shrugged off Benita's grasp and rubbed the back of her neck.

"What do you mean you promised her you'd take a

bath?"

"She took care of my knees, cleaned them as best she could in the car, but she made me promise to soak the gravel out as soon as I could."

Benita tilted her head to the side. "Did she have to tackle Millie to do it?"

"Millie was stressed as hell about getting back to here in time for tea for some reason and other than picking me up when I fell, she was prickly the entire drive home."

"She's been on edge since Sugar got pregnant. You would think she was going to have kittens instead of the cat." Benita unbuttoned the top button of Tessa's shirt and then worked her way down the placket.

Tessa laughed. "Well, Astrid was pretty hardass about taking care of me. It was sweet and confusing. She left it for me to tell the Mistresses about my time working for her."

"And the rest of it?" Benita skewered her with a hard look.

"Yes."

"Good. Now get your ass in the bath." She eased Tessa's shirt off her shoulders.

"You're bossy for a sub." Tessa unbuckled her pants and gingerly lowered them, taking care to avoid her abraded knees.

"And you're easy for a switch." Benita crossed her arms. "Come on, I'll keep you company. I don't have to be anywhere until tonight. You can tell me all about it."

"What's tonight?" Tessa slid her binder over her head and lowered her shorts to the floor. She stepped out of them. She shivered. Gooseflesh prickled her skin as she collected her dirty clothes and deposited them into the hamper. She reached behind her neck and tugged her leather collar around so her numbered tag centered itself in the hollow of her neck.

"We're presenting ourselves to Mistress Astrid."

Tessa groaned. "I thought that was tomorrow night. Fuck me."

"Later. Come on. Let's see what magic we can work with your knees."

*

PETRA RESTED HER hands on the back of the wingback chair by the fireplace. She pointed to an antique telephone. "That's the house line. If you desire anything, the staff will bring you whatever you need."

"Thank you. All I need right now is sleep." Astrid sat on the edge of the bed and slipped off her pumps. She rubbed the ball of her foot.

"I'll leave you then." Petra turned and crossed to the door.

"Petra?"

"Yes?" Petra paused at the door.

"Do you have a submissive selected for me for my audition?"

"We allow the person auditioning to choose their partner. You can select any submissive you choose or pair for each part of the audition. You'll meet the rest of the house submissives tonight." Petra tilted her head and met Astrid's gaze. "We have a volunteer in your case. You're not bound to use her. We'll give her our permission only if you choose her as your audition partner."

"A volunteer?" Astrid lifted her chin. "Is that

common?"

"No. And you're free to change your mind of course. But in my experience, a volunteer often brings a level of commitment to their role not found in random selections." Petra's mouth lifted at the corner.

"Robin volunteered when you applied, didn't she?" Astrid leaned back on her hands.

"Yes. Much to Elaine's consternation. And my delight."

"Who has decided to volunteer for my benefit?"

"Tessa. She's a natural switch so that should make things easier. She doesn't like heavy pain, but unless you've changed your practice, I don't think it will be an issue."

Astrid studied the bedspread, traced her finger over the seam. "Petra, you need to check in with Tessa, make sure she's still willing."

Petra's dark brows drew down. "Did something happen on your trip to the house? I will address it if she was inappropriate in any way."

"No." Petra's shocked expression let Astrid know she had failed to keep the worry out of her tone. "Tessa was perfectly behaved on our trip here."

Petra lifted her eyebrow. "Astrid, I spent many years speaking with people who wanted to tell me things but needed to be prompted. I'm asking you now, as your friend, is there something you need to tell me before we start this process? I would be thrilled for you to work with us, but I have recused myself from the decision because of our friendship."

"You need to speak with Tessa. I won't betray her confidence. I am comfortable with her as my partner for the audition, but you need to confirm with her she still feels the same now that I'm here."

"I will. And if you need to discuss anything, or have any questions about the process, I'm available."

"Thank you." Astrid stood. "I'm sure it will not feel so fraught on the other side of a nap."

"I'll leave word you're not to be disturbed." Petra crossed the room. She wrapped her arms around Astrid and gave her a quick hug. "I'm so glad you're here. I've missed you."

Astrid relaxed and leaned into Petra's gentle affection. "I don't even have words for how grateful I am for this opportunity. It's not the same without a house to back you. Worrying about security and working out of hotel rooms, no matter how posh, gets old."

Petra released her. "It did for me too. Get some rest. I'll see you at tea." She crossed the room, turned, and waved once before she closed the door.

Astrid strode to the door, turned the deadbolt knob, then flipped the bar lock in place. The solid click of the lock soothed her. Alone. At last.

She poured herself a glass of water and sipped it as she toured her suite. The hand-loomed wool carpet centered in the room was thick and luxurious on her bare feet. The hardwood floors gleamed, as did the furniture. The faint smell of lemon polish hung in the air. A queen-sized tester bed was placed near the floor-to-ceiling window. Heavy, burgundy-colored drapes hung in the window. In the sitting area, two matching wingback chairs and side tables were next to a gas fireplace. On the far side of the room was a dressing area with an armoire, beside a vanity with a chair.

Astrid opened the double doors of the armoire. Her clothes hung neatly on hangers. All her personal kink items, her crops and paddles, were arranged on a set of hooks on the door. Normally she liked unpacking her own things, had grown accustomed to it since disbanding her escort service. She had not had her own submissive in years, but Rowan House had a reputation for full service, and she appreciated their attention to detail.

In the bathroom, she located her toiletries bag. Through gritty eyes she stared at the deliciously decadent claw foot tub. She ran her hand along the cool porcelain and stifled a yawn. Later. When she could be sure she wouldn't fall asleep in the soothing water.

After a quick shower, she brushed her teeth before she left the bathroom. She loosed the thick twisted rope curtain ties that held the curtains in place and pulled them closed before she slid between the crisp sheets naked. The mattress was the perfect blend of hard and soft. In the dim light she stared at the canopy over the bed. Gold and red stars in swirling patterns stood out against a dark-blue background. Astrid clasped her hands over her chest, closed her eyes. The events of her arrival played out in her thoughts.

Tessa's exuberance, Elaine and Martha's quarrel, and the way both of them clearly submitted to Lucia's command played in a constant loop in her mind. Petra and Lucia had made it all seem so normal to leave the bickering sisters behind as they escorted Astrid to her room. Lucia's coolness had been a sharp contrast to Petra's warmth.

Her mind flitted back to Tessa. Memories of their time together swirled in a fast-paced mental montage.

Tessa had excelled as an escort, easily assimilating to the role. She had absorbed every lesson Astrid had taught her. She learned how to assume the celebrities' identities her clients had sought in record time. Tessa's natural talent as a performer had made her stand out.

Astrid had cherished taking her in hand. Not quite a virgin but Tessa's limited experiences and hunger to embrace her kinky side had been exquisite. A memorable lover, shy at first, Tessa had taken to the business quickly.

Tessa had learned not only the give and take of dominance and submission, along with other kinks, she was also a more than capable actress. She had been able to project the image and personality of the celebrity she was impersonating to perfection. Adept at memorizing her scene lines, her ability to ad lib when necessary was what had set her apart from other escorts.

A natural switch, Tessa was willing to take control or surrender it, instinctively knowing what a client needed or wanted. She had been Astrid's most requested escort.

Cherished memories of performances they had given for those clients who preferred to watch surfaced, and Astrid pressed the heels of her hands to her eyes, stemming the tears hovering behind her eyelids. Their interactions had been genuine, as much a treat for Astrid as for her clients. A bitter taste rose in her mouth as she relived the moments when she had put in motion the end of her business, ceased to exist as Roxanne Faust, and assumed her identity as Astrid Lepler.

She had done everything she could to protect her workers and herself from the Widow's efforts to seize control of her business. And regretted running from the Widow every day since. Fifteen years later and here she was, about to audition for a place in a house instead of having her own empire, a worker herself instead of Mistress of her own service.

Worry shoved her rage aside. Astrid turned to her side, plumped her pillow with her fist. She curled her knees to her chest, peered over her shoulder to check to see if she had set the bar lock. Satisfied it was securely fastened, she closed her eyes and let sleep take her.

Chapter Four

"HOW WAS SHE? I mean besides taking care of your knees? Did she seem happy to see you? Pissed off you were here?" Benita perched on the edge of a small stool next to the bath.

Tessa leaned back in the warm water. "I don't know. She was kind in a Mistress way. If she was surprised, she sure hid it."

"Maybe Mistress Petra talked to her? Turn around, I'll get your back."

Tessa turned and leaned forward, clasping her knees. Benita scrubbed the soapy cloth over her skin. "I've never told Mistress Petra anything about my past. No one but you knows all of it. That feels so good, thank you."

"Enjoy it, because in a few minutes I'm going to get the gravel out of your knees." Benita finished washing Tessa's back. "Done." She passed the washcloth to Tessa.

"Ugh. I can't believe I wiped out like that. So much for a smooth entrance." Tessa rubbed the soapy cloth over her breasts.

"Anyone can trip. And she was kind to you. She could have been a real bitch about all it."

"She was always kind to all of us." Tessa turned her head to meet Benita's gaze. "Maybe I made it all up in my head that she cared for me more than the others."

Benita cupped Tessa's chin. "No matter if she did or didn't. That is past. This is now. What happens going forward is what's important, right?" She smoothed her thumb over Tessa's lower lip, then kissed her. Benita held her gaze a moment before she released her.

Tessa lifted her chin. "Right." She passed the cloth back to Benita and propped her feet on the edge of the tub. "Do your worst."

"It won't be so bad. My brothers were always skinning their knees in the street. I'm an expert."

Tessa gripped the side of the tub, braced for the burning pain she was sure would accompany Benita clearing her knees of the last bits of gravel and grit.

"Benita? Tessa?" Petra called from outside the bathroom door.

"In here, Mistress." They answered in unison.

Petra opened the bathroom door. "Am I interrupting?"

"Only Benita about to torture me. Not in a good way." Tessa inclined her head toward Benita.

"Tessa fell picking up Mistress Astrid. The gravel needs to come out, or it won't heal properly."

"Thank you, Benita." Petra held her hand out for the cloth. "I'll take it from here. I need to talk to Tessa. Leave us."

"Yes, Mistress." Benita rose from the stool and passed Petra the cloth. "See you in a bit, Tessa."

Tessa eyed Petra's face. Her calm demeanor and jet-black eyes gave nothing away.

"I think mechanical debridement is barbaric." Petra turned from Tessa and opened the medicine cabinet. She plucked a bottle of hydrogen peroxide from the shelf. She stalked over to the tub and sat on the low stool next to it. "Astrid asked me to speak to you. Do you still wish to be her partner for her audition?"

"Yes."

Petra gripped the back of Tessa's leg. "Ready?"

"As I'll ever be, Mistress." Pain, bright and sharp, bloomed as Petra poured the peroxide over Tessa's knee to dislodge the last bits of grit in her skin. The burning ebbed as the bubbling stopped.

"That should do it. Most of it was fine grit anyway."

"Mistress Astrid cleaned out the larger gravel in the car." Heat rose in Tessa's face. "I've not been honest, Mistress."

"About?"

"I know Mistress Astrid from before." Tessa's ears and cheeks burned. She shifted in the tub and the water sloshed dangerously close to the edge.

Petra's expression remained neutral. "And you didn't see a need to mention this when you volunteered? Why?"

"I didn't know if it would be proper or if Mistress Astrid would want me to."

"I admire your desire to not violate Mistress Astrid's confidence, but I will remind you, you are pledged to this house. Honesty is part of your agreement."

Guilt wormed its way under Tessa's skin. "I worked for her, she—she was my first Mistress."

Petra smoothed her hand over Tessa's shoulder.

"Were you pledged to her?" The tenderness in her voice broke Tessa.

"No," Tessa choked out.

"But you wanted to be?"

"Desperately." She turned away from the understanding in Petra's eyes.

"Did she know?"

Tessa lifted her shoulders and left them fall, unable to answer Petra's question.

"Nothing is more painful than rejection. Are you sure your volunteering is good for you? There is no guarantee she will receive an offer, nor that she will accept if we make one."

"I know, Mistress." Tessa chewed her lip.

Petra rose from the low stool. "I'll need to discuss this with the other Mistresses."

Tessa swallowed on a dry throat. "I'm sorry, Mistress."

"Don't be. You did what you thought was in Mistress Astrid's best interest. As your Mistresses, we are pledged to keep you safe. Even from yourself." Petra held out a towel. "Out now. Let me put some ointment on your knees."

Tessa stepped from the tub into Mistress Petra's care.

*

TESSA SHIFTED HER weight back and forth on the balls of her feet, the motion soothing as she waited for her Mistresses' verdict. The ballroom was warm, and a trickle of sweat ran the length of her spine. She knotted her fingers together behind her back. From under her lashes, she watched as they filed past her.

Under their collective consideration, a calm energy spread over Tessa. She was safe. They would make a decision based on their collective judgement with her best interest at heart.

"Tessa, eyes to us." Mistress Lucia's dulcet tone lifted Tessa's heart. She swept her gaze over the other Mistresses' faces before she brought her gaze to Mistress Lucia's.

"Mistress Petra has shared with us your history with Mistress Astrid. While we are unhappy you were not more forthcoming about your past, we understand your motives."

Tessa rested her chin on her chest. Nothing was worse than disappointing her Rowan House family. She lowered herself to her knees, ignoring the pain of her abraded skin. She bent until her forehead touched the floor. "Forgive me, Mistresses, please." Tessa bit the inside of her cheek to keep the tears that threatened at bay.

The toes of Lucia's red pumps entered her field of vision. "Stand."

Tessa lifted her head from the floor and stood. She widened her stance, clasped her elbows behind her back. She kept her gaze fixed on the floor. She stared at the toes of Lucia's scarlet pumps, so shiny she could see her red-hued reflection. A shiver chased up her spine as she waited for Lucia's judgment.

Lucia clasped Tessa's chin and forced her head up. Eyes stormy, she pinned Tessa with her gaze. She slid her hand to Tessa's shoulder. Tessa winced at the strength of her grip. Lucia delivered a single sharp slap to her cheek.

Tessa's skin burned, her nipples tightened, her body

responding to her punishment.

"Forgiven. You will be allowed to serve her for her audition if she chooses you. Do not test our generosity in the future."

Joy surged in Tessa's chest, and she swallowed the ache in her throat.

"Never forget who you're pledged to again." Lucia bent and brushed a kiss over her lips.

Tessa absorbed Lucia's attention, the love she saw reflected in her eyes, savored Lucia's correction and the connection. "Thank you, Miss. Please, Miss, may I be allowed to show my gratitude to the other Mistresses?"

Lucia pursed her lips as she glanced at the clock in the ballroom. "Make it quick. We haven't much time before Mistress Astrid and the others arrive."

Tessa lowered herself to her knees. Holding tight to her pain, she pressed her forehead to the toes of Lucia's shoes before she crawled to the dais and did the same for Martha and Elaine. Her knees ached. Her abraded skin burned, and she clung to it as her penance, part of her gift to her Mistresses. When she arrived at Petra, she kissed the toes of her pumps and risked lifting her gaze. Petra lifted a brow, leaned down, and clasped Tessa's nipple in an iron grip. Tessa gasped as a surge of desire flooded her body.

Petra's gaze burned as she stared into her eyes. "Do not make us regret this decision."

Tessa trembled in her grasp. "No, Ma'am. I'll make you proud, Ma'am."

The clock chimed the hour and the doors to the ballroom opened.

"See that you do." Petra released her. She pointed to

a spot on the floor next to her chair and an empty seat. "Sit tailor style, take the pressure off your knees." Tessa crawled over and sat between the two chairs.

Astrid strode in, dressed in 1940s styled belted black pants and billowy white top. She carried a coiled rope in her hand. She lifted it in salute to the other Mistress as she took her place in the chair next to Petra's.

Tessa lowered her gaze. A thrill raced through her when Astrid's pants leg brushed against her bare skin as she sat down. Petra's hand on her shoulder steadied her and she leaned into it, resting her shoulder against the frame of Petra's chair. She would not embarrass the house by initiating contact. Only Astrid could do that. *Please let Astrid do that.*

The rest of the staff filed in and lined up along the walls of the ballroom. Robin and Myfanwy entered. Robin sat on the floor between Elaine and Petra's chairs. Myfanwy received a kiss from each of her Mistresses before she sat on the floor between them that made Tessa ache with jealousy. From under her lashes, she watched Elaine toy with Robin's hair, before she leaned down and cupped her chin and kissed her. Petra rested her hand on Robin's shoulder and kissed her cheek before she leaned her forehead against her. Her mouth moved as she whispered to Robin, eliciting a blush from the fair-skinned woman. Tessa ached with jealousy. What would it be like to be so cherished? By not only one but two people?

Gas lamps bathed the room in a golden glow. Benita, Sharon, June, Danica, Evelyn, and Meredith were naked save for their collars. Their tags twinkled in the light. Benita's hair was styled in flowing waves that begged to be touched, her make-up on point. Tessa's clit stiffened as she took in Benita's appearance. They had not had time to take the edge off their desire before the salon. Want surged through Tessa as she stared at Benita.

Spun up from the punishment she had received from Mistress Lucia, her nipples drew tight with need. Even if Astrid didn't want company tonight, they had no other guests at present. Benita would be there after the salon. She would understand Tessa's needs and let her embrace the dominant side of herself.

Martha stood. "Nicely done. I appreciate how prompt you all are. Tonight, we welcome Mistress Astrid. She is to be given the same respect you accord any of us while she is auditioning for a position here. You all remember, I'm sure, how fraught auditioning can be. I remind each of you to behave. If you act in any way unbecoming to Rowan House, there will be consequences—and not the kind you will enjoy. I'll let Mistress Astrid explain her work. Pay attention, you may or may not be called upon to assist her. Make me proud."

Tessa pressed her lips together. What would happen if Astrid chose someone else? Her stomach twisted. A cold sweat broke out along her hairline.

Astrid stood as Martha sat down next to Lucia. She inclined her head in acknowledgement of Martha's introduction. "Good evening. Tonight, I come to you as Mistress Astrid"—she paused a beat—"but tomorrow, I may present as an actress or celebrity or literary character in my repertoire. As a Mistress, my services are to provide my clients with one of two things, either a private interaction with me acting in character as we test their sexual limits, allowing them to live out their fantasies, or I act out a scene of their choice with a partner. Think of it as live action fan fiction as it were. Any questions?"

Benita raised her hand. "I'm Benita, Mistress, and how do you handle requests for celebrities outside of your race?"

"I don't do black face or brown face or make myself appear as another race. As a white woman, I have limited my celebrity choices to women I resemble physically."

Benita lifted her chin. "Thank you."

"You're welcome, Benita. What are your specialties?"

"I like it all, Mistress. My limits are no race play, no scat or water scenes."

"Lovely." Astrid tapped her finger to her lips.

Astrid's obvious interest in Benita rocked Tessa to her core. A vision of Astrid taking Benita welled up, and her desire pooled beneath her.

Astrid resumed her seat when no one else asked questions. Tessa zoned out as the rest of the women introduced themselves. Each one stated their preferences and hard limits with flirtatious flair. A treat for the eyes, the woman of Rowan House embraced their roles. Pride swelled in Tessa's chest. She was part of this, part of a family of women unafraid to be who they were, who embraced their true nature.

Astrid shifted in her seat, drawing Tessa's attention away from the front of the room. She was so close Tessa could feel the warmth of her body. Her delicate perfume teased Tessa's senses. A spicy cinnamon scent, it had haunted Tessa's dreams for years. She closed her eyes and inhaled deeply.

The women finished their introductions and left the ballroom quietly. Tessa squirmed, earning herself a sharp look from Petra. She stilled. Why she had not been called on to introduce herself?

A hand on her shoulder startled her and she glanced up. Astrid held her gaze. "Your turn." She wrapped her hand in Tessa's hair and pulled her to her feet. "I promised the Mistresses and their pledged submissives a private showing."

Tessa's pulse sped up as Astrid shifted her grip to her upper arm and urged her down the two steps of the dais.

"Remain standing and present yourself." Her voice had taken on a low timbre.

Tessa straightened her shoulders. She clasped her elbows behind her back and widened her stance. Her skin was cool where her desire slicked her thighs. She kept her gaze focused on the ballroom floor.

"Look at me." Astrid placed the coil of rope under Tessa's chin.

Tessa met her piercing gaze.

"You have been given permission to participate in my audition. Do you consent to it? I will not ask again."

"I do, Mistress."

"Limits?" Astrid teased the bright white coils over Tessa's breasts.

"No heavy impact play, no edge play, no scat or water scenes, no race play."

Astrid drew the soft rope over Tessa's clit. "Safe word?"

Tessa gasped at the contact. "Sunset to stop. Yellow to slow down."

Astrid added gentle pressure as she moved the rope back and forth over Tessa's clit. The barely-there sensation drew a moan from Tessa.

Astrid's knife-edged smile was her reward, before she

drew the rope away from Tessa. It was dark in places. "So wet. For me?"

"Yes, Mistress."

Astrid set the rope aside. She cupped Tessa's face in both hands. She rubbed her thumb over her lower lip. "Liar." She slid her hands lower and locked both of Tessa's nipples in an iron grip. "Not just me, is it? You were looking at Benita as if she were an all-night buffet and you were desperate to eat. You wanted her, still want her, don't you?"

Tessa gasped. "Not just her, Mistress."

She tightened her grip, and Tessa yelped.

"I did not ask for anything more than a yes or no answer. So I'll ask again. You want her, don't you?"

"Yes, Mistress."

Astrid released her. Tessa bit her cheek to keep from coming with the sudden rush of blood back into the tips of her nipples.

Astrid turned to the dais. "Would it be possible to bring Benita back to join us?"

Tessa blinked. Martha opened her mouth to speak.

"Not a problem. Robin, my love, fetch Benita." Elaine spoke over Martha and shot her sister a devilish look, daring her to disagree.

Tessa lowered her chin to her chest, mind spinning out as she waited, her body aching for release.

*

ASTRID SHIFTED HER attention back to Tessa. Her chin rested on her chest, her shoulders rigid. Her nipples jutted from her small breasts. The scent of her desire perfumed the air. And yet, Astrid could sense her hesitation.

"Look at me." Astrid stepped in front of Tessa, blocking her from the Mistresses' view. "Do you want this, Tessa?" Astrid held her gaze and moved closer and whispered into Tessa's ear. "If not, we can stop now. I'll choose another. There is no shame in changing your mind." Astrid stepped back and fondled the end of the rope as she met Tessa's gaze and waited for her answer.

"I want this, Mistress." Tessa's voice was strong, her eyes clear.

"Then put your hands behind your back." Astrid stalked around her until she stood behind her.

Tessa clasped her hands above the small of her back. Astrid tied the end of the rope around them. She passed the rope up and over her shoulders, between her thighs and back over her shoulders. Then she walked around Tessa slowly, paying out the rope, laying it in coils that covered her neatly, taking care to expose her breasts. She finished behind her and tied off the rope in a loop, giving herself a handle to control Tessa. She stepped close and pressed her nose under Tessa's ear. The scent of warm skin, mixed with Tessa's desire, filled Astrid's senses. "Bend over."

Tessa obeyed, her thighs taut as she folded neatly in half, displaying the defined muscles of her ass and legs. Astrid placed a hand on her hip to steady her. Saliva pooled in Astrid's mouth as she trailed a finger down Tessa's wet swollen center. She licked her lips as she studied her body. Astrid smoothed her hands over Tessa's ass and thighs. "My, you do spend some time in the gym, don't you?"

"Yes, Mistress." Pride edged into Tessa's voice.

Astrid's nipples peaked with desire as she smoothed her hands over Tessa's thickly muscled body, delighting in the contrast of sensation of firm muscle under soft skin. She rubbed her body over her back, draped her body over her, reached round to plump and tease Tessa's nipples. Tessa had been waif thin in college, not the hard-bodied woman who surrendered to her now.

"Pick a number between one and twenty."

"Fifteen, Mistress."

Astrid straightened. She gripped the rope and swatted Tessa's ass twice. She soothed her skin with light strokes of her palm before she reached between her legs. Wet heat enveloped her fingers as she pushed deep. Tessa groaned and struggled to widen her stance. Astrid gripped her hip to steady her.

"Watch the clock. If you come before fifteen minutes is up, you won't get to play at all. With Benita or me." Astrid feathered her fingers over Tessa's clit. Tessa whimpered. Astrid savored the sweet sound before she thrust her fingers deep. Warm heat enveloped her. Tessa shifted on her feet, opening her stance wider. With determined strokes she fucked her while she held tight to the rope binding her.

Tessa trembled, her body shaking. "Mercy, Mistress."

"Shh. Show me how well-behaved you are." Astrid kept her pace. The door opened. Benita followed Robin into the room. Her heavy breasts swayed as she strode in.

Astrid inclined her head toward Benita, not stopping her torment of Tessa. "Benita, join us."

Benita's gaze shifted between Tessa and Astrid as she walked toward her. "What would you have me do,

Mistress?"

"Tessa was, shall we say, stirred during our introduction." She stroked hard over the spot that made Tessa buck her hips and moan. "Come here. Stand in front of her, legs spread."

"Tessa, suck her clit. She doesn't come until I say, understood?"

Tessa's moan reverberated off the high ceiling before she answered. "Yes, Mistress."

Benita crossed the floor quickly and took her position. Tessa lifted her head.

Tessa trembled under Astrid's hands as she continued fucking her.

Benita buried her hands in Tessa's hair. "Open up, Bebê." She pushed herself into Tessa's mouth.

"Five minutes left, Tessa."

Tessa groaned, her body vibrating with the sound. Benita rolled her hips, grinding herself against Tessa's face, a fierce grin on her face.

The muscles in Tessa's arms stood out in relief against the coils of the rope. Astrid feathered her fingers as she fucked her. The salacious sounds of their scene surrounded them. Astrid leaned down and whispered in Tessa's ear. "You are so beautiful like this." She traced her tongue over the shell of Tessa's ear. "If you're a good girl, I'll let you taste me too. Make Benita come for me. Now."

Tessa applied herself, the wet sounds of her attention to Benita's clit loud in the ballroom.

Astrid straightened. "You may come as you wish, Benita."

Benita panted. "Thank you, Mistress."

A low groan drew Astrid's attention to the dais. Robin

was on her knees, face buried in Elaine's lap, while Petra's head was bent to her nipples. One hand on Robin's head, her other wrapped in Petra's hair, Elaine stared at Astrid with a wolfish smile.

Astrid shifted her gaze from Elaine's taunting expression, unprepared for the vision of Lucia kneeling, wrist deep in both Martha and Myfanwy as they lay side by side before her. A rush of heat rocketed through her body. Her clit throbbed. Astrid returned her focus to Benita's face. Eyes closed now, she panted, mumbling to herself in Portuguese. Astrid glanced at the clock, shifted her hips until she could rub against Tessa's ass.

Three minutes. Only three minutes, then Astrid could hear Tessa's sweet cries as she came undone. The pull and drag on her clit was exquisite as she rocked against Tessa. Her back muscles bulged and flexed as Tessa stiffened her legs to support Astrid and Benita. A high-pitched scream split the air as Benita came, bucking against Tessa's face.

Driven by Benita's cries, Astrid fucked herself into orgasm on Tessa's ass. Pleasure spun out, spiraling from her belly as she came.

The clock struck the hour. "Come for me, Tessa. Now," Astrid ground out as she drove herself on to another orgasm.

Tessa shouted her release, her body squeezing tightly around Astrid's fingers. She bucked against Astrid, as Astrid rode her firm ass. She curled her fingers over her sweet spot, drawing another cry and a gush of satisfaction as Tessa filled her hand. Jolts of pleasure laced through her as she shuddered through aftershocks surrounded by the cries and shouts of the women of Rowan House.

Chapter Five

TESSA HELD TIGHT to her control as Astrid came, her sharp cry and shudder testing Tessa's limits. She panted, held back, waiting for Astrid's permission, desperate for her release. Close. She was so close. Benita's body blocked her view of the clock. Her world became Benita's clit in her mouth and Astrid's touch. She relaxed into serving. A willing vessel for their pleasure. Her soul thrilled, her body thrummed with the sensation of being the center of their attention. Benita's fingers tightened in her hair, the tug and pull on her scalp delicious. Tessa worked to extend Benita's pleasure as she denied her own, desperate to please Astrid.

Exquisite tendrils of sensation gripped her body as Astrid edged her expertly. The combination of Benita's familiar sweet taste in her mouth and Astrid's hands on her body was heaven, or at least what would pass for it in this life. Benita shifted her grip, cupped the back of Tessa's neck. She swore softly in Portuguese, mumbling as she came again. Her salt honey taste flooded Tessa's mouth.

Tessa licked and sucked her thick clit, pushed her tongue deep, feathered her tongue over her, driven by Benita's cries and Astrid's moans.

The last echo of the clock chime sounded. "Come for me, Tessa. Now." Astrid gasped as she rocked against Tessa's ass.

Given permission, Tessa screamed her release. Pleasure gripped her, held her down and shook her. She trembled as Astrid wrung another orgasm from her. Shaking, she cried out as a gush of liquid satisfaction coated her thighs.

Tessa closed her eyes, floating on the waves of sensation roiling through her. Astrid withdrew her hand slowly, setting off a series of aftershocks of pleasure as she eased herself from Tessa's body. Tessa buried her face against Benita's soft belly, bereft at the loss of Astrid's touch.

Benita smoothed her hands over her shoulders, her touch reassuring, grounding.

"Steady her, Benita. Tessa, stand up slowly." Astrid's gentle tones soothed as she assisted Tessa to standing. Tessa kept her eyes closed, unwilling to expose herself, fearful of what she would, or wouldn't see in Astrid's eyes. Her throat ached. Astrid unwound her bindings. She bit back her cry as the last of her bonds slipped from her body.

"Look at me, Tessa." Astrid spoke softly, close to Tessa's ear, as she rubbed her hands over her shoulders.

Tessa opened her eyes and met Astrid's gaze. Her eyes were glittering ice-blue pools above her flushed cheeks. She gathered Tessa in her arms, cupped the back of her head, and kissed her. Tessa relaxed into her embrace, her hands opening and closing at her sides, her palms burning to touch Astrid.

Astrid's searing kiss branded her soul. Tessa would never belong to anyone the way she belonged to Astrid. Fifteen years or one hundred, Tessa was hers. Tessa shivered in Astrid's grip. Benita pressed against her back, warming her. Benita kissed her shoulder and rested her cheek against her back.

Astrid broke their kiss. "Follow me." She led them both to the fainting couch arranged off to the side of the ballroom. Tessa frowned at the empty dais.

Astrid followed her line of sight. "They left to follow their own desires." She pushed Tessa onto the couch, sat next to her before she clasped Benita's hand and tugged so she was beside her. Astrid nuzzled Tessa's neck, then she turned and kissed Benita.

Tessa's heart squeezed hard as she watched Astrid take her time kissing Benita. They had worked with many clients together, but this was more than that, more than an audition. She watched to see if Benita was as captivated by Astrid's kisses as she had been. Benita reached for Tessa's hand as she kissed Astrid. Tessa caught her hand and held tight. She squeezed once, a quick check-in. Benita squeezed back, reassuring Tessa she was happy with what was happening between them. Tessa rubbed her thumb over Benita's knuckles, then let go of her hand.

Astrid slid her hand over Benita's belly. "Spread your legs for me."

Astrid's command, wrapped in the honeyed tones of her voice, set off a new wave of want. Wetness surged between Tessa's thighs and her clit ached as she watched Benita open her legs.

Astrid pushed inside slowly, rubbed her thumb over

Benita's clit. Benita's eyes were dark pools of want, her pupils wide. Astrid then pulled her fingers free. She licked her fingers, her tongue darting over her hand, savoring the taste of Benita. "So sweet." She swept her fingers over Benita's clit and thrust them in again. Benita's lips parted as Astrid slid her fingers from her and offered them to Tessa.

Tessa leaned forward. She greedily sucked every taste of Benita from Astrid's hand. Astrid pulled her fingers from Tessa's mouth and patted her cheek.

"I promised you a treat if you did well, didn't I?"

"You did, Mistress." Tessa gripped the edge of the couch.

She stood and stripped off her clothes, tossing them into a heap with a Domme's indifference. Tessa swallowed her whole with her gaze as Astrid stood before them naked.

Astrid swept her fingers over her clit, drew them away. They glistened in the lamplight.

"Would you like a taste?"

Saliva pooled in Tessa's mouth. "More than anything, Mistress."

Astrid sat on the couch and spread her thighs. She crooked her finger. Tessa leaned forward. Astrid placed a hand on top of her head and pushed her into the lush wet heat between her legs. "Lick me."

Tessa's nipples tightened and her body hummed with pleasure as she sucked and licked Astrid's labia. She worked hard to collect every bit of sweetness on her tongue.

"Benita, you look hungry. Why don't you put your gorgeous mouth to use?"

"Thank you, Mistress." The couch swayed and dipped.

Benita planted her hands on Tessa's hips. She leaned down and pressed a kiss to the dimple at the top of her ass. "Move in front of her on your knees and raise your hips for me, Bebê."

Tessa kept her mouth on Astrid as she moved to the floor and knelt between her legs. Benita patted her thigh. Tessa widened her legs as Benita worked her way under her. Benita's hands clasped her hips, urging her lower. Tessa groaned as Benita's warm mouth closed over her. She teased her tongue over her clit. Tessa gasped with the sensation. Benita hummed as she sucked and licked. The vibrations had Tessa clinging to her control. She would not come before her Mistress. She worked her tongue in tight circles over Astrid's clit. Her thighs tensed under Tessa's palms.

Astrid bucked her hips into Tessa's mouth. "There. Right there." Iron fingers on her neck held her in place as Astrid's satisfaction burst over her tongue and ran down her chin.

Astrid yanked her hair and arched her neck. "Look at me when you come."

Given permission, Tessa held her gaze as she rocked on Benita's face. "Give it to me, Bebê." Benita spoke against her. She swirled her tongue over Tessa's clit and finished her with a flick of her tongue. Fierce tremors shook her. She trembled as she came in Benita's mouth while staring into Astrid's eyes. Time stopped as the loose threads of Tessa's life pulled tight. A web of pleasure and affection spun out between them, drawing them close, holding them in place. Astrid stroked her hair and cupped her face as she rubbed her thumb over her lower lip. Tessa leaned into her touch and closed her eyes. Benita nuzzled the crease of her leg and kissed the insides of her thigh. Tessa sank into their care. How would she keep from unraveling outside their scene?

*

"ENOUGH." ASTRID MOVED away from the intense sensation. She pushed at Tessa's shoulders.

Tessa moved away, lifted off Benita's face, and sat back on her heels. Benita rolled to her knees and sat next to her, her face shiny with Tessa's pleasure.

Tessa's forehead wrinkled and her eyes widened. "Did I hurt you, Mistress?"

"No. Come up here." Astrid shifted until she laid on her back. She held out her arms wide. Tessa moved onto the sofa. She positioned herself with her back against the cushions and rested her head on Astrid's chest. "You too, Benita."

"We're going to need a bigger couch, Mistress." Benita pressed her lips together in a thin line.

"Hush. There's room."

Benita shifted her gaze to the floor and remained kneeling.

"Do you require more than my request?" Astrid reached out and lifted Benita's chin with one finger.

Benita met Astrid's gaze. Tessa reached over and touched Benita's shoulder. Astrid sensed her tension dissolve under Tessa's touch.

"No, Mistress."

Benita laid on her side with her leg over Astrid and

Tessa's thighs. Her breath teased against Astrid's breast as she rested her head on her shoulder. She savored the feel of Tessa and Benita in her arms, delighting in the press of their weight as their bodies tangled on the couch. The women's breathing synced as they snuggled together.

This was the part Astrid missed the most with her paying clients. They were always in a hurry, eager to leave, ready to pretend they had not paid for intimacy. Would it be so if she worked here? Benita's reluctance to join, her willingness to forgo aftercare with Astrid pricked her pride. A thread of anxiety wormed its way into her bliss.

Her soul remembered Tessa. And Benita was part of Tessa, that much was clear to Astrid even if it wasn't clear to them. Benita's reticence to join them until she had been encouraged by Tessa was a clear clue to their relationship beyond their pledge to Rowan House. Astrid stroked her fingers over their shoulders. A shiver rocked Tessa's body. Astrid frowned. She reached for the blanket draped over the back of the couch, stretched her fingers out. Their tips brushed the edge of the blanket, unable to grip enough to pull it over them.

Benita snagged the coverlet and pulled the soft fabric over them as she murmured to Tessa in Portuguese. Benita's words were incomprehensible to Astrid, but her tone was clear. The love between them was palpable with Tessa's whispered answer.

Astrid stifled the feeling of being shut out, clamping her mouth shut and refusing to disturb the intimacy between the two women. She shoved her worries and bent feelings aside, closed her eyes, and held on to the near perfect experience just a little while longer.

Chapter Six

BENITA LAY CURLED in Tessa's arms, her breathing even. Tessa watched her face as she slept. The curve of her cheek, her lush mouth slack in repose as familiar as her own features. For the last six years they had shared a room and their bodies with each other, whispered their hopes and dreams in the dark. Tended each other's wounds, physical and emotional.

How many nights had they lost themselves in each other? Or spent an evening quietly reading, or watching a silly movie in the game room? Tessa glanced at the calendar, willing time to stop. Benita would leave soon. Go home to her family.

A familiar ache settled in her chest. The twelve weeks Benita visited her family every year were the hardest. How many nights had Tessa watched her pack? Benita would chat excitedly about seeing her family, revel in the time she would spend in the sun, all while Tessa pretended she would not be miserable without Benita for three months.

Last night had been magical and confusing. Astrid

had enjoyed them both, participated in aftercare, then dismissed them. Tessa had managed to hold it together until they were in their room. Benita had seen through her in a second, taken her to bed and held her until her tears had dried. As sweet as it was to be with Astrid again, she had dismissed Tessa as easily as she had walked away from her before.

Benita stirred, shifted until she faced Tessa. She snuggled into Tessa's chest. "What time is it, Bebê?"

"Noonish, I think."

"*Raios me fodam*! I was supposed to help Veronica in the barn this morning." Benita scooted off the bed and bolted into the bathroom. Water splashed in the sink.

Tessa rolled off her side the bed. "She'll understand."

"I hate not showing. *Caralho*, why didn't I set an alarm?" Benita spoke around brushing her teeth.

Tessa winced when she straightened her knees. "I don't remember skinned knees hurting this much when I was a kid."

Benita flew past her, yanked open her dresser drawer. She drew a pair of panties on, followed by T-shirt and jeans. She sat on the end of her bed and pulled on her socks. "What are you scheduled for today?"

Tessa shrugged. "Interview with Astrid. And then whatever she commands after that. I'm excused from any other duties."

Benita stood, grabbed her hoodie from its peg by the door. She turned back to Tessa. "You okay, Bebê?"

"Yeah, just tired."

Benita pursed her lips. "No. Don't do that. This is me."

"I'm feeling some kinda way because she dismissed

us. And that's on me."

Benita crossed the room in three quick steps. "You need to stop. She came here because she wants a position here, and because she's Petra's friend. She had no idea you were here. It's not like she was expecting you. You need to let go of what you think she's here for." Benita rose on her toes and kissed Tessa's cheek. "Any *idiota de merda* who walked away from you without explanation is not deserving of your tears."

Tessa laughed at Benita's insult to Astrid. "What would I do without you?"

"A lot of jillin' off." Benita swatted her ass before she walked to the door. "See you later, Bebê."

The door closed and Tessa collapsed onto the bed. She rolled to her side, pulled the blankets up over her shoulders, and curled her knees to her chest. What would she do indeed?

Chapter Seven

ASTRID WIPED HER mouth with her napkin. Petra held up the French press. "More?"

"Yes, please." Astrid pushed her cup toward Petra.

Elaine leaned forward on her elbows. "Tell me again, Astrid. How is what you do different than what any of us do when a client wants to role play?"

Astrid sipped her coffee before she answered. "Do you now, or have you ever had an actress or other celebrity you had a crush on? Someone you would in all likelihood never meet in person. Instead of a generic fantasy, say of a queen seducing a loyal retainer, the client can ask for Charlize Theron as Andromache the Scythian to seduce her. Or the client might ask for a more explicit version of Therese's first experience in *Carol* performed for them. That is the difference."

Elaine pursed her lips. "We cater to our client's wishes. They fill out an extensive questionnaire before they come. Just because we don't assume another's identity, is it really that different, enough to warrant charging what you suggested in your proposal?"

"I offer a bespoke engagement, complete with costumes, and voice work that deepens the experience for them. I bend reality for them. I let them live out their dreams." Astrid studied Elaine's expression, searching for clues for what she could say that would drive home how her interactions with clients delved deeper into their most secret fantasies. "If there were no limits, Elaine, what would you like to see? Who do you fantasize about? Aside from your lovely partners?" She met Elaine's hard-edged glaze with one of her own.

Elaine cocked an eyebrow. "Why me? Why not ask Lucia, or Martha?"

"Because you are here, and they are not. Nor have they asked me to justify my life's work." Astrid lifted her chin. "Is my question too personal? Makes you feel exposed?"

Elaine sniffed. "Certainly not."

"Then what would you like to see? You've seen my file, what will it be?"

Elaine's eyes narrowed and her mouth twisted into a sharp smile. "*Atomic Blonde*. I'd like to see a more explicit version of Lorraine and Delphine's first time together. The scene in the back part of the bar is one of my favorites. I loved their interactions and adored the taunting banter between them and the power dynamic. Lorraine is an unapologetic ass-kicking, powerful, sexy woman. Bold. Fearless. She truly cared for Delphine. I was pleased the filmmakers showed the rough love between them, but the movie was ridiculously chaste for my taste. I'd have loved to see more powerplay. Maybe Lorraine punishing Delphine for putting herself in danger."

"Excellent choice. I'll need three days to prepare."

Elaine quirked her mouth. "Three days?"

Astrid gestured to the remains of their meal. "How long did it take you to prepare the gravlax? Which was excellent by the way. Would it have tasted as perfect as it did if you had rushed it? Been palatable if you served it after only one day in the cure?"

"Point taken." Elaine placed her hands flat on the table. "Friday then?"

"Yes. Will it be a private showing, or will Martha and Lucia be there?"

"We make all the decisions jointly, so yes. They'll be there, along with our Robin and Myfanwy as well. Let the staff know what you require for your scene."

"Thank you." Astrid folded her napkin and placed it next to her plate.

Petra reached over and placed her hand over Elaine's. "If you'll excuse us, I'll take Astrid on a tour of the house so she can select the best place for her audition." She turned her attention to Astrid. "Were Tessa and Benita satisfactory last evening?"

"They were adequate." Astrid kept her tone and voice neutral.

Elaine shook off Petra's hand and lifted her chin. "We have the finest staff anywhere and 'adequate' is all you have to say about them?" She glared at Astrid before she shoved her chair back, stood, then turned on her heel and walked away from the table muttering to herself.

Astrid watched Elaine as she retreated, mentally packing her bags. She could not imagine Elaine ever voting for her to become part of Rowan House.

Petra scooted her chair back from the table. "Don't

mind Elaine. She's frustrated with"—she glanced away briefly before she brought her gaze back to Astrid's face—"many things." She held her hand out. "Come on, let me show you the rest of the house."

*

TESSA RINSED HER hands in the wash sink. "That all of it?"

Robin passed her a side towel. "Yes. And why are you here helping me with cleanup? Aren't you assigned to Mistress Astrid?"

"I am." Tess dried her hands. "She hasn't called for me. Mistress Petra took her on the house tour."

Robin's eyebrows lifted. "She did? Oh, hell." She untied her apron and hung it on the hook near the door. "Elaine will have a total case of the ass over it." She sat down at the kitchen table.

Tessa pulled a chair out and studied Robin's face. "Is there trouble in paradise?"

Robin pushed a stray curl away from her face. "Only the kind you'd expect from being a throuple with two headstrong Mistresses. It was fine until Petra pledged to us. I think Elaine is worried Petra will become bored with us and leave us. Although she'd never admit it to a soul, not even me, she's afraid of losing her."

"To Mistress Astrid?" Tessa's stomach twisted. She noted the tight lines around Robin's eyes and the set of her jaw. She leaned forward and whispered, "Are you worried?"

Robin blew out a breath. "No. Not really. I only worry Elaine's jealousy will provoke Petra into breaking up with us."

"Does Elaine think Mistress Petra would break her promise?"

"No." Robin lifted her chin. "She offered herself to us." Robin picked at her nails. "I wish we'd just left things as they were. Elaine was calmer when Petra was not pledged to us. Petra is still in the place of needing and wanting to interact with clients, as she was when we first started our relationship. Elaine worries Petra believes we—I have not truly accepted her pledge because she has not given up seeing clients."

Tessa's heart ached at Robin's despondent tone. "From what I've seen of Mistress Petra, she'd never break a promise. And why would she invite Mistress Astrid to audition if she were going to quit Rowan House? Why invite her best friend to work with her and then leave?"

Robin met Tessa's gaze. "If Petra was going to leave, don't you think she'd want to make sure we had a Mistress to take her place?"

Tessa chewed her lip. "That can't be true. Can it?"

Robin shifted her gaze to the floor. "Goddess, I hope not."

Chapter Eight

ASTRID FLIPPED THROUGH her scene notes for her audition. A sharp rap at the door sounded in her room.

"Come in." Astrid placed the stack of papers on the table between chairs.

Tessa stepped into the room. She closed the door gently before she kneeled, head down, palms up.

"Get off your knees and get over here." Astrid shifted in her chair. Her dressing gown pulled open to reveal her thigh. She didn't bother to pull it back in place, enjoying Tessa's hungry expression. The moment stretched out until Tessa glanced up and into her eyes. Her light-brown skin turned a dull red as a blush spread over her cheeks.

Astrid held her gaze, delighting in Tessa's consternation at being caught looking. "We will be performing a scene between Lorraine and Delphine from *Atomic Blonde*. Have you seen the film?"

"Several times, Mistress."

"No. When we are alone, you will call me Astrid. Unless we are performing a scene or are in front of the others, at which time you will refer to me as Ma'am. I am not your Mistress, is that understood?"

"Yes, Astrid."

"Very good."

"We will improv as far as sexual interaction goes, but we will stay in character. Take this." She passed Tessa a Blu-ray copy of the film. "Watch this at least five times between now and my audition on Friday. I want you to understand both characters as they are written. They don't get a happy ending in the movie, so we will make sure they do for our performance."

Tessa's brows drew down. "I haven't performed like this in years, Astrid. I'm not sure I can be ready by Friday."

"Would you like me to choose someone else?"

"No! For fuck's sake, I'm just trying to be honest. I don't want to fuck up your audition."

Astrid narrowed her eyes. "Come here."

Tessa stepped close to Astrid. She was taller than Astrid, and her proximity forced Astrid to look up.

"On your knees. I may not be your Mistress, but you will not speak to me that way."

Tessa made no move to bend her knees. "I'm not the girl you once commanded." A muscle jumped along her jaw. "And you just said you're not my Mistress, not that you ever were."

Stung, Astrid lifted her hand and gripped Tessa's chin. "No. No, you're not that girl, are you?" She stared into the depths of Tessa's amber hued eyes. "What's your plan, Tessa? Piss me off enough I choose another to help me? Benita perhaps? So you can watch? Or are you hoping I'll let you fuck you me like you want to right here, right now, instead of making you wait until Friday?"

The slight flare of Tessa's nostrils tipped her hand.

"What is it you're trying to provoke?" Astrid slid her hand to the back of Tessa's neck. "Fighting?" She lifted on her toes and brushed her lips over Tessa's mouth. "Or fucking?"

Tessa opened to her, took over their kiss, her tongue teasing and provocative.

Desire caught low in her belly as she deepened their kiss. She leaned into Tessa, melding her body to hers. A harsh groan escaped Tessa and she wrapped her arms around Astrid, lifted her off her feet. The sensation of being taken raced through Astrid. She wrapped her legs around Tessa's narrow waist. She nipped her lower lip, stopping short of drawing blood. Tessa growled into her mouth.

Tessa turned with her in her arms and crossed the room in three strides.

She tossed Astrid onto the mattress and fell on top of her. Her teeth grazed Astrid's skin, sending ripples of desire along her spine as she nuzzled Astrid's neck. Tessa raised her head and peered into Astrid's face, her eyes silently searching for consent.

Astrid held her gaze, lifted her chin. "Do it."

Tessa yanked the belt to Astrid's gown open.

Astrid gripped Tessa's shoulder, dug her fingers into the sweeping curves of her thick muscles. "What are you waiting for?"

No subtle touch, just a quick thrust, and Tessa buried herself in Astrid's welcoming body.

Astrid gasped with the sensation. She tugged Tessa closer and kissed her. Lips, tongue, and teeth clashed, their kiss savage. "Fuck me," Astrid panted, surrendering to her desire to give up control within the safety of Tessa's arms.

Tessa's lips pulled back, a taunting expression on her face. "So wet for this."

"For you. For you, Tessa." Astrid rocked her hips up to meet Tessa's hard thrusts. Pleasure gathered low in her belly, as the heel of Tessa's hand rocked against her clit as she fucked her. Her body caught flame when Tessa lowered her head, captured her nipple, and sucked hard.

"Give it to me. Now." Tessa bit down on her nipple.

Astrid screamed, her hips bucking wildly as she sought more of Tessa's roughness.

Tessa slowed her thrusts, teasing and curling her fingers over Astrid's sweet spot, stroking gently. "I've waited fifteen years to hear you scream like that. The first year you were gone, I went to sleep every night hoping I'd have a message from you in the morning." She thrust deep and slow, each stroke drawing out Astrid's pleasure. "Why? Why did you leave me behind, Roxanne?"

Astrid stilled, reached up, and placed her fingers across Tessa's lips. "No. As far as the world knows, Roxanne is dead. And I left to keep you safe." She traced the thick scar on Tessa's cheek. "It seems I failed. I don't expect you to forgive me—what I did was unforgivable—but try to understand I had no choice."

Tessa edged Astrid, the sensation intense, pleasure bordering on pain. "And if you had to do it again?"

Astrid lowered her hand and clasped Tessa's wrist. Tessa stopped stroking but remained inside.

Astrid met her gaze. "I'll never regret trying keep you safe, but I will always regret the time we might have had."

She cupped her face with one hand. "I thought if I ever saw you again it would be on a stage."

Tessa leaned her brow against Astrid's forehead. Her eyes glittered. "This is my stage. Will you come for me?"

Astrid slid her hand from her wrist. She locked her legs around Tessa's hips. "Just for you."

Tessa thrust hard and deep, her fingers curled and stroked over her sweet spot, drawing sharp cries from Astrid. Astrid thrashed her hips, arched her back and came, clenching around Tessa's fingers. She clung to her as waves of pleasure rocketed through her body, each more intense than the last, as she screamed her release. As the echoes of her screams died away, Tessa eased her down, gentled her thrusts as she pressed kisses to Astrid's throat. Astrid closed her eyes, pressed her face into Tessa's neck, savored her care, her love, and cursed herself for ever letting her go.

*

THEY LAY IN Astrid's bed, sheets crumpled beneath them. Tessa smoothed her hand over Astrid's body, mapping the changes their years apart had brought. A series of scars and a small incision marked her belly. She palmed her lush curves. "Gall bladder?"

"Yes. How did you know?"

"Benita has the same set of scars."

"Are you in love with her?" Astrid tucked a lock of Tessa's hair behind her ear.

Tessa leaned up on her elbow and flattened her palm over Astrid's silky skin. "Maybe. She's my best friend with amazing benefits."

Astrid arched her brow. "What does that mean? And unless I'm mistaken you have an extensive group of women whose 'benefits' you enjoy if Petra's stories are true. You are, or you aren't in love. And it doesn't bother me either way."

Tessa lay back down. "I know." She rubbed her brow as a dull ache settled in her heart.

Astrid rolled on top of her. Bracing herself with her arms, she leaned down and kissed Tessa. A gentle kiss. Tessa sank into the utter sweetness of it, reveling in Astrid's attention, shoving aside Astrid's claim of not caring if Tessa loved another.

Astrid broke their kiss to trail her lips along Tessa's jaw. "It's not because I don't have feelings for you."

"Feelings? If you had any feelings for me at all you would never have left me behind." Tessa pushed at Astrid's shoulders.

Astrid sat up and straddled her. "I had no choice. Would you have preferred prison to having your freedom these last fifteen years? Or for me to surrender the entire service to the Widow?"

"I would have preferred a choice." Tessa met Astrid's blistering glare with one of her own.

"Did you ever stop wallowing in your own feelings long enough to think maybe I didn't want to go to jail? That maybe I thought you had enough sense to choose a career other than the one I'd shown you? That you'd get off your ass and follow all those dreams you told me about?" Astrid scooted off the bed. She turned her back to Tessa. She snatched her robe off the floor and pulled it on. "Forget it. Go. Now. I don't know why I thought you'd understand. This was a mistake."

"Coming here? Or agreeing to have me as your partner for the audition?"

"Right now, all of it." Astrid turned to her, her mouth pulled into a thin line as she tied her dressing gown.

Tessa held on to her anger. "Fine. But I've had a good life, Astrid. Most of it. I have more than I'd ever have had if I'd kept chasing stupid pipe dreams of headlining on Broadway or starring in a movie. More than I'd ever had than if I'd stayed in Oildale, surrounded by roustabouts and burnouts. I would have been one of them, working my ass off to put food on the table and have a roof over my head. Rowan House is my home. I am loved. For who I am. I love working here. I love making people's wildest fantasies come true. I love every single minute of it. And you gave me that. You opened the door, helped me understand who I am. I've never regretted a single moment of what I do."

Astrid remained silent. Arms crossed, she stood with her back to the fireplace. Her hair was mussed, her face still flushed from their time together and their argument. All Tessa wanted to do was kneel, crawl to her, press her head to her feet and beg forgiveness, to beg Astrid to come back to bed and let her worship her. And at twenty she would have done it.

Tessa shoved off the bed. She stopped long enough to straighten out her clothes and pick up the Blu-ray disc on the table. "When do you want to rehearse this scene?"

Astrid rested her hands on her hips. "You still want to help me?"

"I serve Rowan House. I volunteered. My backing out now would cause problems with staffing."

Astrid narrowed her eyes. "Is that the only reason?"

"No." Tessa shifted her gaze, studied the toes of her boots, clamped her teeth on her lower lip. Her anger melted away, melancholy shoving it aside. It didn't matter. She didn't matter. Astrid would choose another if Tessa told her the truth, and that would be worse, so much worse.

"Meet me at eight in the large playroom."

Tessa walked out and closed the door softly.

Chapter Nine

ASTRID SETTLED THE thin straps of her short black dress over her shoulders and studied her reflection in the full-length glass. She adjusted her platinum-blonde wig and used a tissue to smear her eyeliner until she was satisfied with her makeup. Her four-inch heels would make up the height difference between her and Tessa. She closed her eyes, focused inwardly on projecting Lorraine Broughton's reserved power. She conjured a vision of Lorraine fighting, her deadly skills on display. The lead character of *Atomic Blonde*, Lorraine was a symbol, a fearless MI6 agent, a strong woman unafraid of who she was. Lorraine owned her power, as much as she owned her sexuality. A bold beacon of sexual energy, she drew the innocent Delphine to her, as in control as a Mistress, before becoming ensnared in Delphine's sweet and honest love. Astrid opened her eyes. She slid into Lorraine's character, embracing her essence as an old friend. Dangerous. Deadly. Savage in her affections. Her body responded, her nipples tightening in anticipation. The chase, even when imaginary, was always thrilling. She smoothed her hands over her skirt.

The door to the playroom clicked open. Tessa strolled in wearing a tight-fitting striped top that accented her modest cleavage. Thin leather bands circled her neck above her Rowan House collar. A black miniskirt short enough to reveal her fishnet hose were held up by garters completed the illusion she was Delphine.

"Nice costume on short notice. The wig is excellent."

"June hooked me up."

"No leather jacket available?"

"The only leather jackets available were Benita's, which was too small, and Millie's, which was too big."

Astrid strolled around Tessa. "Nice you thought of flats. The illusion of size difference and the earnest vulnerability of Delphine is key to this scene. Are you prepared?"

"I think so. I've rehearsed some with Benita."

"Do you want to take it from after the kiss in the hallway? The 'Politics of Dancing' scene?"

Her gaze skittered away from Astrid's. "I don't want to do the part with the gun play."

Astrid studied the tense set of Tessa's shoulders. "Agreed. I think the hallway from their kiss is a nice place to begin. We'll see where it takes us, shall we?"

She pressed play on the music system and the pounding beat of Re-Flex's "The Politics of Dancing" surrounded them.

"All right." Tessa backed against the wall of the room. She rested her chin on her chest, closed her eyes briefly before she lifted her chin and met Astrid's gaze.

"Scene." Astrid focused on Tessa's face.

Tessa's expression transformed as she projected the desperate need of Delphine. Her eyes and the faint quiver of her lower lip combined into a delectable combination of fear and desire as she met Astrid's gaze.

Astrid gripped Tessa's throat with one hand and squeezed hard once before she slid it up and cupped her chin. She dug her fingers into Tessa's skin, delighting in the rise and fall of Tessa's chest as she sank into the scene.

Astrid inhaled the scent of Tessa's skin. The delicate smell of sweat, soap, and a hint of fear underlying it all. She tightened her grip. Tessa's skin blanched under her fingers, sending a wave of want rippling through her. She kissed her, savaging Tessa's mouth before she turned her to face away. She forced her roughly against the padded wall of the playroom. Tessa's hand scrabbled against the wall, her quiet gasp setting Astrid on fire.

Astrid pressed against her back, trapping her against the wall. She wrapped her hand around her throat. Tessa's pulse pounded against her palm. Astrid savored the feel of her hard body, the gift of her surrender. Having Tessa at her mercy opened the gates and a torrent of desire raced through her as she tapped into her character's ruthlessness and her own wants to fuel the scene.

Tessa groaned, pushed her hips back against her. Astrid slid her hand down, palmed her breast, and plucked at her nipple through the thin shirt.

"I'm afraid they'll find us," Tessa whispered as she arched her head back and tilted it to the side. She reached back and dug her fingers into Astrid's hip.

"Shh. I'll keep you safe." Astrid bit and sucked at the tender skin of Tessa's neck as she rucked Tessa's skirt up. Bare skin greeted her. She skated her fingers up Tessa's thighs, slick with want. The heady scent of desire rose between them. Wet heat coated her fingers as she plunged them deep. She tightened her grip around Tessa's throat, holding her still as she nuzzled the soft skin under her ear. She traced her tongue over the delicate shell of her ear before kissing and nipping the tender skin underneath. The music surrounded them, the heavy beat matching the beat of the pulse in Tessa's throat under her fingertips as Astrid stroked hard and fast.

The illusion was complete. Astrid savored the sensation of power, Tessa's complete surrender, and the raw energy pulsing between them. Tessa moaned softly, spread her legs as wide as the skirt would allow. She trembled under Astrid, her body clutching around Astrid's fingers.

"Please." Tessa panted and shuddered.

Astrid thrust harder. "Give it to me."

Tessa filled her palm as she gasped her release. She fell back and collapsed against Astrid. She held Tessa up, supported her as her body shook and trembled. Astrid waited until the subtle rhythmic clutch of Tessa's body faded before she eased her fingers from her. She turned Tessa to face her. Astrid kissed her, sipping from her mouth, savoring the feel of her plush lips. Tessa teased her tongue over Astrid's lower lip before she broke their kiss.

Tessa held Astrid's gaze as she sank to her knees. "Let me." She ran her hands up her thighs until her fingertips brushed the hem of Astrid's skirt. Tessa pressed her nose between the junction of Astrid's thighs and exhaled. Her breath was warm through the thin material of her dress. She mouthed Astrid over the dress, the barely-there pressure over Astrid's clit exquisite. "Let me taste you. Please,"

Tessa whispered.

Her quiet request at the end ignited a raging fire of need in Astrid's belly. "Do it. Now." She rested her hand on the crown of Tessa's head.

Given permission, Tessa shoved up the short dress. Her fingers were hot against Astrid's skin as she slid her panties down her legs. Astrid lifted each leg clear. Tessa dropped the sodden underwear into a heap on the floor. Tessa shoved the skirt up. Her calloused hands were rough against the tender skin of Astrid's thighs. Tessa's mouth closed over Astrid, warm and wet.

The first stroke of her tongue had Astrid scrabbling for a hold on the wall. She braced herself on her arms and looked between her legs. Tessa peered into Astrid's eyes as she worried her clit with hard flicks of her tongue.

Astrid fell into her amber gaze, trapped by Tessa's exquisite attention and the adoration reflected in her eyes. Tessa slid her fingers up Astrid's thigh, teased her opening briefly before she plunged inside. Astrid gasped as Tessa pursed her lips, sucked hard as she fucked her, fast and dirty, driving her into a devastating climax. Rolling waves of pleasure crashed over her. She closed her eyes as Tessa continued to fuck her. She came hard, her legs shaking.

"Again," she ground out, desperate for Tessa to take her again, for the illusion of being treasured, of being someone somebody would risk their life to protect.

Tessa applied herself, giving Astrid what she wanted. Astrid stiffened her legs, relaxed into Tessa's grip, trusting her to support her as she shouted her release to the ceiling.

Their coarse breathing was loud in the room, the

soundtrack having ended long ago. Tessa nuzzled her thighs, placing one last kiss on her clit, sending a screaming aftershock through Astrid's body before she stood. She kissed Astrid's cheek, then the corner of her mouth before she brushed her lips over Astrid's.

Astrid gripped her shoulders, held her tight and kissed her, savoring the taste of herself on Tessa's mouth. She eased back to peer into Tessa's eyes. There it was, all the longing, all of Tessa's need for Astrid to see her, truly see her as more than a devastatingly good fuck. She held her gaze, traced her fingers over her cheek. "End scene."

Tessa remained still in the circle of Astrid's arms, her hands resting on Astrid's waist. She tightened her grip, her strong fingers digging into Astrid's hips. "Is it?"

"Is that a request?" Astrid placed both hands on Tessa's chest. She flicked her thumbs over her nipples.

"I think Lorraine would want more. I know Delphine would."

"Would she?" Astrid thumbed Tessa's nipples through her shirt, teased them into hard points before she gripped them tightly.

"Yes." Tessa panted.

"She'd want Lorraine to fuck her again, wouldn't she?"

"Yes."

"All right." Astrid tugged on Tessa's nipples, eliciting a moan. "Come with me."

She released her and pointed to a padded bench. "Over it, lie down so your middle is supported and you can see yourself in the wall mirror."

Tessa obeyed, pulling her skirt up to expose herself as she lay down. Her fishnet stockings and suspender belt framed her succulent ass. Astrid's palms itched to warm it.

She kneeled next to the bench and placed her hand in the middle of Tessa's lower back. "You shouldn't have followed me, Delphine. Shouldn't have put yourself in danger." Astrid swatted Tessa's ass. The echo of the smack reverberated off the walls. "You should be home, safe. Not risking your life for me." Astrid paddled with her hand. Tessa's soft cries and deep groans drove her on. She kept her strokes light, in keeping with Tessa's limits. Astrid smoothed her hand over Tessa's skin, warm from the spanking. "Why are you here?"

"I couldn't help myself." Tessa's teary confession melted Astrid.

Astrid bent over, kissed the dimple at the top of Tessa's ass before she trailed kisses up her spine. "On your back."

Tessa lay on the wide bench with her legs on either side. Astrid savored the sight of her, the way her skirt was rucked up, her ripped hose and smeared eyeliner. She moved to the end of the bench and sat between Tessa's legs. She feathered her fingers over her thick clit, bent to lick a long stroke over it before she slipped inside. Searing heat enveloped her fingers, as Tessa's body opened to her.

The muscles of Tessa's thighs stood out as she spread her legs, offering Astrid more access. Her clit stood proud, glistening with wetness. Astrid licked the stiff tip as she worked more of her fingers in. Four wide, she sucked Tessa's clit in time with her strokes.

Tessa gripped her shoulder. "All of you. I want all of you."

Desire flowed from Astrid, wetting the bench under

her. She held tight to the desperate note in Tessa's voice, turned her wrist, tucked her thumb, and pushed forward.

"Take it. Take what you want." Tessa panted and reached down. She wrapped her hand around Astrid's wrist. Her rough voice seared Astrid's soul.

Astrid rocked forward as Tessa kept her hand in place, moved with her, a fixed point in the universe of their scene.

"For you," Tessa cried out. Her body clenched hard, then bloomed around Astrid's hand, welcoming her with a rush of liquid heat. Tessa's shoulders lifted off the bench as she came, muscles rigid, her nails digging into Astrid's wrist.

*

TESSA HELD TIGHT to Astrid's wrist as she came, curled into the pleasure. "For you." A gush of desire spilled from her, the release shaking her to her core. Tessa shuddered through her orgasm until she was spent. Her mind spun out. She left Delphine's character and dropped back into herself. She grasped for something to hold on to as she released Astrid's wrist, severing their connection. A gaping hole opened in her soul as the impact of the scene hit her full force. In the years since her time with Astrid she had not experienced a connection with anyone like this. She dug her hands into the padded bench.

"Slow your breathing." Astrid worked her way gently from Tessa's body. Tessa tensed, unwilling to open her eyes, not quite ready for the return of reality. An aftershock rocked her as Astrid eased her fingers free. After a gentle kiss on her clit, Astrid left the bench. The tip-tap of her pumps echoed in the room. Tessa shivered as the heat drained from her body.

Astrid placed a soft blanket over her, cupped her face. "Don't try to sit up without me."

"Yes, Mistress." Tessa bit her lip, annoyed with herself for slipping back into old habits. She braced for Astrid's correction. After a long minute she opened her eyes. The ceiling mirror reflected the far side of the room. Astrid stood in front of the counter next to the small refrigerator with her eyes closed and her hand over her mouth. After a moment, she lowered her hand and opened her eyes. Tessa studied the set of her shoulders as she poured water for them.

Astrid crossed the room and placed the water glasses on the floor. Tessa met her gaze.

"Ready to sit up?" Her voice was cool, steady.

Tessa gripped the edge of the blanket. "Yes." She lifted her leg over and pushed up off the bench. Astrid gripped her arm to help her. She steadied her before she picked up the glass and offered it to Tessa.

"Drink. Fisting takes a lot out of a person." Astrid steadied her before she picked up the glass and offered it to Tessa.

The tender tone of her voice washed over Tessa as she took the glass from Astrid's hand. She sipped the cool water. Her throat ached, raw from their session, and the strain of stifling her tears. Tessa kept her eyes focused on the blanket over her knees. The silence between them thickened.

Astrid pushed her hair back with one hand and picked up her glass. She stood and paced the room with long strides, occasionally pausing to sip her water. Tessa focused on her pumps, counting her steps as she waited for Astrid to speak. A chill settled in her bones, and her hand ached where she clutched the blanket.

After she had drained her water glass, Astrid walked to Tessa. "Do you feel prepared?"

Tessa frowned. "What?"

"Do you feel prepared for our performance? I liked your improv and agree it makes the scene stronger."

Tessa inhaled sharply, her mind spinning with Astrid's whiplash change in demeanor, stung by her cool appraisal of the performance. Astrid offered her nothing more than a perfunctory glass of water and a warm blanket, standard aftercare, the same as you would offer any client. Tessa avoided Astrid's gaze. How stupid she was to think there was more between them. Their connection had been an illusion.

"Glad you liked it." Tessa set her glass aside, yanked the blanket clear of her body, stood, folded it neatly, and placed it on the bench before she pulled the wig free of her head. She strode to the door, watching Astrid's reaction from under her lashes.

Astrid cocked her head to the side. "Where are you going?"

Tessa turned to her, kept her hand on the door handle to ground herself. "My room. We're done, aren't we? Or did you want to rehearse more?" She lifted her chin, braced herself, waiting and wanting Astrid to reprimand her for her tone, for failing to use her honorific.

Astrid stilled. Her icy gaze pierced Tessa. Her lack of correction was more painful than a slap. "No. I've seen enough. Be in the ballroom at the appointed time tomorrow."

Tessa blinked back the tears she was unwilling to shed in front of Astrid. "I'll be there."

Chapter Ten

"I'M IMPRESSED." MARTHA filled Astrid's cup from the French press between them.

"It was hot, I'll give you that." Elaine lifted her chin toward Astrid. "You and Tessa were marvelous. I understand now."

"I'm pleased you enjoyed it." Astrid sipped her coffee, her gaze fixed on Lucia, waiting for her evaluation. Under the table she rolled her napkin in between her fingers, holding on to her training, willing herself calm. The clock on the sideboard chimed the hour. Astrid spooned cherry jam onto her plate. She plucked a slice of bread from the toast rack as she settled into the silence. She would not break, would not ask for Lucia's opinion. Lucia forked a bite of her eggs into her mouth and chewed slowly. Astrid watched from under her lashes as she smeared the dark-red jam on her toast.

Lucia finished her eggs, wiped her mouth, took a sip of water before she spoke. "While I enjoyed your performance, I have some concerns."

Astrid placed her toast on her plate, leaned back in her chair. "Which are?" She met Lucia's cool gaze.

"I'm unsure if it is good for you to continue working with Tessa."

"Why?" Astrid lifted an eyebrow. "Did you find her performance lacking?" She clenched her jaw, stifling her anger.

"No." Lucia leaned forward. "Her performance was magnificent." She stared into Astrid's eyes. "Heartfelt, if I'm any judge." She tapped the top of the table. "And that is why you should choose another for the next audition. Tessa has true feelings for you. Unless you have intentions of returning them, you should not encourage her. It is not in her best interest."

Astrid lifted her chin. "Do you honestly think I am not aware of her feelings for me? That I missed it? What kind of a Mistress do you think I am?"

"The kind who would do well to remember she is applying for a position and shouting at a potential future employer is unbecoming." Lucia sat back in her chair, pinning Astrid in place with a glare that could cut stone.

Astrid inhaled sharply. "My apologies. I have spoken to Tessa about this. I made it clear I am not seeking anything more than a position here. She insisted she continue as my partner for the audition. Stated she did not want to cause issues with staffing and made it clear to me she was only continuing for the sake of the house." She shifted her gaze to Martha and Elaine. "Although, as I expressed to Tessa at our initial meeting, maybe this whole adventure is a mistake. If I had known she was here, I would not have applied."

"Do you truly wish to withdraw your application?"

Lucia reached across the table, laid a cool finger on the back of Astrid's hand. Her touch grounded her, reminded Astrid of what she might have if she were able to win a position at Rowan House.

Astrid met Lucia's gaze. "No. No, I don't. But I don't want to cause harm to Tessa."

Robin cleared her throat. "Permission to speak, Mistresses?"

Elaine nodded her consent. She lifted her hand in acknowledgement of Lucia and Martha, who also nodded, signaling their agreement.

Astrid met Robin's gaze.

Robin clasped her hands together in front of her waist. "It would be more painful for Tessa to be denied participating in Astrid's audition." A rueful expression spread across her face. "I don't expect any of you to truly understand, but for a submissive, especially a submissive in love, if Mistress Astrid chooses someone else now, Tessa would forever believe she had done something wrong, and that was why Mistress Astrid set her aside."

"My sweet wise girl." Elaine picked up Robin's hand and pressed a kiss across her knuckles before she hauled her into her lap. She wrapped her arms around Robin. Robin leaned her brow against Elaine's forehead, tucked a lock of Elaine's hair behind her ear, and kissed her.

Astrid blinked. She looked away from the tender moment between Elaine and Robin as she turned Robin's words over her in her mind. And there it was. The why. The reason Tessa had held on to Astrid in spite of her abandonment. Why it was still as raw for Tessa as the day Astrid left. Could she ever make it right?

"Thank you, Robin, for your insight." Lucia turned to

Astrid. "I'll allow you to continue with Tessa for as long as she wants to continue. But know this, until she ends her commitment to Rowan House and declares she is your submissive she belongs to us, to Rowan House. We will do whatever we need to do to keep her safe." The deadly tone of her voice raised the hairs on the back of Astrid's neck.

Gooseflesh rose on her arms under Lucia's frosty glare. "I understand Rowan House's commitment to its submissives very well." Astrid stood and pushed her chair closer to the table. "Robin, thank you very much for your wisdom. It made a good many things clear to me." She inclined her head toward the group. "Excuse me, please."

Chapter Eleven

"COME ON, TESSA, show me what you've got." Millie grinned and waved her forward.

Tessa watched the larger woman's feet as they circled each other on the mat. Taller and heavier than Tessa, Millie presented a challenge to Tessa's Krav Maga skills any day. On a day when Tessa's mind was unfocused, doubly so.

Millie took two steps closer. Tessa shifted to the left, staying out of her line of force. She spun and kicked out at Millie's leg, attempting a sweep. Millie shifted direction, rounded on Tessa, grabbed her by the neck in an arm bar. Tessa inhaled sharply, went limp to drag Millie down, shifted her weight, and shoved hard at her elbow. They crashed to the floor. Tessa rolled atop Millie, raised her fist, and feigned a punch to her throat.

Millie held up both hands. "Well done. I thought I had you."

Tessa lifted clear and held out her hand to Millie. "That arm bar is wicked. I wasn't sure it would work."

"Your execution was perfect. I want to go over some weapon defenses. Do you have time?"

Tessa shook out her shoulders and glanced at the training room clock. "Sure. I'm not due to see Astrid until this afternoon."

Millie strode to the storage cabinet and picked up the training weapons. She placed the orange wooden knife on the side of the mat. She held up the pistol, a bright-yellow mockup of a 9mm Glock. "Let's do the pistol first." She passed the pistol to Tessa.

"Remember, out of the line of fire, control, disarm, get away, and if that's impossible, disable." Millie backed away from Tessa.

Tessa pointed the imitation firearm at Millie's face. In seconds Millie had the gun from her hand and Tessa was looking at the ceiling of the training room. Millie had retreated to the far side of the mat with the pistol in her hand. Tessa rolled to her side and pushed herself to sitting. "How the fuck are you so fast?"

"Practice. I've done it so many times, my brain doesn't have to work out the steps as I do them. It's like walking, or swimming. Once you know how to do it, your body just takes over."

Tessa stood and held her hand out for the gun.

They spent an hour, each taking turns as they worked on their techniques. Sweat stung Tessa's eyes. "One more and then I'm done."

"Are you scheduled tomorrow?" Millie wiped her face with the sleeve of her T-shirt. She replaced the training weapons in the cabinet. "I want you to work on this some more."

"Not as of now."

Millie's concerned expression let Tessa know she'd failed to keep her tone neutral.

"What's up with that anyway? Most Mistresses want their audition sub to attend them all the time. We didn't see June for days at a time when Mistress Andrea applied. Still can't believe she turned us down."

"Not everyone wants what we have here." Tessa shifted her gaze to the worn canvas mat. Her eye landed on faint reddish-brown stains, reminders of missed cues and accidental injuries in the training room. "I don't know. I should step aside. Let someone else serve her. She doesn't seem to want me."

"Hey."

Tessa looked up and into Millie's face.

Millie's brows knit tightly. "You're an amazing person, no matter what she thinks. She should fuck right off if she doesn't get that."

Tessa lifted her shoulder. "I know that here—" she pointed to her head. "But here—" she put her hand over her heart. "Here, doesn't want to listen."

Millie crossed the room, laid her broad hands on Tessa's shoulders. "I'm not the best at love advice. Have you talked to Mistress Lucia?"

"I'm afraid if I do, she'll force Astrid to pick someone else." Tessa rested her forehead against Millie's chest. "And I couldn't watch that. Even thinking about it makes my stomach ache."

Millie moved Tessa back and peered into her face. "What the hell will you do if they offer her a position? Would you feel that way if she was seeing clients?"

Tessa chewed her lip. "I don't know."

"How do you deal with it with Benita?"

"What?" Tessa shrugged out of Millie's arms and stepped back.

"Don't look so freaked out. We all see it even if you don't. We set our watches by how you mope when she leaves to visit her family. I know you care for her deeply, even if you haven't said the L word to her. And she would kill for you. You both seem to be handling the client part just fine. Why is it different with Astrid?"

"It just—it just is." Tessa chewed her lower lip. Why? Why was her heart so fucking stubborn when it came to Astrid?

Millie placed her arm around Tessa's shoulders and walked her toward the door. "You need to figure the why of that. We don't want to gain a Mistress and lose the best librarian we've ever had."

Tessa snorted. "I'm the only librarian you've ever had."

"Come on. Myfanwy promised me she'd save us some chocolate orange muffins."

*

RAPID POUNDING ON the door shattered the afternoon quiet. Astrid started and narrowly missed stabbing her eye with her lash brush. The dark color smeared over her cheek. She swore, plucked a tissue from the box, and scrubbed at her cheek as she crossed the room. She flung the door open. "What the hell is going on?"

Elaine stepped forward, crowding her and forcing her back from the door. She closed the door behind her and leaned against it to close it. "I need to talk to you."

"Now?" Astrid dabbed at the mascara on her cheek.

Elaine rested her hands on her hips. "No, tomorrow, I just thought I'd ask today."

"Oh my goddess." Astrid turned away and strode back to her dressing table. "You're just as impetuous and dramatic as Petra described you." She sat before the mirror and scowled at her reflection. With a new tissue she swiped at the stubborn mascara. "What is so urgent you practically break my door down knocking?"

Elaine came over and stood behind Astrid. She held her gaze in the mirror. "How long have you known Petra?"

Astrid rubbed makeup remover over her face, applying extra to the dark smudge on her cheek before wiping it away with tissues. "Why?"

Elaine turned away and paced the room.

Astrid continued to clean the makeup from her face as she watched Elaine in the mirror.

Elaine paused in her pacing with her back to Astrid. "Are you here to woo her from Rowan House?"

Astrid tossed the tissue to the top of the vanity. She stood, crossed the room, grabbed Elaine by the shoulder, and spun her around. She peered into her face. "Are you high? Or drunk?"

Elaine lifted her chin. "I am neither. And it is a legitimate question."

Astrid rested her hands on her hips. "If you were a smaller woman, I would attempt to shake some sense into you. Why would you think so little of Petra? Or me?"

Elaine pushed her hair back with both hands. "Fuck. I don't know. This all made sense in my room."

"Elaine, listen closely because I am only going to say this once. I am here because I'm tired of working from hotel rooms. I'm sick of always looking over my shoulder, trying to stay one step ahead of the Widow and two steps ahead of the law. I want the security of a house, this house in particular. Petra told me about Norway."

Elaine pursed her lips. "That was a unique situation."

"I also know Petra would die before she ever dishonored her pledge to you and Robin. What have I done to make you think I would ever try to come between the three of you?"

"Nothing. Really. It's just—Petra feels distant, far away from me right now. I'm afraid she's bored with us."

"Us?" Astrid studied Elaine's expression.

"Me."

Astrid strolled back to her dressing table. "So mix it up."

"How?" Elaine followed her, stood behind her chair.

"You were once the most in-demand Mistress in the world and you're asking me for advice? You're a legend."

"I am sincere. I've seen how intrigued she has been with your audition. I hear it in her voice every time she talks about you. Even Robin is enamored with your performances. I want to do what you do, but just for her and Robin."

Astrid tilted her head. "Well to start, you'll have to suppress your larger-than-life personality. Set aside your ego and become the character you are playing. Learn to respond and react as they would."

"You make it sound so simple."

Astrid picked up her foundation brush and applied it to her skin. "It is deceptively simple. But to do it well, to become someone else, to leave reality behind, and create a scene that feels true to your partner or client, that is the trick of it." She blinked and considered her application before she set the brush aside. Astrid met Elaine's gaze in the mirror. "I've spent so much time being other people, some days I don't know who I am until I look in the mirror."

"Is it hard? Not being yourself?"

Astrid shifted her gaze away from Elaine's keen gaze and shrugged her shoulders. "Does it matter?"

"It should. Don't you want people to acknowledge you, for you? What kind of Mistress doesn't care if her subs acknowledge her?"

Elaine's disapproving tone rankled. Astrid picked up her concealer and dabbed it over the dark circles under her eyes, avoiding Elaine's gaze in the mirror. "A very busy Mistress. Are you finished wasting my time with ridiculous accusations or is there something specific you wanted to know?"

"How do I start?"

"Is there a movie Petra asks to watch always? One that she always chooses if given a chance? Start with that. Watch it, over and over until you can recite it. Absorb the characters' reactions, practice them, how they say things, how they move. Then use your imagination. Play with it. You've done generic scenes with themes, consider this an upgrade, or embellishment of that."

Elaine's brows knit. "You won't say anything to Petra, will you?"

"No. I'd rather my best friend didn't know her partner worried she was unfaithful and accused me of trying to seduce her."

"Ouch. I apologize. Forgive me, please, for doubting your intentions." Elaine's sincere expression matched her contrite tone.

"Forgiven." Astrid hardened her stare. "Now get out. And don't ever question my loyalty again."

*

ASTRID HUNCHED HER shoulders against the chill air as she hurried down the path leading away from the house. Wind swirled random leaves across the bricks. As she walked, she replayed her performance with Tessa in her mind. Tessa's detachment had been palpable. The sincerity and emotion from their rehearsal had not resurfaced. She had been going through the motions, a skilled enough actress she had fooled Martha and Elaine. Both had been enthusiastic about the performance, but Astrid had sensed Lucia's reserve. Worry nipped at her as she contemplated her upcoming mind-fuck audition.

She arrived at the building housing the gym and the sauna out of breath. She reached into her pocket for the key to the building. Nothing. She patted her other pockets to no avail.

"Fuck me." Astrid slapped her hand on the door and spun on her heel. She bumped into Benita, knocking the smaller woman off balance. She grabbed her shoulders to steady her. "Sorry."

"Where are you going in such a hurry?"

Astrid released her and swept her hand through her hair. "I was going to check out the sauna."

"Mmm, saunas are my favorite. So hot and steamy."

"Yes, well, I've lost the key somewhere along the way."

Benita held up an orange tag with a key dangling from it. "This key?" Mischief danced in her eyes.

"Exactly that key." Astrid held out her palm for it.

Benita closed her hand around the fob. "What's my reward for finding it?"

"You want a reward?"

Benita lifted her shoulder and let it fall. "Seems only fair. I saved you a long walk back to the house and having to tell Elaine you lost the key."

"Elaine has no power over me." Astrid reached out and grabbed Benita's wrist.

Benita twisted in Astrid's grasp, feigning resistance. "So strong. Are you going to punish me?"

Astrid tightened her grip and pulled Benita until her soft curves were flush against her. "Are you testing me? Want to see how far you can push me?"

"Maybe?" Benita bit her lower lip. "Maybe I want to find out for myself what Tessa sees in you."

"What would your Mistresses say to that?"

Benita pressed closer and walked her fingers up Astrid's arm. "If you tell them I teased you"—she wrapped her arm around Astrid's neck—"and then touched you without you giving me permission, I might receive a paddling. Or if I'm really lucky, Mistress Petra will remind me of her skill with a single tail." Benita's seductive tone combined with her open desire had Astrid reconsidering her afternoon plans.

"You're quite the pain slut, aren't you?"

"Want to find out?" Benita whispered.

Astrid bent her head to Benita's mouth and kissed her. She melted into her embrace. Astrid crushed her mouth with bruising kisses. Benita kissed her back fiercely. Desire pooled between her thighs. Astrid swept her hand down, unzipped Benita's jacket. She slipped her hand inside and palmed her breast over her soft shirt. Her nipple hardened under her palm. Astrid rolled Benita's nipple between her thumb and forefinger. Benita dug her fingernails into the back of Astrid's neck. Astrid nipped Benita's lower lip, then soothed the spot with her tongue.

Benita's tight groans filled Astrid with want. Her proactive and calculated pushback was delicious and seductive. Astrid cupped Benita's generous ass, squeezed hard once, then swatted it. Her palm stung from the blow and Benita squealed. Her lips brushed Astrid's ear as she moaned her approval. Astrid smacked her ass again, muffling Benita's cries with a deep kiss. Astrid broke their kiss.

"Is that all I get?" Benita pouted.

Astrid pinched her ass hard. "Greedy, aren't you?"

"You have no idea." Benita wrapped her fingers in Astrid's hair and urged her into another kiss.

A loud cough made Astrid start. She broke off their kiss but held tight to Benita.

Petra stood on the path. "Sorry to interrupt, Astrid, but Benita is needed in the stable. Benita, Elaine is tending to Bruno's hoof and requires your assistance."

Astrid released Benita. "Of course."

Benita smirked as she passed Astrid the key. She twitched her hips before she rubbed her hand over her ass. "Enjoy your sauna, Mistress Astrid."

Petra rolled her eyes. "Stable. Now."

Benita ducked her head as she bolted past Petra but failed to stifle her laugh.

Chapter Twelve

"LET'S TAKE IT again, from the part where Carol leaves the bathroom and Therese is in front of the mirror. This is the payoff scene. We have watched them skate the edges of what they both want from the beginning of the movie. They are dealing with balancing their desires and fear of being rejected by the other at a time when women were denied agency in so many ways. Carol and Therese are both pushing back hard against their expected roles in society. The amount of trust it takes for anyone to ask for what they want sexually is immense, doubly so in this case because it is Therese's first time exploring her sapphic desires. In the same way a first-time client comes to us with a delicious combination of fear and desire, Therese knows what she wants from Carol and she has summoned her courage to ask for it. Use those client experiences to power Therese's character."

Tessa retied her black flannel robe. "Can we do the full scene this time? I'm afraid I'm going to get hung on the dialogue if we keep stopping at the lamp scene."

"All the way?"

Tessa drew the robe ties through her fingers, avoiding Astrid's gaze in the mirror. "Yes. Unless you don't want to."

"Tessa."

Tessa raised her head, turned to look at Astrid.

Astrid met her gaze. "I'm fine with doing a full run through. But I really want to work on this part. As sexy as the rest of the scene is, this first kiss is provocative. It is the key to the entire scene. We know Therese is a virgin. This scene is an incredible moment. When she asks Carol to take her to bed, it sets up everything after. Her eagerness and bravery in asking for what she wants, the way she rushes to the bed, almost running but not quite. I need you to not look like you know what you want, but still project confidence. I want you to remember what it was like to ache to be kissed by a woman, to dream of a woman touching you, even if you didn't know exactly what, or how things would go, or where it would lead. I need you to remember the zing that knocks all thoughts of anyone else from your mind. You need to project wanting someone so badly you don't care about the consequences."

Tessa closed her eyes, unable to meet Astrid's gaze. She had lived this scene with Astrid. Begged her to take her on as a submissive. How could Astrid be so calm about it? Tessa had never had a lover before Astrid, never experienced much beyond sloppy kisses with boys, and fumbling sweaty petting in parked cars. And now she and Astrid were going to reenact a precious moment in her life for others to experience? Tessa trembled, raw with emotion and fear.

Astrid rested her hand on her shoulder. Tessa kept

her eyes closed and leaned her cheek against the back of her hand. "Sorry, Astrid."

"Are you sure you want to continue?"

Tessa's heart squeezed. "Yes. I can do it. Give me a minute."

"Look at me, please."

Tessa opened her eyes. Astrid was a breath away. "When you came to me the first time, it was your first time, wasn't it?"

Tessa swallowed on a dry throat. "Yes."

"You were very brave. Do you remember what happened? What started our conversation?"

Tessa flushed. "I tripped and spilled a drink on you because I was staring at you."

"Yes. Red wine. All over my white pumps. You kneeled at my feet and attempted to dry them with a napkin. Do you remember what happened next?" Astrid cupped Tessa's chin, then ran her thumb over her lower lip.

"It made it worse. I offered to pay for them."

"Do you remember what I said?"

"That I was gorgeous on my knees, that my ass looked exquisite in my jeans, and if I really meant it, to meet you after my shift." Tessa focused on Astrid's ice-blue gaze. The world receded and she was twenty again, captured by the quiet power rolling off Astrid, ensnared in her charm and intensity.

"And you did. You got into my car. And in the back seat of that hired car, you let me kiss you, and then begged me to take you to my home, agreed to be mine for the night."

Tessa's clit throbbed with the memory of her first

night with Astrid, her mind awash in sensual memories. "I didn't go back to my apartment for three days."

Astrid brushed her lips over Tessa's mouth. "I need you to project the feeling you have right now." She pulled back and stared into Tessa's eyes. "That's what I need to see for this scene, the young woman who was so eager to be with me, she stripped naked in the back of my limousine and let me finger her, before she buried her head between my legs. The brave woman who let me give her a first taste of what love between women could be. Can you do that for me?"

Tessa inhaled slowly and exhaled, basked in Astrid's attention. "I can. I'm ready."

Astrid kissed her forehead. "That's my girl."

Tessa flushed with her praise, her heart squeezed tight. Astrid did remember, in exquisite detail, their first night together. Tessa had not been just another woman to Astrid.

*

"SCENE." ASTRID ADVANCED toward Tessa as she sat facing the mirror. She rested her hand on her shoulder and met her gaze in the glass. Her eyes locked on Astrid's and in that moment the fifteen years since their first night together evaporated. Her mind seized on Tessa's transformation. Her body surrendered to the memories of them.

Tessa turned, lifted her chin, her expression open, hopeful. Astrid bent to her mouth, slid her hand inside the flannel gown. She palmed her breast. Tessa arched into her touch.

Astrid groaned as she devoured Tessa's mouth. Tessa

opened to her, gave herself over to Astrid's greedy mouth. She broke the kiss, panted, her mind grasping for dialogue, for anything to ground her. Rehearsal, this was a rehearsal. "Take me to bed." Tessa stood, clasped her hand, and led Astrid to the bed. She lay back on the narrow mattress.

Astrid sat on the edge of the bed and tugged at the ties to the robe wordlessly. Tessa arched up to shed her robe as Astrid slipped hers off her shoulders. Tessa lifted her hands over her head and clasped the headboard. "Please."

Astrid smoothed her hands over her body, as if for the first time. And wasn't it? The first time she wasn't rushing through their scenes to keep from becoming mired in her feelings. She let go and gave in to her unscripted desires. Tessa squirmed as she touched her, arching into her hands.

Tessa's knuckles shone white where she gripped the headboard. Astrid slid her hand behind her head, clasped her neck as she took her mouth again. Tessa's tongue teased over her teeth, tentative at first, then bolder as she kissed back, leaving Astrid breathless. She thumbed Tessa's nipples as she broke their kiss.

Astrid stayed silent, afraid to break the spell. The scent of their desire rose, surrounded them. Astrid pressed her nose to the notch of Tessa's collarbones and inhaled the warm scent of her skin before she pressed another kiss to Tessa's mouth. Tessa's rough breathing was loud in her ear as Astrid bent to her breast. She took her nipple in her mouth. The soft crinkled flesh became turgid under her tongue.

Tessa whimpered as Astrid sucked hard, before switching to the other breast. Her mind tripped back, remembering what it had been like to introduce Tessa to pleasure beyond anything she had experienced before, to watch her unravel under her touch.

She scooted up into the bed and lay over Tessa. The sensation of having her under her ricocheted though her body. Tessa's eyes were wide, her mouth open as she panted. Astrid trailed her fingers over her belly, stopping to swirl a circle around her navel. She leaned down, kissed her deeply as she dipped inside, slid a single finger deep.

A groan rattled Tessa's chest as Astrid teased her finger in and out, gently, slowly, as she had done their first time together. Tessa's body clamped down on her finger, tightened. Astrid slid her thumb over Tessa's hard clit. A burst of wetness flowed over her hand as Tessa came with a filthy groan, her body trembling under Astrid's touch.

Desperate to taste her, Astrid slid down the bed, eased her finger from her body, and covered her with her mouth. She slid her hands under her ass, used her thumbs to hold her open as she licked slowly from her center to her clit. Tessa's muscles tensed under her hands as he she feasted on her, teasing her tongue over her labia, before she settled into licking slow circles around her clit.

Tessa's keening cry split the quiet as she came, her body curling up, shoulders lifting off the bed as she spilled her pleasure into Astrid's mouth. Astrid closed her eyes with the sensation of past and present melding. She held tight, pursed her lips, and sucked hard as Tessa thrashed under her. Another scream of satisfaction, then Tessa was pulling at her shoulders, dragging her up in the bed, her mouth everywhere she could reach as she rolled Astrid over on her back.

Her eyes glazed with passion, she clasped Astrid's

hands and forced them over her head as she rasped, "I want—"

*

"WHAT DO YOU want?" Astrid rubbed her thumb over Tessa's fingers.

"I want to taste you." Tessa nibbled at Astrid's lower lip. "Please."

Astrid shifted under Tessa, spread her legs wide as she held her gaze. "Take what you want."

Tessa settled her body between her legs. She let go of Astrid's hands, braced herself on her hands as she drew her body over Astrid's curves. The tips of their nipples brushed, sending a sharp wave of want crashing through her. Tessa lowered herself. She prowled down Astrid's body. Her hard nipples pressed against Astrid's body, her thighs were slick with desire, and need drummed a steady beat in her soul.

She took her time as she moved lower, lingering over Astrid's sublime breasts. She cupped their heavy weight and circled her nipples with the flat of her thumbs. With tiny nips and barely-there kisses, she explored their generous curves. Astrid's thick brown nipples were a contrast to her pale white skin. Tessa captured one in her mouth. She paused, letting her mind drift back over the years as she relived the first time she was allowed to give Astrid pleasure. How dizzy she had been, when she had finally been given permission to touch Astrid's tantalizing breasts.

Astrid groaned, cupped the back of her head, and pushed more of her breast into her mouth. Tessa opened her mouth, licked and sucked, greedy for more. She pressed Astrid's breasts together, nuzzled the soft channel between them. Astrid rocked her hips, her wet heat marking Tessa's belly. She wrapped her legs around Tessa, her heels settling on her back.

Tessa kissed her way down the gentle curves of Astrid's body. She brushed her mouth over the close-trimmed wet curls covering her clit before she settled between her legs. With both hands, she cupped Astrid's succulent ass. Her heels rested on Tessa's shoulders.

Tessa pressed the flat of her tongue over Astrid's clit, savoring the sweet taste of her excitement and the slick slide of her tongue over the hard bud. A memory surfaced, the first time she had given Astrid an orgasm, the sense of accomplishment and wonder, the rush of power as Astrid had surrendered to her.

She rubbed herself against the mattress as the coarse sounds of Astrid's breathing drove her on. She circled her tongue over her clit before she pushed her tongue inside, eager for more of Astrid. With long licks she gathered all the sweetness she could on her tongue. She opened her eyes, lifted her gaze. Astrid's eyes were closed, her hands wrapped around the lower rail of the headboard, her knuckles blanched white. Tessa moved her tongue in slow circles around her clit. Astrid's heels dug into her shoulders, urging her on.

Tessa covered her with her mouth. She teased the hood back and flicked her tongue softly over the thick clit.

Astrid's hip bucked, she groaned. "Finish me. Don't make me wait."

Tessa gripped her ass tighter, holding her in place as she deliberately slowed her motions, savoring the soft string of curses flowing from Astrid's lips as she begged her to continue, to make her come, to take everything.

It was a gift to Tessa's ears, one that stroked her need to exert power and control. She embraced it, the subtle role reversal tripping all her triggers as her switch nature rose up, seized what Astrid was offering with both hands. Astrid's heels drummed against her back as she writhed under Tessa's tongue.

Her chin and face were wet, slick with Astrid's want. At the precise moment Astrid shattered, she slid her thumb deep and stroked in and out. Astrid clenched around her thumb as she bucked and rocked against Tessa's face. Tessa followed her movements, held tight and continued to lick and suck her clit while she fucked her, guided by Astrid's moans and murmurs and requests for more. Astrid shook and trembled under her, muscles straining, deep groans and tight cries filling the room as she came again and again. Each surge of sweetness covered Tessa's chin and wet her hand.

Astrid patted her shoulder. "Enough. Oh, enough." Her knees fell wide and she released Tessa from her legs.

Tessa lifted her head. Astrid gazed into her eyes. With trembling fingers, she touched Tessa's cheek, then let them drift down to her lips. She wiped a thumb over her lower lip, gathered the wetness there. Astrid lifted her hand, rubbed the slickness over her nipples. Tessa launched herself upward, latched onto Astrid's nipple, and sucked hard as she rocked her pelvis into Astrid's hips. Astrid slid a hand between them. Tessa hollowed her stomach to give her room. She opened herself. Tessa lowered her body until their clits aligned. A shiver shook her frame at the contact as need rocketed through her with the first slick slide.

Astrid groaned and gripped her ass, pulling Tessa to her firmly. She held her in place as Tessa ground out her own pleasure with Astrid's hard nipple in her mouth. Sharp nails dug into her ass as Astrid urged her on.

Her belly tightened, and pleasure spiked through her with each roll of Astrid's hips. The sweet drag of clit on clit drove her on, as she fucked herself to her release, each thrust of her hips bringing her closer. Sweat stung her eyes as her orgasm bore down on her.

"Give it to me. Let me feel you come on me." Astrid panted as she rocked with Tessa.

Tessa popped Astrid's nipple from her mouth. Wet salacious sounds surrounded them. With a shout Tessa shattered, stroked on as pleasure spiraled out from her core. Astrid rolled her hips, teasing more from Tessa as she ground against her.

She lifted her legs and wrapped them around Tessa's hips, locking her heels over Tessa's waist. Tessa lifted her head, savored Astrid's wide-eyed gaze.

Astrid's lips peeled back as she gripped Tessa's shoulders. She dug her nails into Tessa's skin, the pain sharp and exquisite, reminding Tessa who was in charge.

"Fuck me. Now." Astrid's eyes were dark pools surrounded by a fine rim of blue.

Tessa shifted to her side, lowered her hand, and slid three fingers wide into Astrid's welcoming heat. She curled her fingers up, grazing them over Astrid's sweet spot.

"There. Right there." Astrid closed her eyes, her mouth open in a delicate *O* as she came with a gush and a silent scream. Tessa kissed her throat as she slowed her strokes, pulling more shudders and sighs from Astrid. She leaned back to look into Astrid's face. Her eyes were open, the blue brilliant as she met Tessa's gaze. A sensation of past and present melding washed over Tessa. Time blended into one long fuck--the years between them seemed a moment, their connection undeniable, stretched thin but never broken.

Astrid cupped her neck and drew her in for a kiss. She brushed her lips over Tessa's. Her brows drew down and she traced her finger over Tessa's mouth. "I missed you. Every single night we have been apart, I wondered, hoped you were happy wherever you were. I'm sorry. So sorry, my girl, for leaving you without telling you goodbye. You did nothing wrong. You were, are, the perfect lover. A sublime submissive any Mistress would be proud to call hers." She slipped a finger under Tessa's collar. "Rowan House has in you what every Mistress dreams of."

"Thank you, Ma'am." Tessa bit her cheek, the pain distracting her from her fears. Was Astrid saying goodbye? Praising Tessa to let her down easy?

Astrid smoothed her hand over her hair. "There is wild fear in your eyes. What are you afraid of?"

Tessa laid her head on Astrid's chest, pressed her ear against her chest, savoring the sound of her heartbeat. She held tight to the steady rhythm, closed her eyes before she spoke. "Of you leaving. Telling me what I want to hear so that I'll let you go when the time comes."

Astrid cupped Tessa's head and held her tight to her chest. "I'm not leaving, yet. I've a good chance of winning a position, don't you think?"

"And then what? I'm pledged to Rowan House." Tessa pushed herself out of Astrid's arms.

"If I'm offered a position here, wouldn't I also be expected to pledge to Rowan House?"

"Mistresses keep their independence. They are not expected to pledge. Their only pledges are to their personal submissives. Haven't you noticed Robin and Myfanwy wear different collars?"

Astrid sat up, clasped Tessa's hand, and kissed her knuckles. She peered into Tessa's face. "How does that work? Do they still see clients?"

"No. Well, Petra still sees clients. The rest don't."

Astrid rubbed her thumb over the back of Tessa's hand. "Are you wanting to stop seeing clients?"

"No. I like the adventure. And the fun of making people feel wanted and—"

"And loved?" Astrid arched her eyebrow.

"Accepted."

"What if I were offered a position here? Would you want to pledge to me?" Astrid laced their fingers together.

Tessa stared into Astrid's face. "And if you're not offered a position? What then?"

Astrid lifted her chin. "I wouldn't ask you to share my life if I can't keep you safe. No good Mistress would ever ask a submissive to risk their life for their own desires."

Tessa yanked her hand free from Astrid's grasp. "You still don't get it, do you? I don't care. I'd take a bullet for you. I'd lie down on broken glass so you wouldn't cut your feet." Tessa held Astrid's gaze. "And don't lie to me, or yourself, that you wouldn't do the same for me."

Astrid looked down and away before she returned her gaze to Tessa's face. She lifted her hand and traced a finger over Tessa's cheek. "That is why if I have to leave Rowan House, you can't go with me."

Tessa jerked back from her touch. "Fuck you. Fuck you and every other noble-minded Mistress who ever ground a submissive's heart under their high heel under the ruse of keeping them safe." She snatched her robe from the bed. "Get someone else for the rest of your audition."

Chapter Thirteen

"WHY? WHY NOW?" Elaine crossed her arms over her chest and leaned back in her chair. Her glower would have made a lesser woman cringe. It only added to Astrid's resentment. Elaine's arrogance stung.

Petra placed her hand on Astrid's shoulder, her touch grounding in the face of Elaine's simmering anger.

"As I said, I don't feel it's in Tessa's best interest to continue as my partner for this part of the audition." Astrid straightened her shoulders and met Elaine's glare with a cool stare. "I don't want to cause her distress. I feel continuing in the role will harm her emotionally."

Martha frowned. "You need to tell us more, Astrid. While we appreciate your concern for Tessa, we have no secrets from each other at Rowan House."

Elaine snorted. "What my sister means is, eventually we'll find out anyway. Tell us your side of what has transpired. If there was some problem with Tessa's behavior, we will address it."

"No. Tessa is perfect, utterly perfect." Astrid inhaled

deeply and exhaled slowly before she continued, "The fault lies with me. I had planned Therese's first experience scene from *Carol* as my mind-fuck audition, not considering that in this case, art would imitate life too closely."

She scanned the faces of the three Mistresses, gauging the effect of her words, assessing her audience. "It is not news to any of you that Tessa and I knew each other from before her time at Rowan House. We had more than a business relationship. What neither of us has admitted to any of you, is I was Tessa's first Mistress as well as her first experience with a woman. While rehearsing the scene, I overstepped with her, said things that should have remained unsaid. I hurt her. She has asked—" Astrid shifted her gaze from Elaine's harsh glare to Lucia's concerned expression. "—no, demanded, I find another sub for the last part of my audition."

"Astrid." Lucia's gaze pinned Astrid in place as if her feet were spiked to the floor. "Why didn't you tell us this when Tessa volunteered to be your sub?"

"I believed she and I had moved on from our time together. I was mistaken." Astrid's gut tightened. "My feelings for her are just as strong as they were. And she has expressed to me, on multiple occasions, she is still angry and hurt that I left as I did."

"And why did you end your relationship with her? You've not given a complete explanation. We need one now, and the truth if you want to continue your interview process." Lucia gestured to the chair on the other side of the wide desk she sat behind. "Sit. Tell us, now, the entire story, or your audition process will end this moment."

Sweat dampened her hair line. Astrid swiped at it with the flat of her wrist. Petra squeezed her shoulder once before she left her side to take a seat in the far corner of the room. Astrid sat across from the three women who would decide her fate.

"My birth name is Roxanne Zimmerman." She crossed her legs and straightened her shoulders. "Who, according to any records you will find, died tragically in a swimming accident off the coast of Belize. The body was never found. Fifteen years ago, as Mistress Roxanne, I ran an exclusive celebrity lookalike escort service. We were unique in that while my workers were all trained as sub-missives, most were switches. I met Tessa at a party. She was working for a catering service while she finished her theater arts degree." Astrid shifted in her chair and knot-ted her fingers together. "She spilled a glass of wine on my shoes and offered to pay for them to be cleaned. Smitten with her wide-eyed delectable innocence, I invited her to come home with me." Astrid paused as memories swamped her mind. "I trained her in the art of submission and taught her how to embrace her dominant side. With her incredible acting ability, she became my most in-de-mand escort. She has an uncanny ability to deliver exactly what a client needs even on those occasions a client doesn't know themselves."

Astrid swallowed the ache in her throat. "For three years, Tessa worked for me, all while pursuing her career in music and theater. She kept her own apartment, but shared my life, staying with me every moment she wasn't working." She blinked back angry tears. "It was going well. I had a client list that was expanding and money was roll-ing in. I had borrowed money from the Widow to start my service. I paid it all back with the ridiculous interest she charges ahead of schedule. That attracted her attention.

She gave me an ultimatum. Surrender my lucrative business and myself. Let her take control of my workers and give her my client list. She threatened to expose me to the police. She wanted to take possession of my workers, keeping the ones she fancied for herself, and planned to sell the others. She took Clarice, one of my workers, to make her point." A shudder rocked her body. "I still don't know what happened to her."

She paused until the ache in her chest subsided. "I had a very well-connected client who was able to provide me with a new identity. He assisted me in my escape to Belize. Once I was there, I became Astrid Lepler. Before I left Los Angeles, I broke off all contact with my workers, destroyed every record of my operation. I had a third party pay them in cash what they were owed and as much extra as I could afford."

"But Tessa was not just a worker." Martha's anger was palpable. "You walked out on her without an explanation? Left her to fend for herself knowing the Widow might abduct her?"

Astrid lifted her chin. "No. The Widow never obtained my worker list. She pretended to be a client, duped me into sending her Clarice. My workers were safe once the records were destroyed. Are you telling me you would have put Lucia or Myfanwy at risk? That I should have fought the Widow?" She held tight to her fury at Martha's judgment. "I am not privileged to have a sister at my back willing to kill for me—" she focused her glare on Martha. "—nor did I have family money to spend on protection. Or fucking anyone else who would have fought with, or for me. Until you face the Widow, alone, don't you dare tell me what I did was wrong." Astrid stood and swept her gaze over the group. "Now, does that satisfy everyone? I took a chance coming here. Now you know all of it do you understand why I never said anything? Why I want to be here? I am sick to death of worrying I'll step out of some hotel room some day and end up dead. Or worse."

"Tessa knew who you were and didn't tell us?" Lucia's tone was even.

"She recognized me. And kept my identity secret. She doesn't know why I left other than my vague explanation it was to keep her safe. She doesn't know all the details. Until today, I haven't told anyone all of it." Astrid glanced at Petra. "Not even you, Petra." She gripped the back of the chair as her anger drained away.

Elaine pushed back her chair. "I've heard enough." She walked around the desk and held her hand out to Astrid. "Will you give us a few moments to discuss how we would like to proceed?"

Astrid accepted Elaine's hand and let her lead her to the door. "I'll be in my room."

She inclined her head toward Petra before she left. In the hall, she turned toward the stairs as the grandfather clock struck noon. Astrid lifted her shoulders and let them fall, straightening her posture. She had faced the Widow and survived. She would survive this no matter what the Mistresses of Rowan House decided.

Chapter Fourteen

RAIN SPLATTERED AGAINST the tall library windows. The scattered drops turned into a soothing steady drumming. Tessa gathered the books from the return box and placed them on the wide wooden table. The warm smell of vellichor, the combination of scents that spoke of libraries and well-loved books, washed over her. She ran her hands over the various covers. She rubbed her fingers over a hardback copy of *Through the Looking-Glass*. The embossed cover was torn, and she set it aside for repair. Tessa sorted through the rest of the books. Worn paperbacks lay side by side with leather-covered hardbacks, mysteries nestled next to romances. Natural history volumes jostled for space alongside biographies. An eclectic combination of books as diverse as the women of Rowan House.

With practiced movements she sorted them, organizing them into stacks by their catalog numbers. The click of the door latch opening made her look up from her task.

"Oh no, my book is overdue." Benita flounced past

Tessa. "Want to paddle me?" She flipped her skirt up, revealing her lack of panties.

Tessa laughed in spite of her gloomy mood. "Again?"

Benita placed a worn paperback copy of *The Stone Gate* on the table. She crossed the room and looped her arms around Tessa's neck. "If my college librarian had been half as good as you are at warming my ass, I'd have had better marks."

Tessa snorted. "You graduated Magna Cum Laude from Brown."

"*Sim.* But I wanted to be valedictorian." Benita kissed Tessa's throat, the tender skin under her ear, before she pressed light kisses along her jaw. She leaned back and peered up at Tessa.

Tessa rested her hands on Benita's curves as she studied her tantalizing expression. Benita's warm brown eyes settled on her. Her humor was infectious. It was impossible to be in a bad mood with Benita around. A sharp pang of want rattled her. Benita would leave soon, off to spend time with her family.

Benita shifted her hand under Tessa's hair and played with the curls at the base of her neck. "So. You going punish me, or what?"

Tessa dug her fingers into the soft flesh of Benita's hips, enjoying the flare of desire that sparked in her eyes. "How late is your book?"

"Two weeks?" Benita traced her fingers over the collar of Tessa's shirt.

"Naughty girl. You're not sure, are you?" Tessa used her fingertips to draw Benita's skirt up, exposing her ass.

"*Não.*" Benita huffed her answer. She leaned up, caught Tessa's lower lip in her teeth, tugged gently before she released it.

Tessa held tight to Benita's ass and pulled her hard against her. She kissed her, savoring her passion, the familiar sensation of Benita in her arms, pushing to be spanked, teasing Tessa into giving her what she craved. Tessa squeezed and pinched her skin. "I've an awful lot of work to do before dinner prep."

"Bebê, don't make me wait." Benita pouted. She kissed Tessa's neck as she rubbed her palms over her breasts. Tessa's nipples tightened as Benita untucked Tessa's shirt from her pants. Her knuckles were warm where they brushed over Tessa's skin as she unbuttoned her shirt. Benita nipped her and soothed the spot with her tongue as she nuzzled Tessa's throat.

Tessa lifted her chin, giving Benita access to what she wanted. "Tell me how bad you've been, besides the library book. What else do you need to be punished for?"

"I left the cap off the toothpaste." Benita flicked Tessa's shirt open.

"After all the times I've reminded you?" Tessa pinched hard, drawing a squeal from Benita.

Benita's gaze burned as she thumbed Tessa's nipples over her bra and she peered into her face. "I touched myself."

"Did you?" Tessa held tight and turned them. She backed toward the long leather couch, taking Benita with her. When her calves pressed against the edge of it, she sat and tugged Benita down until she was lying over her lap. Benita rested her head on her folded hands. She toed off her shoes and wiggled until she was centered over Tessa's knees.

Tessa flipped her skirt up, exposing her fine curves.

She slid her hand up the inside of Benita's thigh, teasing her fingertip over her wet folds. "Tell me exactly what you did."

Benita rocked her hips. Tessa brought her hand down with a snap.

"Mmm." Benita sighed. "I licked my fingers."

Another swat.

"I rubbed my clit."

Tessa slid her hand between her legs. "Like this?"

"Oh, *sim*, just like that." Benita panted.

"Did you fuck yourself?" Tessa kept up her slow strokes over Benita's hard clit.

"Sim. I did. Hard."

"Naughty, aren't you?" Tessa pulled her hand free and swatted Benita's ass.

Benita groaned, arched her back, lifted her hips up. "So naughty. Punish me, Bebê."

Tessa spanked her then, alternating her blows, harder and then softer, driven by Benita's tight groans and pleading words until Benita's ass was dull red and Tessa's hand ached.

Benita's thighs were wet, her scent intoxicating. Tessa rolled her over, tore open her shirt, shoved her bra up with both hands. She cupped her breasts, filling her hands with them, circled her thumbs around her fat nipples. Benita's skirt was rucked up around her waist. Sweat dampened her hairline, her face was flushed, her eyes bright. Her shoulders rose and fell with her breathing. Tessa lowered her hand, plunged her fingers into her liquid heat as she lowered herself to her knees beside the couch. Benita lifted one leg, rested it on the back of the couch, and planted the other on the floor. "Suck me, Bebê.

Let me come for you."

Tessa covered her with her mouth. Three fingers wide, she thrust deep, curling them over the spot that made Benita thrash her hips, seeking more. She stared into Benita's dark eyes. Their gazes locked. Tessa pursed her lips, bobbed her head as she sucked Benita's clit. She flicked her tongue over the tip in time with her thrusts, rocking Benita's body with each stroke.

Eyes wide open, Benita bucked her hips into Tessa's mouth. Tessa wrapped her arm around her thigh and followed her movements. Benita screamed as she came, flooding Tessa's mouth and wetting her chin. Her body tightened around Tessa's fingers and blossomed, welcoming her strokes. Reverent moans and soft sighs echoed in the library over the sound of the rain.

Tessa held tight, savoring the light and love in Benita's eyes. She licked gently as she eased her fingers from Benita.

"Come up here, my librarian."

Tessa kissed her way up Benita's body until she lay over her. She sank into Benita's soft curves.

Benita petted her hair, held her tight against her breasts. "We're going to be in so much trouble for trashing this couch."

Tessa's laugh burbled from her. "We are." She laced their fingers together. "Who should we tell? Lucia, Martha, or Elaine?" Her pulse raced as she imagined the punishment each would dole out.

"Why don't we tell your amor?"

Tessa pushed herself up to peer into Benita's face. "You already know about the couch." She waited for her words to sink in.

Benita stilled. She reached up and cupped Tessa's face. The heat of her palm warmed Tessa's heart. "Your other amor, Bebê."

"It won't do any good." Tessa set her teeth on her lips.

Benita slapped her face gently. "None of that. She loves you. I see it. Why don't you see it?"

"She doesn't love me. She never did. She feels obligated. If it had been real, how could she have left me? Even now she is trying to protect me. She keeps secrets from me like I'm the naive young girl I was. She doesn't see me as I am now."

"So show her. Show her what you show me." Benita tugged her back down into a kiss. Bruising and pure.

Tessa soaked up Benita's love like a dry sponge and rained it back down on her, giving over to her as she rolled them over on the wide couch.

Benita sat up and straddled her. "I'm going to make you scream."

"Promise?"

"Promise." She grasped Tessa's belt buckle and yanked it open. She unbuttoned her pants, slid the zipper down. "Lift up."

Tessa obeyed. Benita lowered her pants and briefs to her knees.

The corner of her mouth lifted. "You are so wet." She gathered some on her fingers and showed them to Tessa before she licked them clean. "So sweet." She lowered herself until she lay over Tessa's legs. She nuzzled her belly, tickled the creases of her thighs with her tongue. "Tuck your hands behind your head."

Tessa knotted her hands behind her head. She raised her hips. Desire coiled in her belly as her clit throbbed.

"Lick me. Now."

Benita licked a long slow stroke over her clit. "Like this?"

"Just like that." Tessa strained against her pants, desperate to spread her legs wider for Benita.

Benita blew warm air over her clit. "You're so thick. I love the way you feel in my mouth." She used her hand to expose Tessa's clit. With tiny flicks of her tongue, she teased the tip.

Tessa squirmed as pleasure surged through her. Each touch of Benita's tongue was exquisite torture. She closed her eyes, concentrated on relaxing, not coming too soon. Benita hummed around her, the vibrations making Tessa shudder and shake with the need to come. She fought to hold out. Another touch of Benita's tongue and she lost her battle. Screaming, she came. Tessa grabbed Benita's head, held her there, while Benita continued her gentle touches as she drove her up again.

The echoes of Tessa's screams reverberated off the coffered ceiling. Benita eased back, placed kisses over her clit and her belly. Tessa tangled her fingers in Benita's soft curls and tugged her up. Benita lay over her. She folded her hands on Tessa's chest. Tessa traced the fine lines around her eyes with her fingertip. "I think my soul left my body."

Benita's rich laugh spilled from her. She shook her curls back. "Told you I would make you scream."

"You certainly did."

Tessa craned her neck to follow the sound of the voice. Astrid sat with one hip on the desk, her arms crossed over her chest. Her black riding boots gleamed in the light. A riding crop lay across her lap.

A flush burned Tessa's cheeks. She struggled to move off the couch. Benita shifted her weight, pinning her in place.

Benita turned her head. "Like what you saw, Mistress Astrid?"

"Very much." Astrid lifted her eyebrow. "Tessa, I informed the other Mistresses of your request for someone else to finish my audition." Astrid looked toward the ceiling before she brought her gaze back to Tessa's face. "I also said some things that maybe I shouldn't have. So while I await their decision about my future as an applicant, I had planned on asking you to join me for a ride in the indoor ring so we could discuss how we should proceed if I'm allowed to continue. But I think spending an afternoon in the library with both of you is much more appealing."

Chapter Fifteen

ASTRID SAVORED BENITA'S and Tessa's disheveled clothes and flushed faces. The delicious scent of their lovemaking combined with the rich smell of books. A tendril of desire wove its way along her spine. The heady sensation of her stolen observation of their lovemaking enthralled her. The thought of soothing herself with their sublime submission bubbled up, only to be squelched by her determination to accomplish the task she had set for herself.

"What did you have in mind, Mistress?" Benita toyed with the edge of her skirt, lifting it slightly and exposing herself briefly, her wary tone a complete mismatch for her flirty behavior.

Tessa's pensive expression pricked her heart. Astrid shifted her gaze to the carpet.

"Only whatever both of you are comfortable with." Astrid left her perch on the desk. She sat across from them in a wide wingback chair.

Tessa lifted her chin. "What if we aren't comfortable

with any physical interaction with you?"

"Then that's that. I would never force myself on anyone. Nor would I want to interfere with your time with each other. My original intent stands." Astrid worked on keeping her tone neutral as she met Tessa's hard glare. "I need to talk to you, Tessa. If for no other reason than you deserve the truth about why I left." She inhaled deeply and exhaled slowly, willing herself calm. She could do this. Had to do this. Now, before she was forced to leave. She owed Tessa that much. Owed her so much more than she had given the woman before her, who had confessed her desire to be Tessa's pledged submissive.

Astrid observed Benita as she clasped Tessa's hand in both of hers and held it to her chest. A lover's gesture. The love between them palpable with the intimate body language and tender glances between them. And yet Tessa had asked, said, she wanted to pledge to her.

Did Tessa not see Benita's love? Astrid's heart ached for Benita, for the two of them. They had what anyone could ever want, another person who loved you for everything you were, not just what they wanted you to be. She picked at the seam of her pants as she waited for Tessa to respond.

"Why now?" Tessa lifted her chin. "Why couldn't you tell me before?"

Astrid laid the crop across her knees. "Because I thought I might have time to tell you later, after, if I—no matter. Because I wasn't ready. I may not be here after today and I want you to know all of it."

"Benita's not leaving." Tessa lifted her chin in challenge.

"I wouldn't want her to." Astrid straightened her

shoulders. "I don't think lovers should keep secrets."

Tessa snorted. "Like you're an expert on love? Like I'd take any relationship advice from you? And what does it matter now? If you're leaving don't let the door hit your ass on the way out."

Astrid flinched. "I didn't say voluntarily." She tucked a wayward lock of hair behind her ear. "I have the feeling after my conversation with the other Mistresses that when I return to my room my bags will be packed and Millie will be waiting to escort me off the property."

"Let her speak, Bebê." Benita lifted Tessa's hand and pressed a kiss to the back of it. "You owe it to yourself to listen."

Tessa pulled her hand free from Benita's grasp. She scowled at Astrid as she righted her clothes. She stood and pulled her briefs and pants up. After her trousers were belted and her shirt buttoned, she sat next to Benita. Tessa crossed her arms over her chest. "Fine. So tell me. Tell why you left. Make it make sense to me."

"I can't do that." Astrid rolled the crop over her knees. "I can only tell you the truth. Tell you what my intentions were. What you do with that information is up to you."

Tessa quirked her mouth, lifted her hand, and made a *go on* gesture. Her expression shuttered. Where her eyes had once held warmth and love, visible every time she looked at Astrid, there was nothing. Astrid shivered under Tessa's cold gaze. She braced her elbows on her knees and spun her story. She told Tessa everything. All of it. From the moment the Widow had contacted her until she had assumed her current identity, details of her life on the run, and how she had come to apply at Rowan House, skipping nothing.

Tessa's expression never changed, her flint-hard gaze fixed on Astrid's face. She held her shoulders rigid, her feet flat on the floor in sharp contrast to Benita.

Benita's expressions morphed with each part of Astrid's tale. Shock, anger, horror, and in the end tenderness when Astrid had finished her story. Astrid turned her attention to the shelves that lined the walls, unable to tolerate her pitying expression.

The rain outside had slowed, a drizzle now instead of a downpour. Astrid peered out of the window as dark clouds scuttled from the sky. Her back ached from her position. She stood, stretched her arms over her head. She crossed to the floor-to-ceiling windows with her back to Tessa and Benita. The silence clawed at her. Screaming or tears would have been less painful than Tessa's continued silence. Did she think it all lies? That Astrid was fabricating the Widow's threats to her life in order to excuse her behavior? The chill from the window seeped into her body. Would Tessa ever speak? Acknowledge she had heard, even if she didn't want to understand.

Remorse settled over her like a sopping blanket. Wet and heavy, it bore down on her. Tessa's response would be what it would be. No more no less. And Tessa would have Benita at her side to help her navigate her feelings. Astrid and their time together would become a bad memory.

Astrid chewed her lip. What would it be like? To have a lover who was a sanctuary from the world. She had thought she and Tessa were moving toward that when she left her behind. Astrid had entertained herself imagining what might be with Tessa and Benita more than one night since her arrival at Rowan House. A fanciful dream.

Her actions had squelched whatever chance she had ever had for a relationship with someone who truly loved her, loved her for who she was, not who she could pretend to be. She loved Tessa. Loved her now, even more than before. The strong woman Tessa had become was even more beguiling than the girl Astrid had fancied.

Astrid stared out of the window. In the distance, the clouds covered the mountains, promising more rain. The dark scuttling clouds matched her mood. Unaccustomed to self-pity, she shoved aside her hurt at Tessa's continued silence. She seized her anger at the Widow and held tight. Hate for the woman bubbled steadily in her soul. Another opportunity with Tessa lost because of the threat of the Widow. Astrid would do whatever she needed to do to protect Tessa. Even if that meant grinding her own heart under her heel.

Astrid knotted her hands together behind her back. A drop slid down the pane of glass. Astrid tracked its path until it bumped into other drops, grew larger as it raced to the edge of the glass before disappearing from her view. The click of the library door opening and closing made her turn. Only Benita remained.

Astrid pressed her lips together to keep from calling Tessa's name, willed herself not to chase after her.

"Give her time, Astrid. Tessa's never been in a bad situation." Benita stood and buttoned her blouse and smoothed down her skirt. "She's had a charmed life. Never had to worry about anything but herself. She doesn't understand hard decisions. The Widow is nothing but whispered tales to her." Benita crossed the room. She stopped a few steps away and rested her hands on her hips. "She loves you. Don't doubt that. I see it in her eyes every time she's with you or talks about you. And you love her, no matter what you tell yourself. I sense it between you."

Astrid's heart squeezed hard. "You love her, too, Benita. Any idiot with eyes can see she loves you as well. Why aren't you pledged to each other?"

"Because she hasn't asked." Benita's harsh tone stung.

"Sorry." Astrid studied Benita's expression, the stark pain in her eyes.

"Oh, she does all the little things that make it seem like she loves me. Acts like she does. But she's never said the words to me. Ever. Every year when I pack for my vacation she mopes. But never once has she asked me to stay. Or to go with me." Benita lifted her shoulders and let them fall. "We are friends. Friends with plenty of benefits." A wistful expression crossed Benita's face as she moved closer to Astrid. "And even if she did love me like that, I can't be everything she needs. She can't give me all I desire in a Mistress. She lets me get away with things. She's a top but no Mistress." Benita rested her hands on her hips and raked her gaze over Astrid. "I need a Mistress who can handle my top from the bottom style. Someone who won't let me get away with anything. I'll work with you for your last audition. If you get to stay."

Astrid met Benita's bold assessment with one of her own. "Thank you. But why?"

"I love her. If you go, she'll be miserable. I want her to be happy." Benita stepped closer, rose up on her toes, and dared to press a kiss to Astrid's cheek before she lowered herself. She peered into Astrid's eyes as she flattened her hand over Astrid's chest and flicked her nipple with her thumb. "And I want to be happy."

Astrid caught her hand, squeezed her wrist hard before she twisted her hand behind her back. She pulled Benita hard against her and wrapped her hand in her hair, yanking her head back to expose her throat. The banked fire of desire within Astrid exploded with want. Need sparked in her soul, a fierce desire to punish Benita for touching her without permission.

She squeezed her fingers tighter and tugged her arm higher, rewarded by Benita's sharp intake of breath. Astrid reveled in the sensation of Benita's nipples hardening under the thin shirt where her body pressed against Astrid.

"Testing me again? Trying to piss me off so I'll fuck you?"

Benita closed her eyes briefly and relaxed in Astrid's arms, a subtle surrender as she gave in to Astrid's grip. "What are you going to do about it?"

"Not give you what you want. Make you wait, until you understand I make the rules, Benita." Astrid tightened her grip in Benita's hair. She bent her head and brought her lips close to her ear. "I can't wait to take you apart and put you back together." Astrid released Benita, savoring her heavy-lidded expression.

Benita widened her eyes and met Astrid's gaze. "Mmm. That's what I need, Mistress. Someone who won't let me get away with anything. Someone who will melt me down like a candle when I push them." She brushed her lips over Astrid's mouth and backed away. "Maybe someone like you."

"That's three."

Benita lifted an eyebrow. "Three."

"Three times you've touched me without permission. What do you think to gain by pushing me?"

"Everything." Benita stepped out of Astrid's reach before she turned and left the library.

Astrid touched her lips. A flare of hope and desire burned through her.

*

"GIVE ME WHATEVER else you need prepped." Tessa poured the diced carrots into a bowl. A kettle of vegetable stock bubbled on the stove, the scent soothing. Tessa relaxed into the intimacy of the kitchen. Its familiar sounds and smells were a balm for her battered heart.

She had spent last night alone, sleeping on a couch in the large playroom, too embarrassed to return to the room she shared with Benita. Her guilt had blossomed after she spent the morning avoiding her. She had waited until she had left for her barn shift to shower and change.

Robin had lifted her eyebrows when Tessa had appeared asking for work, but she had not questioned her, simply passed her the list of prep that needed to be accomplished for the day. As much as she loved her library work assignment, when Tessa needed solace, the kitchen was her temple.

Robin pushed three onions toward her. "Last thing. I need the two small ones cut into thin half-moons, and the large one small dice. Make the half-moons pretty. They're going on top of the onion poppy bread."

Tessa took up the onions and placed them on the cutting board. She focused on her task. The familiar ritual of helping Robin prepare food settled over her, grounded her as she turned Astrid's story over in her mind. The hair on the back of her arms rose as she thought about Clarice, the woman the Widow had snatched to send a warning to Astrid.

It could have been Tessa. Or even Astrid herself. Dread saturated her as she thought of the stories Benita told of her time on the streets before Rowan House. She paused in her chopping to stop her spiral. It would be different if someone tried to snatch her now. Her training with Millie left her feeling more than capable of protecting herself. And anyone else who needed it.

She glanced up at Robin. Her chef coat sleeves were rolled back. In the overhead light, the faint scars of her former addiction littered her arms—hard evidence of Robin's struggles and the reality of being trafficked. Guilt tugged at Tessa. She had never known any of what so many of the workers at Rowan House had experienced. Astrid's training and sheer luck had led her to a Rowan House audition. She had been spared all of it. She had the privilege of shedding her homophobic family and living a safe and happy life where she was cared for and loved just as she was. The Mistresses and her clients made her feel irresistible, special, treated her as a valuable person. They cherished her for who she was, and how she made them feel.

"Don't worry." Robin cut the dough she was kneading in half and tossed flour on the work bench.

"Easy for you." Tessa peeled the papery skin from the onion.

"Not always. But Elaine's not going to let Astrid leave here unless Astrid requests it. Petra wants her here. And that means Elaine will do whatever she has to, to make it happen."

"Even going against Lucia and Martha?"

"If she puts it to them the way I imagine she will, they won't defy her." A half chuckle escaped her. "The only person she defers to is Petra."

"And you."

Robin flushed. "Okay, yes. But that's not deferring so much as respecting my opinion and spoiling me."

Tessa sliced the onions in paper-thin half-moons. "I need to talk to Astrid. And Benita. I'm so embarrassed. I'm an ass for flouncing out of the library. I slept in the large playroom last night because I couldn't even face Benita."

"You're not an ass. From what Elaine shared with me, Astrid was acting with your best interest in mind. As far as things with you and Benita go. She knows you. She gets it when you need to be alone to work things out." Robin shaped two loaves and placed them on the bench in front of her. "You have my onions?"

Tessa gathered the delicate half-moons into a pile and slid the cutting board toward Robin. "Here. Are they thin enough?"

"Perfect." Robin placed the onion slices over the bottom of the forming basket and settled the bread dough on top of them gently.

Tessa watched her work. "Your bread is always so pretty." She chewed her lower lip. "Astrid lost so much. To protect me. I can't even imagine what it cost her to disappear."

"Thank you. Not just you. Don't take all of that one. Anyone who operates a service knows the risks. Astrid did what she did to protect you and the others as well as herself."

"Will Elaine really be okay with her staying?" Tessa set the knife aside and wiped at the tears the scent of onions stirred.

"Why don't you ask me what you really want to ask me?"

Tessa picked up the large onion and cut it in half. "I don't want to pry."

Robin covered the loaves with a damp towel and placed them into the proofing cabinet. "It's not prying. And it's all good between us. Now. Elaine and Petra and I are solid." She crossed the room and washed her hands. Tessa sliced the final onion in half. She turned each half, cut it lengthwise before she sliced it crosswise, creating small dice.

Robin came to stand across from her. Tessa paused and glanced up.

"Elaine has been—" a bright red blush covered Robin's face and her eyes sparkled. "—exceptionally attentive in the last few weeks. And Petra has been so—it's been as if we were on our honeymoon again."

"You have to tell me everything, please. I love good sex stories. And yours are always the best."

"How much time do you have?" Robin glanced at the kitchen clock. "I don't have anything else to do until half three."

"As much time as you need to tell me all the delicious things you three have been up to." Tessa finished with the onion in front of her. "Let me clean this up and make us some coffee."

"Want a lemon tart? I have two I've saved."

"Yes. Please."

Robin bustled over to the chiller. Tessa studied her

back. So petite, submissive to the bone, so many would underestimate the quiet strength that radiated from Robin. A wave of affection washed over her for her friend.

"Hey, Robin?"

"Yes?"

"Thanks."

Robin turned from the refrigerator with the two plates in her hands. "Of course, I know lemon is your favorite."

"No. For the other. For just being you. For helping me stay calm."

"You're welcome. But you have to promise me something."

"Can I hear what it is first?"

"No."

"Okay."

"Good. Now promise me no matter what the Mistresses decide you will talk with Astrid and tell her everything you just told me."

"Why would she listen to me? I've acted like a selfish bratty ass."

"No. You acted on the information you had to go on. You believed you had been abandoned. Done something so wrong your Mistress turned you away without explanation. Now you know the truth you can have an honest conversation with her." Robin placed the plates on the table. "It took Petra to get Elaine and I to acknowledge how we felt about each other. You need to talk to Astrid. And Benita. You've been dodging that too. You need to tell them both about how you feel. Or you'll have regrets and questions the rest of your life."

Tessa covered her face with her hands. "I hate talking.

I never know what to say. And then I panic and just bolt." Robin reached across the table and peeled Tessa's hands from her face. She held them tight as she spoke. "Just tell the truth. For once. To yourself and to them. Trust them to love you enough to listen. Because they do." Robin released her and pushed the coffee press toward Tessa. "Use the red tin. Petra had it shipped from Vietnam and it's amazing."

"You could write an advice column." Tessa slid the red tin close to the press.

"It'd take time away from my cooking. And my Mistresses." Robin touched her collar, decorated with a large R with Elaine and Petra's initials intertwined. The kettle clicked off. "Hurry up now or I'll have to skip some parts."

Chapter Sixteen

ASTRID STARED AT her book unseeing. Her eyes burned. She left the bed and made her way to the chair by the fire. She tucked her feet up under her gown before she pulled a lap robe over her legs. The mantel clock chimed three. Her stomach rumbled and she pressed her hands against her belly, annoyed with herself for skipping dinner. Unwilling to call for her meal, she had satisfied herself with her last protein bar. That was long gone as was her stash of other snacks she had stowed in her luggage.

The low gas flames danced and flickered. The subtle ache in her belly grew annoyingly strong. No way she would be able to wait until breakfast. And no way she could fall asleep. She stood and stretched before she picked her robe up from the bed and donned it. One pair of slides later and she was on her way to the kitchen.

The house was quiet, the whisper of her slippers over the carpet loud to her ears. She held tight to the railing on the staircase. The glow of nightlights along the baseboards lit her way as she traveled to the kitchen. She had no idea if it was forbidden but how much more trouble could she be in? The superb meals she had been served since her arrival would be high on the list of things she would miss most if they turned her out.

Tessa would be at the top. Once again snatched from her by a turn of events Astrid was not in control of. Some Mistress she was. Unable to hang on to a submissive or control her own life.

The last hallway was unlit and as dark as her thoughts as she carefully worked her way to the kitchen doorway with one hand on the wall. The swinging door creaked on its hinges as she pushed it open. In the kitchen, she groped a path along the wall until she found a panel of switches. She tried them all before she found one that lit the kitchen table.

A chill settled over her as she opened the wall cabinets in search of something to satisfy her until breakfast. In a cabinet over the kettle, she found a tin of biscuits. She placed them on the counter and popped the lid. Her mouth watered as the rich scent of vanilla and chocolate rose from the box.

"You need to leave the chocolate ones for Elaine or there will be hell to pay."

Astrid yipped and spun toward the sound.

Dressed in a short sleeve chef's coat and checked pants, Tessa smirked as she leaned against the doorframe.

"You scared the hell out of me. What are you doing here?"

"Since I excused myself from your service my normal work assignment is here. I promised Robin and Myfanwy I'd do today's baking." Tessa crossed the kitchen, opened an oven, and peered inside, before she closed the door and switched it on. She repeated the procedure with the second oven.

"You're a chef? I thought you were the librarian?" Astrid pulled a plain biscuit from the tin.

"I'm many things. Most of us have two positions and we can all fill in anywhere we are needed. Although we work hard to keep June out of the kitchen. She hasn't figured out the smoke alarm is not a timer. I didn't go to cooking school, but I can hold my own in a kitchen." Tessa moved to the sink and filled the kettle. She replaced it on its base before switching it on.

Astrid munched her biscuit as Tessa moved around the room, turning on more lights and gathering supplies. "So tell me, please. I want to know. What happened after I left? How did you end up here?"

"Why now?" Tessa pressed her lips together.

"I might not get another chance." Astrid plucked a second biscuit from the tin.

"If you're going to spoil your breakfast with biscuits, at least get a plate and stop scattering crumbs over my counter." Tessa snagged a plate from a cabinet and shoved it in Astrid's direction along the counter.

Astrid selected two more biscuits from the tin, avoiding the chocolate ones. She placed them on the plate. After replacing the lid, she returned the box to the cupboard.

"Sit down so you're not in my way." Tessa inclined her head toward the wide kitchen table. She pulled a canister from the cabinet. "Coffee?"

"I don't want to make extra work for you."

"I'm making it for myself. If you want some tell me, else I'll just fix enough for me."

"Coffee would be wonderful." Astrid placed the plate

on the table and sat opposite Tessa.

Tessa worked efficiently setting up the pot. While the kettle heated, she assembled her ingredients and created an egg wash. Wordlessly she set the bowl and a silicon pastry brush on the bench top. The muscles in her forearms bunched and flexed as she lifted full trays loaded with several loaves of bread in shaping baskets. Returning to the cabinet, she carried two half trays of rolls to the bench and lined them up next to the other trays. Astrid took advantage of Tessa's focus to study her as she worked, delicately unmolding the bread from their forms. The tip of her tongue peeped from between her lips as she carefully brushed the egg wash over two round loaves. Delicate half-moon onion slices covered the top in a repeating pattern.

Astrid rested her palms on the table. Wide with thick planks and dark with age, small scratches and nicks covered its surface. A relic as solid and as old as the house. The kind of thing one owned when you weren't moving every three weeks. The kind of thing you had in a home.

Not the kind of thing she ever hoped to have. A home. Nor a level of comfort as solid as Tessa demonstrated, confident in her work and her place. A pit of yawning need opened wide in her soul. How could she ever consider asking Tessa to give up the security of Rowan House for a life on the run with her?

The kettle clicked off, startling Astrid from her rumination. Tessa filled the coffee press before she returned to the worktable. Astrid satisfied herself watching Tessa's deft movements as she turned the proofed bread out onto trays to bake. The decorative swirls of the rising baskets shone after she applied the egg wash. A chime sounded.

Tessa carried the bread trays over to the oven.

"Get yourself some coffee and pour one for me, please. Cups are in the cabinet over the kettle." Tessa placed the trays inside the oven and closed the door gently. She repeated the procedure with the trays of rolls.

"Still take it black?"

Tessa paused and cocked an eyebrow. "You remember?"

"I remember a great many things about you." Astrid poured two cups of coffee and carried them back to the table. She placed one in front of her chair and the other directly across from her. "Did you ever go back to Oildale? Mend things with your family?"

"No. Didn't see the need. My folks wanted to pretend I never existed, so I made it easy for them." Tessa pulled out a chair, placed a timer on the tabletop next to her. "What do you really want, Astrid? Forgiveness? For me to say it's all right and we can start again?"

"No. I expect it's too late for that. What I would like, if you're willing, is for you to tell me about your life after I left."

"What does it matter?" Tessa blew across her coffee before taking a sip.

"It matters. To me. You matter to me. If you don't want to tell me, that's fine. If my being here distresses you, causes you pain, I'll leave you alone. I'll withdraw my application this morning." Astrid shifted her gaze to the clock. "Although I'll wait until a decent time to do it." She stood and pushed her chair closer in to the table. "It was never my intention to hurt you."

"But you did."

"I did." Astrid rested her palms on the top rung of the

chair back. "And I am so very sorry. You deserved better from me."

"Sit down." Tessa sipped her coffee and set her cup aside. "You'd withdraw your application. Give it all up just like that? For me?"

Astrid dragged the chair away from the table and perched on the edge. "Yes." She traced her finger over the wood grain of the table. The scent of baking bread surrounded them. A warm homey smell.

Tessa placed her hand on top of Astrid's, stilling her movement. "I waited. Expected you to call. To tell me where to meet you. I'm not stupid. I figured something had happened to make you run. I'm glad I never heard of your faked death. I'd have gone crazy. Well, crazier than I did." Tessa released Astrid's hand and scrubbed her hand over her chin. "After six months my savings were gone. I took a job with a woman I met at a fetish party. She was a collector of first editions and pretty girls. I was one of five. Her business was international. We traveled the fashion circuit. Worked as party favors. I learned I liked being in charge of a scene as much as I do being on my knees. On a trip to Italy, I met Elaine. I was tired of traveling. Even haute couture and top tier hotels grow old. I said as much during a party. And after a night I'll never forget, Elaine convinced me I could make a lot more money and find what I was looking for at Rowan House. She gave me her card and encouraged me to apply." Tessa paused and sipped her coffee.

Astrid folded her hands in her lap. "And you did."

"Not right away. But I couldn't get her, or what she said out of my head. Four months later I called the private number she had given me."

Astrid touched her face in the location of Tessa's scar. "And the scar?"

Tessa rolled her eyes before she answered. "You've noticed the transoms over some of the doors? I had an unfortunate encounter with one. I stumbled trying to adjust it, hit it with the transom wand, and shattered it. I was lucky one of our guests at the time was a plastic surgeon or the scar would have been worse. Anything else you want to know?"

"Regrets?"

"Only that I didn't leave with Elaine when she first asked me." The timer chimed. Tessa left the table and took the dinner rolls from the oven. Astrid finished her biscuit as Tessa moved the rolls to wire cooling racks.

Astrid sipped her coffee now gone cold. Tessa moved to the second oven, cracked the door open, and stared at the bread. She closed the door and returned to the table. She reset the timer.

Tessa set the timer aside and shifted in her chair. She crossed her arms over her chest. "Are you satisfied? Any more questions you want to ask?"

"When will you tell Benita you love her?"

Tessa's brows drew down. "She knows. Not that it's any of your business."

"Does she?" Astrid stood and carried her coffee and plate to the sink. "Should I leave this here."

"Put it to the left of the sink. And what do you mean?"

"Never assume, Tessa. You of all people should know that. Never assume anyone knows how you feel about them if you're not willing to say the words out loud." The timer chimed. "Thanks for the coffee. And for talking to me."

"That's it? You're just leaving?" Tessa spoke over her shoulder on her way to the oven.

"Unless you give me a reason I should stay."

"Sit your ass back down, Ma'am, and I'll give you two." Tessa placed the bread trays on top of the stove.

Astrid hid her smile behind her hand. This version of Tessa was intriguing. A flicker of hope flared in her chest. "All right." She pulled her chair out and waited while Tessa moved the bread to the wire racks.

Chapter Seventeen

HEAT ROSE IN Tessa's face as she slid the loaves of bread to the racks. She hadn't expected Astrid to stay. Not after she had spoken to her the way she had. And now what was she going to say? Tell Astrid she loved her? That she loved Benita? That she wished Astrid had trusted Tessa enough to turn to her when she was in trouble?

A shiver raced through her as she thought of poor Clarice. Distracted and in a hurry, she bumped her wrist against the edge of the hot pan as she carried it back to the stove top. She swore and yanked away from the pain. The pan crashed to the floor. Before she could turn to the sink, Astrid was at her side.

"How bad is it?" Astrid shoved the tap on full, gripped Tessa's elbow, and pushed her wrist under the cool water.

"I'll live. Fuck, that hurts." Tessa peered at her reddened skin.

"You never did like pain." Astrid let go of Tessa's elbow. "Do you have any burn cream?"

"Still don't. Third drawer down in the chest is a first

aid kit." Tessa kept the burn under the water.

"Got it." Astrid held the blue and white kit up.

"I don't think it's too bad." Tessa shut the tap and dried her arm gently. She tossed a side towel at Astrid. "Put the pan on the stove, please."

Astrid used the towel and placed the tray on the top of the stove.

"The tube is green and white."

Astrid bent over the first-aid kit and rummaged through it. "Is this it?" She held up the squat tube of burn cream.

"Yeah." Tessa sat in her chair and held her arm out. The irregular blotch was an angry red. "Myfanwy is always after me to wear long a long-sleeve coat."

Astrid washed her hands before she scooted her chair closer. "Ready?" She squeezed a bit of the cream over the burn.

"There is some cling film in the drawer, we can cover it with that so it doesn't stick."

Astrid followed Tessa's instructions as she bandaged her burn.

Tessa studied Astrid's hands as she tended to her. Gentle hands. Loving hands. Did she love Tessa? She had never said. Never claimed to in the time they were together.

"There." Astrid sat up straight. She replaced the contents of the first aid kit back inside the blue and white box.

"Thank you."

Astrid left her chair next to Tessa's. Their knees touched. "You said something about giving me reason to stay, if I'm allowed."

Tessa clasped Astrid's hands in her own. "Because I

want you to. Because I want to see if what we once might have had is still possible. Is that enough?"

Astrid squeezed tight. "More than enough."

Tessa released her hands. She lifted them slowly and dared to cup Astrid's face. Astrid held her gaze. "Are you waiting for permission?"

"No." Tessa leaned in and kissed Astrid. She slid one hand behind her neck and held her in place as she teased her tongue over her lips until she opened to her. Astrid moaned and clasped Tessa's shoulders, urging her closer. Tessa broke their kiss. Astrid's pale skin was flushed, her eyes bright.

"If you're going to say no, say it now." Tessa studied her expression.

"If I was going to say no, I would never have agreed to stay."

Tessa knotted her hand in Astrid's hair. "I'm going to have you the way I've wanted to since you got here."

"Are you?" Astrid swallowed visibly.

"Yes." Tessa arched her head back and kissed her throat.

"Right here?" Astrid lifted her chin, giving Tessa access to her neck.

"Right now." Tessa kissed her way to Astrid's jaw before she stood. She stepped back. "Strip. Then bend over and brace your forearms on the table."

Astrid glanced at the clock, her eyes wide.

"No one will be here until six. We have plenty of time." Tessa plucked a thin metal ruler from the kitchen desk and tapped it against her palm. "Quit stalling."

Astrid lifted her trembling hands to the belt of her robe.

"Wait." Tessa held her hand up.

"What?" Astrid paused.

"Something I've always wanted to know."

Astrid lowered her hands. "Yes?"

Tessa crossed the room and gripped her chin hard, enjoying the flare of heat in Astrid's eyes. "Your safe word?"

Astrid held Tessa's gaze. "Mercy."

"Mercy. I can't wait to hear it. Now do what I said."

Astrid toed off her slippers before she untied her robe and placed it over the back of the chair. She inched up the hem of her silk gown, then she stripped it off and added it to the pile. She bent at the waist, slid her panties off, and kicked them to the side. A quick glance over her shoulder at Tessa, then she was leaning over the table, braced on her forearms. She took a half step and widened her stance. Her desire gleamed in the light, on display just for Tessa. The heady scent of her need was enticing and rich.

Tessa grew wet and her clit ached as she watched Astrid obey her commands. "Spread your legs wider. Show me how much you're enjoying this."

Astrid widened her stance. Her glistening labia were a deep pink and swollen. Tessa placed the ruler on the table in Astrid's line of sight before she traced a finger down the wet seam and brought it to her mouth. Astrid gasped with her touch. Tessa stepped close and pushed her hips against Astrid's.

She wrapped her hands around her hips and dug her fingers into her soft curves. "What I wouldn't give for my strap right now. I love how you look like this. There is nothing like fucking a Mistress. Making them beg you to do it. Hearing them shatter under you. Begging for release." She slid her hand lower and teased Astrid's thick clit as she rocked against Astrid's ass, rubbing hard against her. "You'd like that, wouldn't you? You want me to run this scene. So you can be free to just feel." She punctuated each statement with a thrust of her hips. "Before I'm finished with you, you'll beg me to fuck you. Say it."

"Fuck me. Please." Astrid rested her brow on the table, the wood muffling her response.

Tessa picked the ruler and snapped it across Astrid's ass. A bright-red stripe appeared, spanning both cheeks. "Fuck me, who? Who do you want to fuck you?"

Astrid gasped. Her fingers scrabbled against the table. Tessa spanked her twice more.

"You, Tessa. Please fuck me." Astrid's voice quavered.

Tessa smoothed her hand over her hip. "Better. But you'll have to earn it." She bent and kissed the dimple at the base of Astrid's spine. She straightened and laid her hand over Astrid's lower back. Tessa rubbed her thumb along the valley over her spine and pressed down, pinning Astrid against the table. She leaned close and teased her tongue over her shoulder then along her neck before she nuzzled her ear. "Ready?"

"Yes, Tessa." Astrid's breathless response assured Tessa she was.

Tessa brought the ruler down over each cheek, the snap against Astrid's taut flesh loud in the quiet of the kitchen. Astrid moaned and swore softly with each blow. The muscles in her back tensed under Tessa's palm.

"Now count for me."

"Yes, Tessa." Astrid's brow was pressed against the tabletop.

"No. No hiding."

Astrid turned her head to the side. Her hair slid over her cheek, covering her face. Tessa reached down and pushed her gray-streaked blonde hair back. "I want to see your tears."

Astrid swallowed visibly. Tessa hit her twice in quick succession.

"Two." Astrid's eyes were bright.

Tessa drew her fingertips over the red marks on Astrid's ass. She danced away from Tessa's touch, earning her a hard slap on her thigh. "Be still." Tessa cracked the ruler against her ass again.

"Yes, Tessa."

"Now how many is that altogether?"

"Four." Astrid's voice was tinged with tears.

"Six." Tessa brought the ruler down hard, laying another stripe next to the others crossing Astrid's ass. "Are you bad at math, or do you just like being punished?" Tessa swept her fingers over Astrid's clit. Slick heat coated her fingers. "So wet. I had no idea you were such a pain slut. Let's make it fifteen. One for each year I needed you like air." Tessa spanked her then, varying her blows as Astrid counted each stroke.

At fourteen Astrid broke. A sob rattled her chest and tears flowed from her eyes. Tessa smoothed her hand over her cheek, wiped the tears away. She held her gaze. "One more. Can you do that for me?"

"For you, Tessa," Astrid choked out, her voice rough.

Tessa lifted the ruler and brought it down the final time.

"Fifteen," Astrid cried out.

Tessa tossed the ruler aside, stepped behind Astrid,

lay over her, and thrust three fingers deep. Astrid moved her hips, spreading her legs. "Please fuck me, Tessa. I need it. Need you. Please."

Tessa rocked her hips against her as she stroked her fingers in and out. Astrid's steady stream of filthy encouragement drove her on. Tessa slid her hand around her throat, squeezed gently, and kissed her ear. "You are a delightful slut when you let yourself go. Come for me, Astrid, let me feel you come around my hand."

Astrid's body stiffened under her hands. Her muscles stood out as she bucked her hips wildly. She came with a shout. Their cups rattled on the tabletop and the table scraped against the floor with their movements.

Tessa held tight, added a finger, curled them over the spot that made Astrid buck her hips for more. She screamed as she came again, filling Tessa's palm until her delight ran down Tessa's wrist.

Tessa eased her hand from Astrid. She stood and in one motion turned Astrid to her back. She grabbed her hips and lifted her onto the table. Tessa bent her head to the sweet feast between Astrid's legs. She kneeled, ignoring the pain of the tile beneath her knees, and worshipped Astrid with her mouth. Tessa gorged herself on Astrid, savoring her gift of surrender.

Astrid's hands landed on her shoulders. Tessa growled and she moved her hands away. Tessa sucked gently. She slid her tongue over Astrid's labia, gathering all the sweetness she could. Quiet moans and soft sighs transitioned into chest-rattling groans as Tessa satisfied her desire for Astrid to come in her mouth. No roles, no scripts, just the two of them, naked in this moment. "May I come for you, Tessa?" Astrid's voice was breathy. Her body trembled under Tessa's hands.

"Come for me, now." Tessa lapped at her clit, pursed her lips, and sucked.

"Just for you." Astrid clamped her thighs around Tessa's body. Her heels dug into Tessa's shoulders as she came undone under her tongue.

*

ASTRID LET HER legs fall wide and clasped her hands over her head, determined to obey Tessa, to give her absolute obedience and trust. Tessa's grip on her legs tightened, her fingers digging into her thighs as she held tight to Astrid. A relaxed heat built in her belly as Tessa rolled her tongue over her clit in a slow rhythm. She panted as Tessa drove her up again. Astrid worked to relax, focused on letting her orgasm build. She closed her eyes and savored the sensations as her pleasure peaked and waves of pleasure shook her frame.

Tessa gentled her mouth and eased Astrid down from her high. She shivered as an aftershock shook her frame. Tessa pressed a kiss to her thigh. She stood and pulled a chair over to the table. With gentle hands she assisted Astrid off the table and onto her lap. Astrid snuggled into Tessa's shoulder.

"Are you all right?" Tessa wrapped her arms around Astrid's waist. "Did I hurt you?"

"Perfectly. I'd forgotten how much I enjoyed being spanked." Astrid closed her eyes and savored the sensation of Tessa's tight embrace. "Thank you."

"We should get you dressed. Myfanwy will be here soon."

Astrid shifted off Tessa's lap. She picked her gown up from the floor and pulled it over her head. Tessa's chin rested on her chest with her shoulders hunched. Astrid tugged her robe on and tied it. The tick of the clock was an incessant reminder of their limited time together. She rested her palm on the back of Tessa's neck.

"Look at me, please."

Tessa lifted her chin and met Astrid's gaze.

"Where did you go?" She cupped Tessa's cheeks with her hands.

Tessa stood and rested both hands on Astrid's hips. "I don't even know. I'm sorry."

Astrid studied her face, memorizing each line and the color of her eyes. "I wanted what happened to happen. However this turns out. I appreciate this side of you. Did you suppress this when we were together? Were you afraid I wouldn't like the dominant side of you?"

"Yes. I want—I need to tell you —" Tessa's gaze flittered over Astrid's shoulder to the clock and back to her face. Her shoulders slumped. "Damn it. I need to clean the table before everyone else arrives and I then have to help with breakfast and the dinner prep." She rubbed her forehead. "Could we—would you meet me later? I'd like to talk more."

"Of course." Astrid tugged Tessa's chef jacket, straightening the centerline, then smoothed her hands over her shoulders. "What time works with your schedule? Provided they haven't put me out."

Tessa's brows drew down. "Don't say that. You'll be here. I'll be there at half two." She rested her hands on Astrid's hips, her mouth twisted into a half-smile. "Does your ass hurt?"

"Deliciously so. You're so handsome in this outfit. Don't change out of it." Astrid leaned close and brushed her lips over Tessa's mouth. "I'll be waiting."

The kitchen door swung wide. "*Bore da*, lovely, did you have any trouble with the—" Myfanwy pushed through the kitchen door and stopped. She cocked an eyebrow at Astrid and Tessa. She stared at Astrid's underwear on the floor before shifting her gaze to their faces, then to the table. "For the love of all that's holy, you better have that table clean before Elaine gets here."

Tessa's skin bloomed a dull red under Myfanway's glare. She stepped away from Astrid's side and bent to snatch her panties from the floor before she stuffed them into her pants pocket. Chin on her chest, she trotted over to the sink and returned with disinfectant spray and a towel. Tessa sprayed the towel and set about methodically cleaning the table.

Astrid glanced back at Myfanwy, who stood with one hand on her hip and the other over her mouth, attempting to hide her smile. She tipped her head at Myfanwy. "I'll be out of your way in one minute. Tessa?"

Tessa looked up from her where she was scrubbing the table.

Astrid stepped closer to her. "Thank you for the coffee and conversation." She held out her hand.

Tessa's broad grin was her reward. "Anytime, Ma'am. Anytime." She retrieved Astrid's panties from her pocket and deposited them into her palm.

"See you this afternoon." Astrid tucked her underwear into her robe pocket. "Don't be late."

Myfanwy muttered to herself as she filled the electric kettle. Tessa returned to scrubbing the table, her shoulders shaking with suppressed laughter. Astrid left them there, managing to control her giggles until she closed the door behind her.

Chapter Eighteen

EYES GRITTY FROM her late night and ass sore from Tessa's attentions, Astrid adjusted her skirt and straightened her shoulders. Lucia sat at the wide desk reading from a thick gilt-edged book. The curtains were drawn against the chill and gas lamps lit the room. The expansive mahogany wood desk gleamed in the flickering light. Lucia was the only Mistress present. A quiet panic started in Astrid's chest. She pressed her hand to her chest, willing herself calm before she knocked on the doorframe of the office.

Lucia glanced up, slid a bookmark in place, and closed the book. "Come in and sit down, please." Her voice was even, her face a mask of indifference.

Astrid inclined her head in acknowledgement. She perched on the edge of the chair across from Lucia. Dread settled in her stomach as she studied her inscrutable expression. At least they hadn't tossed her out in the middle of the night. Maybe if she were lucky, they'd give her a few days to plan her travel. A list of potential places to stay formed in her mind as well as calls to make to clients. She was sure some of them had missed her. Or at least missed the idea of her. Her bank account was flush so at least there was that. Heat rose in her face. She was about to be dismissed. Denied sanctuary. Why had she ever let Petra convince her to apply? Foolish. She was a foolish woman. And Tessa. Losing Tessa again. The ache in her stomach increased and she held her hands tight across her abdomen.

"Astrid." Lucia's whip sharp tone snapped her out of her reverie. Her brows were knit, concern writ large in her expression.

Startled, Astrid gripped the arms of the chair. "Sorry, what?"

"Are you ill?" Lucia gestured to a pitcher of water and glasses on a tray on the corner of the desk. "Would you like some water?"

"Fine. I'm fine," Astrid lied.

Lucia pursed her lips and pinned Astrid in place with her gaze and melted her determination to remain stoic.

"No. I'm not fine." Astrid rubbed her forehead. "I've wasted everyone's time applying. I'm embarrassed I have caused Tessa distress. I have behaved in a manner most unbecoming for any Mistress. I betrayed your trust and Petra's friendship." Astrid stood and knotted her hands together at her waist. "I appreciate the kindness you and everyone else has shown me. Rowan House is the finest house I have ever visited. If it's not too inconvenient, would it be possible for me to leave the day after tomorrow?"

"You wish to withdraw your application?" Lucia lifted her eyebrow, her tone even.

"No. Not if I'm honest."

"Then why are asking to leave? And you need to be honest with us and yourself from now on. I won't tolerate anything but the truth from you going forward. Is that understood?" Lucia peered into Astrid's eyes as if she were staring straight into her soul.

Astrid rested her hands on the back of the chair. "I thought—you want me to finish my audition?"

Lucia rested her chin on her folded hands. "Are you always this skittish? Yes. We want you to continue. I appreciate your concern for Tessa's well-being. Both in the past and currently. You acted in what you thought was her best interest. Something every good Mistress does, and something that can be at odds with what a submissive wants. Tessa has assured me she is okay with your presence. Although I have denied her request to assist you for the mind-fuck portion of the audition."

"She asked to help me?" A surge of hope and happiness spread through Astrid.

"She did." Lucia shook her curls back. "But I think it will be better for everyone if she does not. I have assigned Benita to you unless you object?"

Astrid lowered herself into the chair. "No. No objection. And thank you for the opportunity to continue. Would it be possible for Tessa to observe the audition?"

"I will allow it." A tight smile crossed Lucia's mouth. "We all make mistakes. I appreciate how much it took for you to trust us with your story. I think you would be a wonderful addition to our staff. I've wanted to move our services toward more couples-oriented offerings." Her gaze hardened. "Do not disappoint me." Her silk over steel voice sent a shiver down Astrid's spine. Astrid had only met Madame Givernay once, but in Lucia's command she heard the echoes of Madame's voice.

Astrid straightened her posture. "I'll do my best not to."

"See that you do."

Her blue-green eyes pierced Astrid's soul. A shiver shook her frame. She set her teeth on her lower lip and held tight to the arms of the chair to keep from sinking to her knees on the floor in front of the desk. She could only imagine what it was like for Myfanwy and Martha to serve Lucia.

Terrifying in her passion, Elaine's stunning beauty and fiery behavior could intimidate anyone. But Lucia's cool control snuffed out any doubt who was the one true Queen of Rowan House. Not even pledged to the house and Lucia's demeanor had Astrid desperate to please her.

Astrid lowered her gaze, acknowledging Lucia for who she was. "Yes, Mistress Lucia." She stood and turned to go.

"And Astrid?'

She turned back to Lucia. "Yes?"

"Don't lie to us again. Ever. Even by omission. We can't protect you unless you are honest with us."

"I won't, Mistress Lucia."

*

TESSA STRAIGHTENED HER uniform before she knocked at Astrid's door. Her mouth went dry at the sounds of movement from the other side of the door. A flush heated her face as memories of their morning romp in the kitchen flooded her mind. Astrid had bent to her will, allowed Tessa to have what she wanted. Without reservation. And now Tessa could think of nothing more than kneeling to Astrid and worshiping every inch of her, to balance her nature. Her desire to submit as strong as her desire to dominate.

The door clicked open. Astrid wore a tight black skirt and a red shirt. Open at the collar, the silky fabric clung to her, displaying her exquisite breasts to perfection. Red strapped pumps, matching the shirt, perfectly completed her outfit.

"Don't loiter in doorways. It's unbecoming." Astrid stepped back and turned away, leaving the door open, not bothering to see if Tessa followed. Her haughty tone sent an arrow of desire straight through Tessa. A shiver chased down her spine.

"Yes, Mistress." Tessa stepped through the door and locked it behind her. She glanced around the room. A spark of joy lit in her chest. No suitcases, no evidence of packing.

Astrid lifted an eyebrow. "Is this how you present yourself to a Mistress? Clothed and standing? Strip and kneel."

"Forgive me please, Mistress." Tessa shed her clothes, folded them neatly, then kneeled, head down, hands upturned resting on her thighs. The position of the house. Calm spread over her. A sense of rightness, of her world aligning, settled in her soul. Astrid was here. Wasn't leaving. And by appearances was ready to assert her control over Tessa. A quake of raw want spread heat through her body.

The whisper of Astrid's shoes over the carpet was loud in her ears. The tips of Astrid's pumps came into view. Tessa fought her urge to bow her head over them and kiss the smooth leather tips. Would Astrid allow her to press her lips to her delicate ankle, her calf, her thigh, then let her worship between her legs? Tessa chewed her lip, working out how to beg for what she wanted. She needed to feel complete, to serve Astrid any way she wanted.

Astrid gripped her chin. Her fingers dug into Tessa's skin as she forced her head up. "You're late."

Tessa swallowed hard. The menace in Astrid's voice rolled over her. Heat spread through her body, her clit hardened, and her nipples tightened.

"And then you failed to present yourself in a manner consistent with Rowan House rules."

"I'm sorry, Mistress." Tessa relaxed into Astrid's hard grip. Waited for the slap she had craved since Astrid arrived. A second later, Astrid's hand cracked against her face. Pain bloomed across her cheek. Her nipples ached. Desire coursed through her as want coiled in her chest. Astrid cared enough to correct her as if she were hers.

Astrid bent and pressed her soft lips to the hot spot on Tessa's skin. "Lucia told me you volunteered to help me with the rest of my audition." She rubbed her thumb over Tessa's lower lip. "I appreciate your desire to help me. Did you know this morning when we met, I would be allowed to stay?"

"No, Mistress."

"About this morning." Astrid released her chin. "Eyes to me."

Tessa lifted her gaze to Astrid's.

"As much as I enjoyed our time, in the future, we will make an effort to be less spontaneous. Or at least pick more suitable locations. And although I was thrilled with our session, Mistress Elaine was not pleased about our activities. She reminded me, in a raving phone call, what a kitchen was for and that there were plenty of other locations more suitable for play."

Tessa failed to stifle her giggle. "Mistress Elaine has an entire drawer full of sex toys and has done things in the kitchen and dining room you would not believe."

Astrid cupped her face and kissed her then. A hard hungry kiss. She circled Tessa's throat with her hand. She rubbed her thumb over the pulse in Tessa's neck, igniting the smoldering fire in her belly. "You'll have to share the details some other time. Right now, my ass is sore, and I'm in a mood. Get on the bed. Face up."

Tessa scurried to obey, watching Astrid from under her lashes. Astrid walked to the wardrobe and yanked it open. From the rack she removed two spreader bars and leather cuffs along with linking chains with clips. The clink and rattle of chains as she approached the bed sent a shiver through Tessa. Her eyes fixed on the cuffs, her clit already swelling at the sight of Astrid holding the restraints.

"I've been prohibited from partnering with you for my mind-fuck audition. However, there has been no prohibition from interacting with you."

Tessa's heart hitched. Her chest ached. "Who? Who are you assigned to work with?"

"Benita." Astrid's gaze pinned Tessa in place. "You will be there to watch. That part of my request was honored."

Tessa set her teeth on her lower lip. "What are you going to do?"

"Right now, I'm going to have you like I've wanted to since the morning I arrived. No more kid gloves. No more letting you top from the bottom. I am finished with that." Astrid lifted Tessa's leg and clipped a cuff around her ankle before repeating the procedure with the other leg. She attached both to a spreader bar. The sensation of being exposed, unable to close her legs, rocketed Tessa's desire. Her clit throbbed and heat spread out from her center. She groaned under Astrid's gaze. Astrid's subtle nod at her response as she moved to the head of the bed and cuffed her arms to a smaller spreader bar had Tessa panting.

Astrid braced her arm on the bed post. "You look divine like this." She pinched Tessa's bicep. "I love all this muscle you have now. So strong." She smoothed her palm down her arm to her chest. Her fingers tightened around her nipple. "You are sublime."

Joy filled her with Astrid's praise.

Astrid released her nipple and yanked open the bedside table. She withdrew a dual-headed dildo and a bottle of lube. Tessa shifted her gaze from the thick toy. Which side would Astrid pick for hers? To fuck or be fucked? Tessa strained against the bars, the delicious sensation of being restrained, at Astrid's mercy, spreading through her.

Astrid stepped back from the bed, unzipped the side of her skirt, and let it fall. Tessa followed her movements, her hands opening and closing as she watched her unbutton her blouse. Her silk shirt fluttered to the floor, revealing a sheer red bra and panty set. Astrid turned away from the bed, bent from the waist, and drew her panties down her legs. She stepped out of them before she reached behind her and unfastened the bra. She straightened, leaned forward, and shimmied out of it. Tessa groaned watching the seductive sway of her heavy breasts. Astrid thumbed her nipples. "Like what you see?"

"Yes, Mistress."

"Bet you wish you could suck them, don't you?" Astrid cupped her breasts in both hands and held them out like an offering.

"Please, Mistress."

"Later. Maybe. If you're well behaved."

Her pumps whispered over the carpet as Astrid strode to the bed, her breasts swaying with each step. She stopped at the bedside and picked up the bottle of lube from the nightstand. After uncapping it, she tilted the bottle. The shiny liquid fell in a stream over Tessa's mons. The liquid spread down over her clit and onto her labia. Tessa flexed her legs, wanting to close them to relieve the pressure and ache in her clit.

Fiery want burned through her body. Astrid dripped more of the lube onto her fingers. Her hand hovered over Tessa's body a moment. Tessa licked her dry lips. Her body quaked with desire. Astrid held her gaze as she slid one finger deep inside. Tessa's groan rattled her chest.

"So needy. Has no one made you wait lately? Do they all just give you what you want when you want it?" Astrid's voice slid under her skin, made her dizzy with desire. With firm quick strokes Astrid spread the lube over Tessa's labia and inside, avoiding her clit, giving Tessa a fraction of the touch she desired.

Astrid fixed her gaze on Tessa's face briefly before she swept it over her body. Tessa shivered under Astrid's intense inspection. Everywhere her gaze landed burned as if she were branding her. Marking her for her own. Tessa swallowed hard.

Would she do that? Mark me as her own? Please let her mark me.

Astrid leaned closer, her breath soft on Tessa's cheek. She closed her hand over Tessa's throat, tightened her fingers, before she brushed a kiss over her lips. Tessa lifted her head, seeking more.

"You are a proper slut, aren't you?"

"I am, Mistress. What are you going do to me, Mistress?"

"Gag you if you don't stop asking questions." Astrid's pleasant tone as she threatened her rocked Tessa to her core. If she gagged her, she wouldn't be able to suck her nipples, or taste her. Oh goddess, she wanted to taste her. Her mouth watered. "I'll be good, Mistress."

Astrid set the bottle aside. "Will you?"

She straddled Tessa's body. Placed her knees on either side of Tessa's head. With two fingers she held herself open. "Lick me." She planted herself on Tessa's face, wrapped her hand in Tessa's hair.

Tessa plunged her tongue in deep. Astrid rocked her hips, fucking herself on Tessa's face. The points of her heels dug into Tessa's ribs, urging her on. Astrid's harsh groans and muted swearing filled Tessa's ears. The soft flesh of Astrid's thick thighs pressed against her ears, muffling the sounds of her pleasure.

Her chest heaved as she applied herself to her task, desperate to have her Mistress come in her mouth. Her Mistress. Astrid cried out and ground herself against Tessa's mouth. A gush of sweetness spilled over her face. Tessa lapped and sucked, catching every bit of her Mistress's gift to her.

She lifted clear of Tessa's face and straddled her chest. Astrid's eyes were bright, her cheeks flushed as she leaned down and brushed her lips over Tessa's mouth. Tessa yanked against the bars, desperate to hold Astrid. To pull her into her arms.

Tessa's body burned everywhere Astrid's body touched her. Astrid's breasts grazed her lips as she stretched and picked up the toy from the bedside table. Tessa lifted her head, captured a nipple in her mouth, and sucked deeply.

Astrid stilled. "Did I give you permission to suck my nipples?"

Tessa released Astrid's turgid flesh. "No, Mistress."

"Are you trying to goad me into punishing you?"

"Maybe, Mistress." Tessa dared a cheeky grin.

"At least you're honest." Astrid dribbled lube over the short, curved side of the toy, designed to hit the wearer's G-spot.

Tessa followed her movements with her gaze.

Astrid kneeled with her legs apart between Tessa's wide-spread thighs. "Look how fat your clit is. So tempting." Her nipples brushed the top of Tessa's thigh. She leaned close, closed her lips over the tip of her clit, and sucked lightly. Tessa arched her hips, needing more. Astrid slid her tongue under the hood of her clit. Pleasure bordering on pain whipped through Tessa and she closed her eyes and yelped. "Mistress. I can't. I'm going to come." Desperate to please her Mistress, she panted, struggling to regain her control.

"Shh, eyes open, watch me." Astrid kneeled up. She let her head fall back to rest between her shoulders as she slid the short side of the dildo deep. Her harsh groan shattered the quiet of the afternoon. "Mmm, that feels so good." Her gaze heavy lidded, she jacked the shaft.

Tessa whimpered. "That didn't help, Mistress."

"Are you worried? Worried I'll just get myself off and leave you here to wait for me? Maybe I should call Benita, leave you like this while we rehearse. Would you like that?"

"No," Tessa shouted, earning herself a sharp slap on the thigh. "I mean... No, please don't, Mistress. Please don't make me wait."

Astrid tilted her head. "You wouldn't want to watch us? Watch me fuck her? Let your desire build until I released you to come at my pleasure or to serve me? Jealous?"

Tessa swallowed on a dry throat. "Not jealous, Mistress."

"No?" Astrid leaned her brow against Tessa's forehead. "I don't believe you."

"No, Mistress. Honest. I wouldn't be jealous. Not of you touching her."

"Of her touching me?" Astrid shifted her hips, grazed Tessa's labia with the tip of the toy.

Tessa blinked the beginnings of tears back. "Yes."

Astrid kissed her gently. The soft touches of her tongue teased Tessa's mouth open. She took her time. Her deep kiss seared Tessa from the inside. Drove away her fear. With tiny movements of her hips, Astrid rocked the heavy shaft against her. The weight of the toy between her legs, brushing over her clit, drove her mad. An ache settled in her body, need drove her, and she arched up, wiggled her hips, attempting to take the toy inside her body.

Astrid slapped her thigh. "Who is in charge here?"

Tessa stilled. Heat rose in her cheeks as the sting of Astrid's correction burned through her. "You are, Mistress."

"Remember that. Now, back to Benita touching me. Tell me why." Astrid moved her hips, slid the tip of the toy just inside, setting the ring of sensitive nerve-endings at her opening on fire. Every movement of her hips increased Tessa's desire. More. She had to have more. She craved Astrid inside her. The pressure and drag on Tessa's clit was exquisite.

Tessa panted, focused on the sensations. "Mistress, I don't think I can stop. Please fuck me. I need you. Inside me, please. Please." She thrashed on the bed, struggled in her bonds.

Astrid pinched her hard on the hip. "Be still. You will wait for my permission. I'll consider fucking you after you answer my question. You will answer me or I will stop. Release you this second. Send you from this room with orders not to touch yourself or anyone else. Are we clear?"

"Yes, Mistress." Tessa set her teeth on her lower lip.

"Now, why don't you want Benita to touch me?"

Tessa shifted her gaze from Astrid's eyes to the shadow between her breasts. "I just got you back. I don't want to share just yet."

"Try again." Astrid gripped her chin. "You love Benita. Deny it and I will beat you with my crop before I send you from here."

"I won't deny it. But that's not why..." Tessa faded out under Astrid's hard glare.

"It's all right, Tessa. You have to be honest." Astrid's tender tone undid Tessa. "It's okay. It's okay to feel how you feel. But you need to tell me the truth. I have a responsibility not just to you but to Benita as well. How are you going to cope with the next audition? Benita has been assigned to me for the mind-fuck session." Her fingers tightened on Tessa's jaw. "Now tell me why you don't want her to touch me?"

"Because she'll fall in love with you. If she hasn't already. She needs the kind of Mistress I can't be. I'm a top, not a Mistress." Tessa rested her chin on her chest and closed her eyes. "I can't lose her, Mistress." Tessa bit back the part about losing both of them. If Benita fell hard for Astrid and she left, Tessa would be alone.

"Truth at last." Astrid kissed her cheek. "Good girl."

"Will you still let me be there?" At least if she witnessed Benita with Astrid she could see for herself if Benita cared for Astrid.

"I don't know if I'll allow it. You said you didn't want to watch Benita touch me."

"Not if I can't touch you too." Tessa held out the half-truth, praying Astrid would believe her.

"You're being ridiculous." Astrid rocked her hips. "Just saying things to get your way. You need a firm hand. I'm appalled at your behavior. You've been given entirely too much freedom. You and Benita both need someone to rein you in."

"Both?"

Astrid brushed a wisp of hair off Tessa's forehead and rotated her hips. "You don't think I could handle both of you?"

Tessa groaned with the sensation. "Mistress, it's cruel you fuck me while we're trying to talk."

"Cruel?" Astrid stroked into Tessa and withdrew almost to the tip. "I'm a Mistress, Tessa. Fairness has nothing to do with it. I will dole out your pleasure as you earn it. You don't like it, use your safe word." Astrid rolled her hips again.

Tessa shouted as the sensation rippled from her center, sent her spinning toward orgasm.

"Do you want me to stop?"

"No, Mistress. Please don't stop. It's cruel you won't let me touch you."

"Ahh. So it's a matter of you getting your way. Again. No. I like it like this. You at my mercy. Under my control. You can't distract me from what I want to do to you with your kisses. Or disrupt my plans by sucking my clit. Spoiled. That's what you are. Absolutely spoiled."

Astrid withdrew and teased the head of the toy against Tessa's labia. Astrid reached between them and flicked Tessa's clit as she shifted her hips and pushed the shaft steadily forward. In one slow, long stroke she pushed until she was flush against her.

Tessa gasped as the head brushed against her G-spot. Ripples of pleasure spread out as Astrid started a slow grind with sweet strokes that touched every nerve inside Tessa. She slid in and out slowly, the drag and tug on her clit delicious as Tessa's pleasure spiraled out of control.

"Mistress. Oh, may I come? Please. I don't think I can hold out." Tessa panted, fighting herself.

Astrid didn't answer. She simply kept up her even strokes, each one bringing Tessa closer to the peak. Astrid bent her head and took Tessa's nipple into her mouth. She licked and sucked before she bit down gently.

Tessa lost the battle. She shouted her release. Astrid's evil chuckle speared her, sending shivers of anticipation through her, and she came again.

Astrid lifted her head, pulled out almost clear before she thrust sharply. "Oh dear. Coming without permission? Now I really do have to punish you."

Pleasure shot though her as Astrid pumped her hips. Stronger now, fast enough to take Tessa's breath away. Her breast rocked with each hard thrust. Astrid opened her eyes, her teeth pulled back in a fierce snarl. She braced herself with one hand and planted the other hand on Tessa's breast. Locked her thumb and forefinger over her nipple. "Move with me."

Tessa unleashed her desire, bounced her hips, and arched up off the mattress. She bucked up into Astrid, taking the toy deep. Her nipple ached where Astrid gripped it. The sensation of being fucked, taken, owned by Astrid spun out in her body and mind. The rub of the toy deep inside her and on her clit drove her on.

Astrid's breasts rose and fell with her motion, the effect hypnotic. Tessa's orgasm built. She shoved it away, waiting for her Mistress, unwilling to fail again. Astrid's pale cheeks glowed red. Sweat dotted her upper lip. Her ice-blue gaze locked on Tessa's eyes.

"With me," she ground out as she released Tessa's nipple. The blood rushing back into the tip set off a fine pain that detonated her orgasm. Tessa yanked against the spreader bars, rocked up and met Astrid's wild thrusts as she came. Her scream of pleasure matched Tessa's as they peaked together.

Chapter Nineteen

ASTRID LOST HERSELF in Tessa's golden-brown eyes as they came, her orgasm sweeter because Tessa had held out, waited for her permission. She slowed her motions, gentling her strokes. A fine sheen of sweat clung to Tessa's body. The spicy scent of their lovemaking filled her senses. An aftershock rippled through her body. She lay over her, closed her eyes, and rested her head on Tessa's shoulder, savoring their connection. In the aftermath of their session, peace settled over Astrid. Tessa shifted under her, rattling the chains of the spreader bars.

"Are you all right?"

"My shoulders are achy, Mistress."

Astrid slowly withdrew, stopping when Tessa whimpered.

"Shh. We need to see to your joints." Astrid shivered with Tessa's needy sounds. Music to a Mistress's ears. She pressed a kiss to Tessa's mouth. An aftershock rattled her as she eased the toy fully from her body.

She placed it on the towel on the nightstand. Tessa's

eyes were closed, her breathing ragged, her chest rising and falling as she came down from their scene. Astrid rolled over and straddled her waist. She unbuckled the cuffs, freeing her wrists from the spreader bar.

Astrid took advantage of her closed eyes to study her sublime features. Her strong jaw, her sensuous mouth with plush lips. The rise of her cheekbones and her light-brown skin, a sharp contrast to Astrid's pale body.

Tessa's confession of her fears had been real, that much she knew. She feared losing Benita above anything. Maybe because she had never known who owned Astrid's heart. No matter. Astrid would find a way to give Tessa what she wanted. What she and Benita both wanted.

Tessa lay spread-eagled, eyes still closed. Her breathing was even now, her chest rising and falling with each breath. Astrid rubbed her shoulders, appreciating the hard muscle under her soft skin. Tessa hummed as Astrid massaged her shoulders before she moved down her body to rub her hips and thighs. With firm touches she smoothed her hands over every inch of Tessa's body. The hard planes of her tight stomach were a delight, as much as the firm long muscles of her thighs. After she unbuckled the cuffs holding Tessa's ankles, she lifted her legs and closed them gently. Tessa let Astrid move and position her, limp as a rag doll. "Any pain?"

"No, Mistress." Tessa's voice was thick.

Unwilling to waste a moment of their time together, Astrid shoved the bondage equipment off the bed.

Astrid rolled Tessa to her side. "Lay face down for me." Tessa obeyed. Astrid took her time massaging her heavily muscled back, thick hips, and exquisite ass. Tessa's tight groans and soft sighs were loud in the room.

The late-afternoon sun highlighted her body. Satisfied she had soothed Tessa's muscles and joints, she lay on her side next to her. She propped her head in her hand and rested her palm on Tessa's back.

Tessa turned her head. Astrid caught a glimpse of her eyes beneath the strands of hair that fell over her face. She pushed Tessa's hair back, tucked a strand behind her ear. "You okay?"

"I will be." Tessa grimaced. "I haven't—it's been a long time since someone handled me. Fucked me. Usually I do the fucking."

Astrid studied her eyes. "Too much? Did I hurt you?"

Tessa shifted to her side and matched Astrid's position. "No. May I touch you?"

"Yes."

Tessa scooted closer. She cupped Astrid's face. Her eyes were dark, the pupils blown wide. She leaned close, traced Astrid's lower lip with her thumb before she kissed her. Tessa's kiss was gentle, a tender touch. "Thank you."

"For what?"

"Reminding me I like both, that it's okay to like both."

Astrid leaned in and kissed her. "It's a good lesson for both of us. I've been playing with lightweights and wannabe subs for too long. I've missed this. So much." Astrid cupped the back of Tessa's neck "Missed you."

Tessa lifted her chin and slipped a finger under the leather collar of Rowan House. The numbered tag glinted in the light as she lifted it away from her throat. "I wish this was your collar."

"I know. And that's enough for now. Let it be enough for now." Astrid kissed her forehead. She rolled to her back. With a tug on Tessa's shoulders, she urged her to rest her head on her breast. They lay like that, wrapped in each other's arms. "Can you reach the covers?"

Tessa drew the sheets and comforter up over them. "I can't miss dinner service."

"The way Elaine spoke to me on the phone. So imperious. I don't know how you stand working with her."

Tessa laughed. "And I bet she was using her inside voice because you're Petra's friend. That's just Elaine. Give her a chance. She's taught me so much since I started here."

"I'm sure she has. Just as I'm sure she has her good qualities according to Petra. And you. As for today, I'll release you back to kitchen duty when I'm damn good and ready."

Tessa snuggled in close, rested her hand on Astrid's belly. "Yes, Mistress."

Astrid held tight to Tessa's well-muscled shoulders. Memories of other days, other nights bubbled up along with a sense of calm. All would be right in her world. She would win a place here, find the sense of belonging she had been searching for since forever. Home.

Chapter Twenty

WIND RATTLED THE windows in the frame of their room. Tessa shivered in spite of the late-afternoon sun spilling across her bed. She cuddled closer to Benita.

"What do you think she has planned for me?" Benita carded her fingers through Tessa's hair as she laced their fingers together.

"No clue." Tessa relaxed under her touch and rubbed her thumb over the back of Benita's hand. "I've not seen her since our afternoon together. How did your interview go?"

"Fine. I guess." Benita's hand stilled. "Are you going to be okay, Bebê? Watching?"

Tessa pressed her face into Benita's shoulder. "Sure."

"You're lying. Your voice always squeaks when you lie."

"It's not like she'd ask you to pledge to her right then and there."

"What?"

Benita shoved Tessa off her, rolled them so Tessa was

on her back. She pushed up and straddled her. "Bebê, what kind of silly talk is that?" She brushed Tessa's hair back from her eyes. "I just met her. And I like her." Benita rested her hands on Tessa's chest. "She's magnificent. But I'm not in love with her."

Tessa held Benita's dark gaze. "But you could be, you could fall in love with her, couldn't you?"

Benita's bitter chuckle startled Tessa. "So? What would that matter? I've loved many people. Before you arrived, I was so desperately in love with Mistress Martha and Mistress Lucia I prayed every night they would ask me to pledge to them." Benita's gaze flittered away from Tessa's eyes.

Tessa studied Benita's face, the slight downturn of her mouth, the tiny line that always appeared between her brows a clue to her state of mind and the sadness that lurked under the always-sunny exterior she showed the world. "What happened? You stopped loving them?"

"No. I'll always love them. But I realized they had what they needed with Myfanwy and with each other. Watching them together it's clear they are quite content and happy. So fucking happy." She lifted a shoulder and let it fall. "I got over it." She cupped Tessa's face and rubbed her thumb over her lower lip. Her soothing touch flowed over Tessa like honey. She pressed a long slow kiss to Tessa's mouth. Determined not to let Benita distract her, Tessa ended their kiss.

Tessa smoothed her hands over Benita's thighs. "How? How did you get over them?"

Benita eyes shuttered. "Does it matter how?" She leaned down to brush another kiss over Tessa's mouth. She deepened it. Her sweet kiss swept every clear thought from Tessa's mind. She surrendered to her, gave over to her teasing tongue and the delicate nibbles of her lips.

Benita eased back, kissed her jaw, her throat before she sat up and peered into Tessa's face. Her eyes gleamed. "I wish I had time to spend with your mouth before the audition."

"Not the rest of me?" Tessa rubbed her hands over Benita's curvy hips before she cupped her ass and urged her closer. Astrid's taunt about Benita not knowing Tessa loved her, how much she wanted Benita to be her own, whispered through her mind. She pushed it away with both hands.

Benita swept her hands down Tessa's shirt and flicked her nipples. "All of you, Bebê."

Tessa wrapped her arms around Benita, held her close and kissed her, trying to say with her kiss what she'd never said. Benita broke their kiss and leaned her brow on Tessa's forehead. Sadness flickered across her face before she smoothed her expression.

"I won't steal your love, Bebê," Benita whispered, mask firmly back in place.

"That's not— I'm not worried about that." Terror rose in her heart. She could do this. She could tell her, needed to tell her.

"You love her." Benita sat up and rested her hands on Tessa's chest. "Still. You do. I see it. Sense it when you're near her."

Tessa lifted her hands and gripped Benita's shoulders. She studied her expression, stared into her eyes. *Tell her. Tell her now. Tell her how you feel. Don't fuck this up.* Benita held her gaze, back straight, mouth set in a thin line.

Benita twisted out of Tessa's grip and left the bed. "Now shoo. I need to get ready for tonight and I don't need you to distract me." She picked up her dressing gown and pulled it on before knotting it tightly at the waist.

"What scene are you doing?" Tessa picked at the bedspread.

"She didn't tell me. Just interviewed me and then told me to meet her in the dungeon at eight. It's mind-fuck, remember? She's supposed to figure out what I need." Benita rested her hands on her hips. "Like I even know."

"The dungeon?" Tessa's mind spun out in a thousand scenarios that could take place in the dungeon. She took in Benita's posture and the slight tremor in her voice. "You're worried." A statement not a question,

"Sim. I am. I hate having my insides on the outside, you know?" She glanced at the ceiling and shook her curls back. "Whatever. It's a scene, right? I can do it."

"I could ask again. See if they'd let me do it. And if you really don't want to, they won't make you. You can use your safe word."

"I know that." Benita huffed out a breath. "It's not that I don't want to do it. I do. Even if she scares the fuck out of me. It's her eyes. It's like she sees everything. Like she can see inside my head. I feel so exposed when she looks at me. That zing of fear gets me. In a good way. I get why you're still hooked on her."

"As you said, like it matters? And fuck that. If she's so good seeing inside people, she would never have left like she did."

"She did what she had to do, Bebê. And how you feel matters. Even if she wanted to ask you to pledge to her, she can't. Not now. This is it. After this it's up to the

Mistresses if they want her to work here. Wait and see what happens, Bebê. Nothing is written in stone." Benita gestured to the clock. "Don't you have to help in the kitchen or something?

"No. I'm not needed today. At least that's what Elaine said." Tessa rubbed her ass. "Right after she paddled me for having sex with Astrid on the kitchen table. And missing dinner service."

"Lucky." Benita quirked her mouth and turned away from Benita.

The mattress squeaked as Tessa rolled to her side on the bed and propped her cheek on her hand. "You really kicking me out?"

"Sim."

"Why?"

"Do I need a reason more than I want some privacy? Now go. I need to get ready." Benita spoke over her shoulder on her way to the vanity.

Annoyed with Benita's insistence she leave, Tessa scooted off the bed. She snagged her jacket from the coat rack near the door and shoved her feet into her boots. She paused with her hand on the doorknob and turned back.

Benita sat at the vanity mirror sorting through the various cosmetics and laying them out on the top. Her shoulders were rigid. She paused in her rummaging, closed her eyes, and rubbed her brow.

Love swept over Tessa, twined with desire. She wanted to touch Benita, to soothe away the worry radiating off her like a flare. Benita loved her. Like a friend. A friend with benefits. A dear fuck buddy, of that she was sure. Not like a lover. She was sending her away. Wanted to be left alone.

What would she do if Tessa said she loved her? Told her how much she wanted to have with her. Tessa wanted more. So much more. Would she say "I love you" back? Or laugh and pat Tessa's cheek, tell her she loved her too, before she abandoned her to go to her family—or worse, before Astrid asked her to be hers. *Tell her. Tell her you love her before it's too late.* Was it too late already? She was strong. She could do this. Had to do this.

"Hey, Benita?" Tessa released the doorknob and turned fully to watch Benita's reflection.

Benita met her gaze in the mirror, her face a mask of submissive indifference. Tessa's heart split wide. She knew that expression. Practiced it herself. Eyes shuttered. Mouth neutral. Posture alert but relaxed. It was the expression all submissives eventually mastered. A subtle shift in demeanor that permitted them to keep a part of themselves for themselves, even as they were willing to give everything else to their Mistress. She never expected Benita to turn it on her. She was gone. Gone from Tessa. Maybe forever.

"Sim?" Benita met her gaze in the mirror.

Fear rose up and grabbed Tessa by the throat. She clamped her teeth on her lip. Not the time to tell her. Not now. And what to say really? Besides she loved her? And what difference would it make? To add to Benita's worry and stress? No. Not now. Maybe not ever.

"I, um, I'll see you later." Tessa turned away and closed the door gently behind her.

*

ASTRID INHALED THE scent of the well-kept barn. The

fragrance of hay and sweet feed, mixed with the subtle smell of leather underlaid with horse, relaxed her. She strolled the length of the building noting how the older portions of the barn with their worn brick floor blended seamlessly where it transitioned into modern stalls and rubber flooring. She exited the rear of the barn. The last of the afternoon sun reflected off the puddles dotting the area behind the barn. She picked her way across the lot to fenced paddocks.

The horses grazed lazily on the far side of the field. In a group they shifted, moving as one over the gray-green grass. Astrid tracked their movements as she shuffled back through her interview with Benita in her mind. Astrid trusted she had been honest in her answers. Determined to excel in her audition, she had pushed her as much as seemed safe for Benita's emotional well-being. The interview had been time well spent.

But could she pull it off? Self-doubt welled up. Would she be able to show Tessa and Benita the love they had for each other was more than either of them acknowledged? Would it be too much? Leave them both hurting and confused?

A mind-fuck session had to be handled so delicately. She turned over various movie scenes in her mind searching for the right one to lead them to confess their honest feelings and desires without destroying their relationship. Her choice could lead them to their greatest happiness or utter devastation of their souls.

Each of them feared the truth. Feared if they were honest their love would be unrequited, believed they were not enough for the other to be happy. Astrid needed Tessa present when she worked the mind-fuck scene with

Benita. It would lead them to the undeniable truth, then Astrid would step back to let the magic happen. At least that was the way it was supposed to work.

A gust of wind pushed the grass over. Astrid tugged her jacket tighter around her shoulders. She balled her hands in her pockets. And then there was Tessa. And her feelings for her. And her interest in Benita. So unexpected. A bitter taste rose in her mouth. She rubbed her forehead. Did she have any business leading anyone in showing their true emotions?

Having Benita as her foil for her audition sent a wave of anticipation through her. A delectable submissive, Benita was not a brat. Her pushback was purposeful. A strong sub who could not stop herself from testing a Mistress's limits. Her confession she liked pain and had no limits stirred Astrid. As much as Astrid loved Tessa, she longed for heavy impact play. It had been ages since she had a submissive who longed for crops and paddles and relished single tails. A submissive who craved heavy pain was a treasure. It had been far too long since she had truly marked a submissive and had the pleasure of seeing evidence of her work for days afterwards. Her hand itched to paddle Benita's shapely ass. Later.

During the audition she would test Benita and Tessa's limits as well as her own. Her soul ached from her last session with Tessa. A moment where they both dropped their masks, stopped pretending they were other people, acknowledged that for better or worse they were bound to each other, heart and soul.

Astrid strolled along the fence line. She stared at the ground unseeing. Across the field a horse whinnied, disturbing her ruminations.

"They're magnificent, aren't they?"

Astrid yipped, spun toward the sound of the voice.

Elaine stood with a halter in her hand, a smirk on her face.

Astrid smoothed her expression. "They are. Which one is yours?"

"Luna, the white mare." Elaine whistled. On the far side of the field a white Arabian lifted her head and charged toward them.

Fascinated with the horse's obedience, Astrid moved closer to the fence. Elaine opened the gate, stepped into the pasture, and closed it behind her. As the horse approached her it slowed until it walked to Elaine. The mare stopped directly in front of her. Elaine closed the distance. She rubbed the horse's nose and cheek before slipping the halter over her head and buckling it in place while murmuring endearments.

Astrid blushed to witness such a sweet moment. This was not the Elaine who had dressed her down over her behavior, nor the woman who had walked out after her confession without a word or acknowledgement to Astrid.

Elaine attached a lead shank to the halter and led the horse back to the gate. "Stand clear. I'm going to call the rest of them."

Astrid took a place out of the way of the gate. Elaine opened the gate and led her horse toward the barn. She whistled again, a different sound, and the rest of the horses raised their heads.

"Open the other gate, please. You'll be fine, just stand behind it when you open it. Marco and Bruno will find their way to the barn." Elaine led her horse into the barn.

Astrid opened the other gate and stood behind it. The

two horses ambled toward her, picking up their pace as they neared the gate.

After the last horse had entered the barn, Astrid followed at a safe distance. Elaine walked along the shed row, sliding the doors in place and locking each stall. "We start all our new submissives in the barn. Do you ride?"

"Not in many years." Astrid tucked her hands in her pockets. "Do you do that with Mistresses as well?"

"We haven't. Mistresses don't typically have other duties."

Astrid followed Elaine. "Lucia manages the library. You manage the dining room. Martha manages the finances and the barn. Petra tells me she's in charge of employee and guest relations."

"Yes. Everyone has their place." Elaine stopped next to a grain bin. "Hand me that stack of tubs, please."

"These?" Astrid pointed to a collection of multicolored tubs.

"Yes." Elaine unlatched the lid and flipped it back. She took the tubs from Astrid and placed them in a row on the top of the feed bin. She began filling them from the various sections of the box. Elaine paused and turned to Astrid. "Shouldn't you be getting ready for your audition?"

"Why are you here?"

Elaine turned back to her task. "I come here to think." She lifted a shoulder and let it fall. "And usually I'm alone. I gave Veronica, our stable manger, the evening off so I thought I would be." She turned and skewered Astrid with a glare.

Astrid met her glare with one of her own. "Sorry. I needed space to think. When I was a little girl, my aunt used to take me to the barn with her. It was a magical place for me then and now. I've never lived any place I could keep a horse."

Elaine finished filling the tubs. She stacked them in the order she had filled them and placed them inside the grain box. She closed the lid and locked it before she turned to Astrid.

"And you're out here daydreaming." Elaine crossed her arms and leaned against the grain bin. "Thinking that if you're hired, you'll be able to have a horse of your own?"

Elaine's taunting tone undid Astrid's finely crafted reserve, severing the last knot of her self-control.

"No. Oh no, I expect that privilege is only for the ladies of the house. The owners as it were. Who am I to think I'd ever have a place here? Fuck you, Elaine. Fuck you, and this whole audition process. Do have any idea how many people have begged me to work for them? Offered more money than you ever could? And yet here I am applying for a job. Like I'm someone without a name and committed following. And if you ever call me up and yell at me over the phone like I'm a child again"—Astrid stepped closer to Elaine—"I will make sure you know exactly who you are dealing with. I don't give a good fuck everyone else in this house cowers when you walk through or bends over backward to appease you. I. Am. An. Adult. A Mistress. And if I were to take a job here, know this. I. Will. Not. Be. Disrespected." Astrid held Elaine's gaze, braced for the explosive yelling she was sure would follow her tirade.

"Feel better now?" Elaine stepped around Astrid and stretched her arms overhead. "Come on."

"Where?" Astrid turned toward Elaine.

"Kitchen. I need a cup of tea and a chocolate biscuit. You seem like you could use one too." Elaine strode away from her toward the front of the barn, whistling "Ride of the Valkyries," not bothering to see if Astrid followed.

Astrid rolled her eyes at Elaine's retreating back. After a brief debate with herself she quickened her pace to catch up with Elaine.

*

"TESSA, WHAT IS wrong with you? Why are you loitering in my kitchen? Do you really want Elaine to get her paddle again?" Robin failed to stifle her eye roll.

"No." Tessa shifted her gaze from Robin's piercing stare. "I don't have anywhere to go. Mistress Lucia has the library for the afternoon."

A sly smile slid over Robin's face. "I know. Myfanwy was counting the hours until she could go to her and Mistress Martha." Robin glanced at the door. "I am serious though. She's in a funny mood. If she comes back from the barn and you're here in direct conflict with her order not to be, she's going to lose it."

"Where should I go? Benita kicked me out so she could get ready. I don't have anywhere to be until the audition. I'm not going to loiter in the dungeon all afternoon." Tessa drummed her fingers on the countertop. "If Elaine's in the barn, I sure as hell am not going there. She might decide I need another lesson and my ass has barely recovered."

Robin smirked. "You're such a lightweight. That was barely a paddling."

"Well, it was a lot for me." Tessa huffed a breath. "We

can't all be pain sluts."

The door to the mudroom scraped open. "Tessa!" Elaine stepped into the room followed by Astrid.

A shiver shook Tessa. "Mistress." She lowered her head and watched the toes of Elaine's boots, braced for herself for the scolding she deserved.

"Since you seem to not be capable of following my order for you to stay out of the kitchen, make us some tea."

Tessa scurried over to the counter. Her face burned. Being scolded in front of Astrid stung. What must she think of her deliberately disobeying Elaine? She filled the kettle and set up the teapot. She turned to face the women. Astrid stood with one hand on her hip. She rubbed her chin as her gaze swept over Tessa. A singular note of excitement swarmed up Tessa's body until it settled firmly between her legs.

"Elaine, would you mind if I addressed this infraction?" Astrid's voice was honeyed with an edge. Tessa trembled. She knew this voice. Knew what was next.

"Not at all." Elaine sat at the table, pushed the chair back, and patted her lap. Robin sat and looped her arms around Elaine's neck. Elaine kissed her. "Are you in the mood to be entertained?"

"If it pleases you, Mistress. But dinner might be late."

"To hell with dinner. You know my sister et al will never make it in time. Hell, we'll be lucky if they show up for the audition."

Robin settled into Elaine's lap. "Then yes, Mistress. I would love to be entertained."

The kitchen door swung open. "Perfect timing. Is there enough for me?" Petra breezed in, planted a kiss on Elaine that curled Tessa's toes, before she did the same with Robin.

"I'm sure there is." Elaine caught Petra's hand, turned it up, and placed a kiss in her palm. "We are about to be entertained."

"Are we?" Petra shifted her gaze around the room. She peered into Tessa's face briefly before she turned back to Elaine.

"Tessa is in need of a reminder that a Mistress's orders are not to be disregarded, even if one fancies themselves a top. We've been entirely too lenient with her. Astrid has volunteered to remind her of her role."

"Wonderful." Petra stroked Elaine's hair and bent to her ear. Her lips moved and Tessa strained to hear their conversation.

The kettle clicked off. Tessa's hand shook as she poured the first bit to warm the pot. She tossed it into the sink. After that she added the tea and the water, biting her lip to keep herself together. "Leave it, Tessa. Robin will serve us."

Tessa turned to the women, kneeled on the floor, rested her chin on her chest, and waited. Fear and desire curled up and settled in her body. This. It had been too long. Her first days at Rowan House had been filled with sessions like this. Lessons learned over Elaine's knee, or across Martha's lap. Worry nipped at her. Would Astrid paddle her? Spank her as she had spanked Astrid?

Astrid's boots came into view. "Get up and strip."

Tessa stood and removed her clothes, folded them, and placed them in a tidy pile on the bench. A fine sweat rose along her brow. The slow tick of the kitchen clock and the ordinary sounds of Robin serving tea acted as a backdrop to the scene. Just a normal day at Rowan House.

With Tessa now the afternoon's entertainment.

"Come here." Astrid moved a chair out from the table. She sat in the chair. Tessa started forward. "On your knees. Now." Astrid's sharp command made her clit thick.

Tessa crawled forward. She pressed her head to the floor. "Turn around. Get on your hands and knees. Elbows on the floor."

Tessa obeyed. Her ears burned. Her desire would be on display. They would see. See how much she wanted this. To be punished. To have Astrid correct her. To be the object of her attention and affection.

Astrid traced her hands over the red marks left by Elaine's paddle. Tessa shied away from her touch, earning herself a slap on the thigh. "Be still. If I have to tell you again, you won't like what happens next."

Tessa moaned with Astrid's threat. This was the Astrid she had missed. The hard-edged Mistress, her true self. Not someone playing a part, too afraid to push a client or overstep a scene.

Astrid's fingers dug into her hips and urged her legs wider. "Mmm, so wet. You are dripping. Your clit is so thick. So needy. I bet you'd like me to do something about that, wouldn't you?"

"Yes, Mistress."

"Do you want to show us? Show us the naughty things you do to yourself, late at night when you're alone."

Tessa swallowed on a dry throat. "Yes, Mistress. If it pleases you."

"It would please me very much. Elaine, would it please you?"

"Yes. Robin?"

"Oh yes. Mistress, it's been a long time since we've

enjoyed a show."

"Excellent." Astrid's pleased tone hardened Tessa's nipples.

Tessa braced herself on one hand and reached between her legs.

"Stop."

Tessa froze in place.

"On your back. Eyes open. We all want to watch your beautiful face when you come."

On her knees, Tessa would have been able to close her eyes, to pretend she was alone in her room. Now they all would see. See how much she wanted Astrid. She hesitated.

"If you need to use your safe word, use it, now. Otherwise, get your ass up and do what I said right now."

Tessa scrambled to shift her to her back.

"Astrid. Might we move to the dining room? That table's larger and I think we'd all have a better view."

"What a marvelous idea. So much more public. A feast for the senses. Tessa, get up. Clasp your elbows behind your back. I love to see your tits on display."

Astrid's coarse words rocketed through her. Tessa stood, pressed her legs together to stem the wave of want that coursed down her thighs. On display. For Astrid. For them all. For anyone who might walk through the dining room. Slick heat flowed from her.

"Lead on." Astrid inclined her head toward the swinging doors leading to the dining room.

Elaine pushed through the doors.

"Robin, do you need any help with the tea?" Petra picked up the tin of biscuits on her way to the door.

"No thank you, Mistress." Robin collected their cups

on a tray and followed the Mistresses.

Tessa took a step toward the doors. Astrid knotted her hand in Tessa's hair and held fast, pulling her off balance. Astrid stared into her eyes, her gaze searching, a caring Mistress's assessment of Tessa's state of mind. Tessa lifted her chin, met Astrid's searching gaze with a wink.

Astrid yanked her hair hard, arching her back before she kissed her breathless. "Stop dawdling." She released Tessa and prodded her shoulder, urging her toward the door.

Tessa took a deep breath, blew it out, and quick-stepped out of the doors to the dining room.

Chapter Twenty-One

ASTRID HELD THE door open and followed Tessa, admiring the proud set of her shoulders as she marched through the opening. With her hands behind her back, grasping her elbows, the smooth muscled planes of her back were defined. The Mistresses had arranged themselves around the table. Robin had poured out tea, and wafts of steam rose from the cups.

"Stop." Tessa stood at the end of the table. She had imagined her on the dining table, but Tessa would be dangerously close to hot tea. Astrid scanned the room for a suitable space for Tessa's performance. A thick-legged sideboard held a basket of fruit and two candlesticks. Its height would allow everyone a clear view and it was sturdy enough to be safe.

"Clear the sideboard and then arrange yourself on it. Be quick." Astrid sat at the table.

"Cream or sugar, Mistress?" Robin poured out Astrid's tea.

"No, thank you, Robin." Astrid sipped her tea as she

observed Tessa. In record time she had removed the objects on the sideboard.

Using a chair as a step stool, Tessa mounted the buffet. "How would you like me, Mistress?"

Astrid set her teacup aside. "Face us. Brace your feet on the top, and clasp your ankles, knees wide."

Tessa followed Astrid's directions. The rich scent of her desire filled the space as she exposed her glistening center to the women present.

Astrid rose from her chair and picked up her napkin. She gestured to the one in front of Elaine. "Might I borrow this?"

Elaine picked up the napkin and passed it to Astrid. After rolling the napkins, she carried them with her. Tessa's eyes followed her movements. Astrid glared at her. Tessa dropped her gaze to the floor.

Astrid stood to the side, made sure to not obstruct her audience's view. "You don't like heavy pain, do you?"

"No, Mistress." Tessa lowered her chin to her chest.

"Pity." Astrid leaned close and inhaled the rich essence that was Tessa as she used the napkins to bind her hands to her ankles. Astrid reveled in Tessa's tight groan as she knotted the napkin. She ran a finger under the cloth. After she was satisfied the knots were not too tight, she strode back to the table and surveyed her work.

Tessa's chest rose and fell with her breathing. Her eyes were wide, her fingers white where they gripped her ankles. Astrid tapped her lip. Creating a scene with what was at hand was a skill Astrid reveled in; nothing stimulated her more. Creating a sensual experience from ordinary objects and in ordinary settings was a test of a Mistress's ability to bring a submissive to hand no matter where they were. Any fool could use a box full of toys and a dungeon, but it took skill to be able to employ only one's body, voice, and whatever else was at hand to discipline a submissive. It was the key to a Mistress's control.

"Eyes closed." Tessa's lids fluttered shut. Astrid stood and stripped off her shirt as she crossed to Tessa. She folded it and placed it over Tessa's face, creating a blindfold. As she finished tying the sleeves into a knot the door to the dining room opened. Benita stopped. Her eyes widened and she slowly backed out. Perfect. No need to delay nor tip her hand by summoning Benita, the ideal catalyst to drive this. Astrid held out her hand to stop Benita. She lifted her finger up to her lips and beckoned Benita to enter the room. Benita hesitated.

Astrid drew her shoulders back, pointed at the floor, and glared at Benita. This was it. If Benita did not obey her, if she turned and left, then Astrid was sure her chances of securing a job were over.

Benita lowered her chin to her chest and sank slowly to her knees on the spot. She crawled to the place Astrid had indicated. She sat, hands on the back of her thighs, palm up. From her position she would have a clear view of Tessa.

Astrid turned away and returned her focus to Tessa. Tessa's muscles strained, stood out in relief as she tested her bonds. Panic radiated off her. Denied a view of the room, exposed to her Mistress's gaze, Tessa's ragged breathing was loud in the room. Astrid laid her hand on her shoulder. "You're not alone. Slow your breathing. Use your safe word if you need to."

Tessa leaned her head to the side, pressed her cheek to the back of Astrid's hand. She turned her head and kissed the skin over her knuckles. Astrid closed her eyes and savored Tessa's trust. "Good girl."

Astrid trailed her fingers down the center of Tessa's body. Her skin was hot. Her breasts soft, nipples hard, her belly firm. She stopped short of touching her clit, swirled her finger over the damp cluster of curls just above the stiff tip. Tessa's desire had puddled under her hips.

Astrid trailed her fingers lower, grazing Tessa's clit. She stopped to tease a moan from her before she pulled her hand away. As she did, she turned to observe Benita. Her shoulders were rigid, her posture perfect.

She walked to Benita's side. She touched her shoulder, drawing her attention. Benita peered up at her. Her eyes were wide, uncertain. Astrid held out her hand. Benita took it and rose to her feet. Astrid cupped the back of her neck. She brought her close, traced the shell of her ear with her tongue before she whispered into her ear. "Not a sound. You will do nothing to signal your presence. Understood? Nod if you do."

Benita nodded in the affirmative. Astrid gestured to her chair. Benita kneeled next to it, bringing her closer to Tessa.

"Tessa?"

"Yes, Mistress."

"I'm going to ask what you think about when you touch yourself." Astrid stood off to the side of Tessa and palmed her breasts. She toyed with her nipples. "Tell the truth, tell it well, and I'll let you touch yourself for our pleasure. Maybe even let you come." Astrid reached over and pinched her nipple hard. Tessa yipped. "Lie to us and you will regret it. Understood?"

Tessa groaned softly. "Yes, Mistress."

Astrid stroked her hand over the outside of Tessa's thighs. "How often do you touch yourself?"

Silence from Tessa earned her a slap on the thigh. "Answer me or use your safe word."

"Nearly every day, Mistress."

"Better."

"Do you put your fingers inside?" Astrid teased one finger inside Tessa, gathered her silky wetness on her fingertips, and smeared it over her clit. "Do you fuck yourself?"

"Yes, Mistress." Tessa panted as she spoke. Astrid watched the muscles of her lovely throat work as she swallowed. Tessa trembled under Astrid's hands. The worn brass number tag dangling from the thin leather collar that marked her as a submissive of Rowan rocked gently in the hollow of her throat. Astrid shifted her gaze to Tessa's face.

"How many fingers?" Astrid circled and teased her labia.

"Two, Mistress." Tessa's knuckles blanched white where she gripped her ankles.

Astrid slid two fingers deep, drawing a shudder from Tessa. Slick heat encased her fingers as Tessa's body welcomed her. "Just two?" She curled her fingers and stroked gently over the raised spot of flesh that made Tessa gasp and rock her hips.

"Sometimes three, Mistress."

Astrid pulled her fingers out, added a third, and thrust deep. "Like this?"

"Just like that, Mistress." Tessa groaned. The sound ricocheted off the coffered ceiling. Astrid cast a glance over her shoulder. Her audience's gaze was fixed on Tessa.

Benita's lips were parted and her body inclined toward Tessa. Astrid moved until her body was pressed against Tessa's thigh, affording them all a better view.

"Please, Mistress. Please fuck me, Mistress, I can't wait. I need—"

Astrid slapped Tessa's cheek. "You want. You need. No. This is about what I want. What I need. Me first, then you. Always. Understand?" Astrid thrust deep, fucking Tessa hard and fast.

Tessa's shoulders heaved and her hips rocked forward. "Yes, Mistress. I can't—" Her body shook. "Please, Mistress, mercy, help me, I can't stop, I'm going to come—"

Astrid slowed her strokes, clipped her fingers over Tessa's nipple, pinched hard.

Tessa screamed long and loud. Astrid pressed her legs together as desire saturated her panties.

"Thank you, Mistress." Tessa panted.

"Never be afraid to ask for what you need." Astrid leaned close and brushed her lips over Tessa's mouth.

A whimper behind her drew her attention. Benita's lip was clamped between her teeth, her eyes heavy lidded. Astrid swept her gaze over the room. Robin was on Elaine's lap, her skirt rucked up, her chef's coat open. Petra stood behind her, her hands on Robin's breasts, pinching her nipples rhythmically. Elaine's hand was busy under Robin's skirt as she met Astrid's gaze. Astrid inclined her head in acknowledgement and turned her attention back to Tessa.

"And what about your clit? Do you jack it like a cock?" Astrid used her forefinger and thumb to do just that. "It's so lovely and fat."

Tessa moaned and turned her head from side to side.

"No, Mistress."

"No? You should try it. It seems you like it." Astrid took her time, drawing deep moans and sharp cries from Tessa as she kept a steady rhythm, fucking her as she jacked her clit.

"How do you touch your clit?"

"With the tips of my first two fingers, Mistress. In a circle." Tessa ground out. "Oh please, Mistress."

"Please what?"

"Please, let me come for you."

"Oh no. I haven't even asked you the good questions yet." Astrid switched her strokes up, slowed them as she moved her fingers over Tessa's clit as she had described. "Like this?"

"Oh, yes, like that, like that, Mistress."

Astrid slowed her attentions as she assessed Tessa's breathing, eased back to draw out her pleasure and her own. This was power. This was what she craved. Raw unfettered control over a submissive. Tessa's breathing evened out.

Astrid leaned close to Tessa and drew her lips over her jaw, to her ear. She teased the lobe with her tongue before she nipped hard. Tessa jerked and cried out. "Now I have your attention. Tell us, what do you think about when you touch yourself?"

*

THE DELICATE SCENT of Astrid's perfume surrounded Tessa. Denied her vision by Astrid's makeshift blindfold, Tessa gasped as Astrid edged her expertly. The sounds of the others, Robin's groans, Elaine's mumbled encouragements, and Petra's dulcet tones as she spoke to Robin added to the scene as she imagined what was happening in the dining room. She set her teeth on her lip and bit down, the pain distracting her from the pleasure building in her body. Hold on. She had to hold on for Astrid. Sweet relief was hers if she would only answer. How to answer? She hesitated, considered her responses. The slap was sharp, riveted her attention to the spot on her thigh that burned.

"You," she blurted.

Another sharp slap, harder than before, forced a yelp from her. She squirmed on the sideboard. The table under her squeaked with her movements. Unable to see where, or if another blow would come, her pulse rocketed. Deprived of seeing Astrid's face, her eyes pained her. How was she to know what to say? What Astrid wanted? Gauge her reaction, mold herself into what her audience wanted? She panted, shoved the panic that bloomed in her chest away. This was Astrid. She'd never hurt her. She was safe. Wasn't she?

"No. Don't tell me what you think I want to hear. I want the truth. Your truth, Tessa, this instant. Or we are finished here. You get dressed. We'll have tea and talk about whatever trifling nonsense you think I want to hear. I'm not a client. I am a Mistress. Your Mistress in this moment and of this house for today. They would not tolerate your reticence, and neither will I." Astrid's iron grip on the back of her neck focused her. "Now tell me. Who, Tessa, who is in your dreams and fantasies?" The iron in her voice matched her grip.

"You. Truly, Mistress."

"Come now. Just me? Surely you have others who

have starred in your fantasies?" Astrid's grip tightened.

Tessa's face burned. "Benita. And Mistress Petra."

Astrid's grip shifted. She slid her hand along Tessa's jaw, gripped her chin. "There now. Not so hard, was it?" Her voice was gentle, cajoling. "And what is it you think about when you're fucking yourself with those long strong fingers of yours? What do you imagine?"

"This. Being exposed. Fucking. Being fucked. Treasured. Being kept. Cherished. Being owned. Forever." The tears started then, flowed down her cheeks, and dripped onto her chest. Tessa swallowed hard, stifled the sob that hovered beneath the surface.

Astrid kissed the side of her neck, then her mouth. Tessa leaned into the kiss, drank from Astrid's mouth as if from a well of cool water on a blistering day. Astrid rubbed the back of her neck. "Very good. You're doing so well. You care for Benita, don't you?"

"Very much, Mistress. I love her, as I love you, Mistress." Tessa squirmed with her confession. *Ha, confession. Everyone knew. Not that it makes any difference. So what?*

"That's very sweet of you to say. But is it your body talking? Are you so desperate to come you'll say anything? Are you lying?"

"No. Mistress. No!"

"Then why have I had to force you to tell me?"

"I would have told you, Mistress."

"Now you are lying. Did you know your nostrils flare, just the tiniest bit, and your voice squeaks when you lie?" Astrid's breath was warm on her cheek. "You'd never confess you loved me. Or Benita." Astrid circled her thumb with her clit. "Because you think you're unworthy.

Unlovable. Don't you?"

Tessa's heart squeezed hard. "But I'm not worthy, Mistress. Not of you, or Benita." Tears raged down her cheeks. "I've lied. All my life. To my Mistresses. To lovers." Her throat ached with her confession. "And I've lied to you, Mistress."

Astrid lifted her chin, cupped her face, and kissed her, brutal and delicious, the kiss of a Mistress. "From this day forward, you will not. You will tell the truth in all things, even when you think someone will be unhappy with your answer. Truth only, in everything. No lying. Even by omission. I consider it a breach of trust between a submissive and a Mistress. And I will not have any sub of mine talking about themselves in the way you just did, do you understand me?"

"Yes, Mistress." Tessa clung to Astrid's words, held them tight. *Her sub. Hers.*

"Now. Would. You. Like. To. Come?" She punctuated each word with a strong thrust, her fingers drawing pleasure from Tessa as her fingertips stroked her G-spot. Tessa bucked her hips, seeking more. The sounds of Robin's release echoed in the room, threatening her control.

"Yes. Mistress. Please. Please let me come for you." Pleasure and pressure built in her hips, her belly.

"Would you like to see everyone's faces when you come? See the effect you have on them? How much they love and care for you? How much they believe you're worthy of their affection and love?"

"Yes, Mistress. Please let me see your face. Let me see your eyes, Mistress. Please, I need to see you."

Astrid withdrew her fingers. Tessa sobbed with the loss of her touch. "Shh. Just a moment. I need to untie you then I'll remove your blindfold," Astrid murmured in her ear. She pressed a kiss to her wet cheek. Her fingers brushed Tessa's skin as she removed her bonds. "Lower your legs gently."

Tessa shifted and lowered her legs. Her hips ached as she changed her position. Astrid stepped between her legs, rubbed her hips. "Any pain?"

"No, Mistress." Tessa savored the heat and closeness of Astrid's body, kept her eyes closed, as she waited while Astrid untied the knot at the back of her head. The silk fluttered against her cheek as Astrid removed the blindfold.

"Let me see your eyes." Astrid's hands rested on the top of Tessa's thighs, grounding her, her anchor, in the storm of emotions raging through her.

Tessa opened her eyes, focused on Astrid's elegant hands where they rested on her thighs. Pale in contrast to Tessa's brown skin. She stood between Tessa and the others, blocking their view, offering Tessa a sanctuary. Giving her a safe place to sort her feelings before experiencing the rest of the group. Tessa had been naked in front of all of them, served all of them more times than she could remember, but she had never been more exposed. Astrid cupped her face and kissed her cheek, her jaw, then her mouth. A soul-soothing kiss, gentle and possessive. Tessa wallowed in Astrid's aftercare, absorbed all of it.

Astrid released her, peered into her eyes. Tessa studied them, fell into the dark-blue pools, drowned willingly in the love she saw reflected there. Astrid slid her arms around behind Tessa's back, pulled her into an embrace.

Tessa relaxed into her arms, rested her chin on her shoulder. She risked a glance around the room. Elaine,

Petra, and Robin were huddled together, Robin between them. Their gentle expressions and the kindness reflected in their eyes filled her heart. A movement at the end of the table caught her eye. Benita sat alone, head down, face shiny with tears. Fear clawed at her chest. How long had she been there? Had she heard Tessa's confession?

The intimacy of her position hit her harder than her confession. They were holding each other as lovers did. Astrid's embrace said more than her words ever had. It was there, all of it for Tessa to take, to have as her own. Benita rose to her feet. Her mouth twisted into a sad smile, spoiling her beautiful face. Her eyes shuttered. The sensation of being shut out, abandoned, hit Tessa full force. Benita turned and left the dining room though the door leading to their room.

Their room. Would she even want to have Tessa there after this? The horror of her confession of love for Benita settled in her stomach. She had heard. Knew now how much Tessa had hidden from her. Benita. Tessa's heart spun as if on a string. It was not to be. She would have one. Maybe. If Astrid stayed. But not both.

She struggled in Astrid's arms. "Let me go."

Astrid jerked free and stepped back. Hurt flashed across her face before she smoothed her face. "Of course." She retrieved Tessa's clothes from the floor. She handed the pile to Tessa, her face a mask of concern. "I'll get you some water."

She turned her back to Tessa and stalked through the doors to the kitchen. Tessa clasped her clothes to her chest as she moved off the sideboard. With her back to Elaine and the others, she dressed quickly. The doors to the kitchen squeaked open. She turned toward the sound.

Astrid returned with a glass of water. She placed it on the sideboard, avoiding Tessa's eyes. After plucking her shirt from the sideboard, she slipped it on and buttoned it before she turned to Elaine. "It seems Tessa is not the only one in need of an attitude tune-up. Where did Benita go?"

Elaine inclined her head toward the hall leading to the dorms. "My guess is her room. Go past the front stairs and dead ahead will be a hallway leading to the door to the dormitory. You're looking for room 210." Elaine paused to sip her tea. "Cold. Of course. After this demonstration, Astrid, I think we don't need to see the mind-fuck audition. I'll speak with my sister and Lucia. Please inform Benita accordingly."

Astrid pursed her lips, opened her mouth as if to speak, then closed it. She touched two fingers to her brow in salute before she left the room. Tessa watched her retreating back, cursing herself for the way she had ended the scene. Astrid strode from the room, her hands clenched in tight fists.

"Tessa."

Tessa shifted her attention to Petra.

"Come here. Sit with us." Petra drew a chair close to their cluster of chairs and patted the seat.

Tessa picked up the glass of water. "Yes, Mistress."

Chapter Twenty-Two

ASTRID STORMED DOWN the hall leading to the dormitory. Benita had left without permission. Trashed her chances at getting hired. She would not even be allowed to complete her audition. And after Astrid had gone out of her way to make sure that Benita knew. Knew how much Tessa cared for her. She scanned the room numbers. Room two hundred ten. She lifted her fist to pound on the door. A muffled sob filtered through the door.

Her anger melted away. Remorse settled in like an old friend. She had miscalculated. Just as she had with Tessa. Astrid rapped on the door and took a step back into the hall. The crying stopped. Astrid shoved her hands into her pants pockets as she studied the six-panel door, shoving aside the temptation to break it down.

The door clicked open. Benita glared at her. Her eyes glittered with the remnants of tears as she crossed her arms and leaned against the doorframe. "Here to punish me for leaving now that you have fucked up everything?"

Astrid stepped back. "No. Well, yes. I wanted to.

Planned on coming here to beat your pretty little ass to remind you leaving without permission is inexcusable."

Benita snorted. "Pretty yes, but my ass hasn't been little in a long time." Her brows knit into a tight furrow. "Why are you not attending to Tessa? She's probably a wreck after that. I thought I was your mind-fuck audition partner."

"Tessa was in the kitchen in direct violation of Mistress Elaine's order. I asked to discipline her. It was an opportunity, I thought, to display my qualities as a Mistress. Not that it helped my case. Elaine has canceled my mind-fuck audition."

"You'll be leaving?" Benita pressed her lips together in a thin line.

"I'm sure. And I wasn't trying to ruin anything. Now you know you can do something about the way you feel for Tessa."

"Why? What do you care if you're leaving?"

"I—I don't know." Astrid shifted her gaze from Benita's accusing stare.

"Don't know, or don't care?" Benita's harsh tone stung.

"If you can't figure that out for yourself, I can't help you with it. Enjoy your evening." Astrid turned away from Benita.

Benita's fingers closed around her arm above her elbow. "You don't get to turn my world upside down and then walk away." Her fingers dug in as she yanked hard and pulled Astrid off balance, spun her to face her. She launched herself at Astrid, gripped her shoulders, and kissed her. Lips hard and bruising, she nipped Astrid's lower lip. Her teeth cut, sharp and clear. The sanguine taste of her fury reignited Astrid's anger and passion.

Benita broke their kiss. "You are the most infuriatingly attractive woman I have met in a long time." Her chest rose and fell with her words. She slid her hands up, cupped the back of Astrid's head, and drew her down into another soul-searing kiss.

Desire flooded her. She grabbed Benita's arms, pushed her against the wall. "What are you doing?"

"What I wanted to do that afternoon in the library." She shrugged out of Astrid's grip, grabbed Astrid's shirt, and yanked it wide. Buttons pinged off the walls. Benita flicked the front clasp of Astrid's bra open. "*Nossa!* Your tits are amazing."

Astrid's nipples tightened as Benita's hungry expression pierced her soul with an arrow of desire.

Benita filled her hands with Astrid's breasts and squeezed hard. "You want me to stop?"

Astrid grabbed her ass and held tight to Benita's luscious curves. "No."

Benita bent her head, nuzzled her breasts before she sucked a nipple between her lips. An electric current of want shot straight to her clit. She ached, still spun up from her time with Tessa. Clit thick with need and want, Astrid ground her hips against Benita. Benita shifted in her arms and turned them so Astrid's back was against the wall. Her fingers scorched the skin of her belly as she scrabbled with Astrid's belt. She flicked the buckle open, thumbed the button free before she slid the zipper to Astrid's pants down.

Astrid rucked up Benita's skirt, anxious to feel her hot flesh in her hand. She gripped the sides of her panties and yanked hard, tearing them free of Benita's body.

Benita slid her hand lower. Her fingers grazed Astrid's clit. A whipcord of pleasure spread through her. "So hard. And thick. Wet."

Astrid lifted her hand and swatted Benita's ass. "On your knees." Astrid shoved her pants and briefs down, exposing herself. Liquid heat wet her thighs.

Benita sank to her knees in the hall. Astrid wrapped her hand in Benita's hair. "Lick me. Suck my clit."

Benita held her gaze as she nuzzled her before swiping her tongue over Astrid. The wet heat of her mouth closed over her clit. She rocked against her, marking her with her desire. Benita pursed her lips and sucked hard, her attention divine. Astrid panted, savoring the image of Benita serving her. She let herself go, held Benita in place. Goaded by her soft moans, Astrid spilled her satisfaction into Benita's mouth. She yanked hard on her hair, pulling her to her feet. Her face glistened, her pupils blown wide. Astrid tore at her skirt, ripping it free from Benita's body. "So spoiled. Everyone lets you get away with whatever you want when you swing your hips and pout. That will not work with me." She swatted Benita's ass hard. The sting in her hand was as pleasant as Benita's sharp cry. "I'm not through with you. Fuck me. Now." She yanked hard, pulling Benita off balance and into her arms. She locked her arm around her waist, holding her close, and swatted her ass again.

Benita gasped. Heat flared in her eyes as she slid her fingers deep and feathered them inside, setting fire to every nerve-ending she brushed over. Astrid closed her eyes briefly to savor the sensation of Benita's touch. She opened her eyes and held Benita's gaze as she spanked her again. The snap of Benita's skin against her palm was as pleasurable as Benita's nimble fingers. "Fuck me," she ground out.

Benita's mouth twisted into a knife-edged smile. "Make me."

Astrid leaned into it then. Spanked Benita until her hand ached, rewarded stroke for stroke as Benita fucked her. The sounds of their tryst echoed in the hall, the slap of skin on skin, mixed with salacious wet sounds of fucking.

"Give it to me, Mistress, please. Let me feel it. Let me feel you come around me." Benita curled her fingers and pressed her palm against Astrid. The pull and drag on her clit was exquisite. With a shout and a last swat on Benita's ass, Astrid filled Benita's palm with her pleasure.

Benita fluttered her fingers inside again, brushing over Astrid's G-spot, setting off another gush of satisfaction. Astrid's knees buckled as she shuddered through her pleasure. Benita threw her weight against Astrid, pinning her against the wall to hold her up.

Astrid closed her eyes, relaxed into Benita's support as she eased her down. An aftershock whipped through her as Benita withdrew her fingers. She tucked her head under Astrid's chin and tightened her arms around Astrid's waist. The silence between them was interrupted only by their coarse breathing. Astrid hugged Benita close, nuzzled her hair, then kissed the top of her head.

"Regrets, Mistress?" Benita's voice was thick.

"Only that I won't be here for more of this." The sensation of water slipping through her fingers shook her as she came down from the high of their scene.

*

TESSA SAT ON the chair between Petra and Elaine. She shivered as the adrenaline left her body.

Petra slid her arm around her shoulders and hugged her close. "Cold?"

"Afraid, Mistress." Tessa set her glass on the table and knotted her hands together to stop their trembling.

"Of what?" Petra petted her head.

Robin placed her hand on Tessa's shoulder. "You're safe with us."

"My body, yes." Tessa swallowed the ache in her throat. "My heart not so much."

Elaine tapped the table, drawing Tessa's attention. "What is the problem? Your feelings for Benita have been clear to all of us for ages. Why is it a problem she knows now?"

Tessa lifted her shoulders and let them fall. "Because as long as I didn't say it, she didn't have to tell me she thinks of us as just friends."

"What are you going on about? Do you really think she doesn't love you?"

"Why didn't she stay? She couldn't wait to leave." Tessa flushed. Her face burned as she remembered her words. "She doesn't want anything more of me than what we have."

"Because she wants to keep seeing clients?" Elaine quirked her mouth at Tessa. "That would be a problem if you both wanted to stop seeing clients."

"I don't want to give up seeing clients. Neither does Benita. Neither of us care about that. It's business. It's the other things. Life outside of Rowan House. She's not out to her family. I think she thinks I'd demand to meet them or something. Or want her to pledge to me. Fuck if I know.

But now, because of Astrid it's all fucked up. Everything." Tessa gripped the hard edge of the table. Willed herself to sit still and not seek out Astrid. Anger settled in the pit of her stomach. Astrid. Fucking up her life again.

Elaine slapped her hand on the table, rattling the teacups. "Fucked up? She did you a favor."

Petra tilted her head at Elaine. "I don't think Tessa feels that way."

"Now it's out in the open, they can talk about it. Secrets kill every good thing. You taught me that."

Petra reached over, lifted Elaine's hand to her mouth. "Thank you, my love."

"Elaine, may I get us all fresh tea?"

"Of course, my sweet." Elaine shifted in her chair.

Robin slid off her lap. "Come on, Tessa. I need your help."

Tessa glanced from Elaine to Petra's face. "With your permission, Mistresses?"

"You are excused." Elaine pinned her in place with her glare. "Do not go to the dormitory."

Elaine's firm tone rang in Tessa's ears. She lowered her chin to her chest. "Yes, Mistress, sorry I disobeyed before." Her stomach twisted. If she had just obeyed Elaine in the first place, she wouldn't be here now about to lose her lover and best friend, and the only place she had ever called home. Because if Benita put her out of their room, broke off their friendship, she wouldn't be able to stay. Tessa mentally calculated her savings. She had enough money invested to not have to work for a few years if she were careful. She could start over. A cynical voice in her head spoke up. *Where?* Where would a scarred, over forty sex worker find work? She rubbed her chest as despair settled in her chest.

"Tessa?" Robin stood at the door to the kitchen. "Coming?"

The kindness in her voice broke Tessa. She swiped at the tears that squeezed from her eyes and strode toward her. Robin held the door wide. Tessa walked into the kitchen, letting the comforting smells surround and ground her.

"That's odd." Robin crossed the room and closed the door to the mudroom.

"What?"

"The door. It was closed. It's always closed."

"Maybe Veronica or Millie came in for lunch and forgot to close it?" Tessa filled the kettle with water.

"No. Elaine gave them the day off. They went to the saddlery today with Danica and Evelyn. They're having lunch there. They won't be back until late." Robin's voice edged up. "Something's off. Look." She pointed to a series of muddy scuffs on the floor. "I mopped this morning." Her normally pale skin grew even paler.

Tessa's stomach twisted. Her palms grew damp as Robin's fear surged and became palpable.

Robin's eyes flitted to the door leading to the back stairs and the rest of the house.

The small hairs rose on the back of Tessa's neck.

"Elaine! Petra!" Robin plucked the largest knife from the block.

Elaine and Petra shoved through the door together.

"What?" Elaine crossed the room in three steps.

"Someone's in the house." She gestured to the door to the back stairs. "Look."

"Start from the beginning." Petra lifted her chin.

"When we came in the back door was open. See? There's mud on the floor and look—" Robin pointed to the door leading out to the back stairs. "I closed and locked that this morning. No one else has been in here."

Elaine's brows knit tightly. "We need a plan. Tessa, you're with me. Petra, you and Robin stay here. Secure all the doors." She gestured to a thick steel bar. "Drop this in place once we are through the kitchen door and set the pin. Call Millie and tell them to get back here. Tell her plan C. You have that?"

"Plan C?"

"She'll know what it means." Elaine kissed Robin. "Don't worry, love. Listen to Petra." She moved to Petra and kissed her. "Stay together." She cupped her face. "Take care of each other and remember what I've taught you."

She pulled a key from her pocket and unlocked a deep drawer. After she opened it, she removed a large rolling pin, dark with age, thick and heavy. She passed it to Tessa. Elaine plucked a set of black gloves and pulled them on. Her eyes gleamed as she seated them between her fingers and flexed her knuckles. Tessa raised an eyebrow.

"Weighted. You should have a pair. Remind me to ask Millie to obtain some for you." Tessa—" Elaine held her gaze. "This is not a drill. Have you ever been in a real fight?"

"Once or twice in grade school. And sparring with Millie and you."

Elaine tapped the rolling pin with her index finger. "There are no rules. And we cannot afford mercy. They'll not show you any. If someone attacks you, end it. If this means what I think it means, they won't stop until we're all eliminated."

A frisson of fear and anger spread through Tessa's body. Her hands were damp on the rolling pin. Her simmering anger bloomed hot. "If they start anything, I'll finish it."

"Good."

"Elaine?" Robin's knuckles were white where she gripped the knife. "What about the others? June and Fallon?"

"We're going to the library first to check on Martha and the others. If we see them on the way, we'll send them here. Only open the door for them or us."

Robin nodded her understanding with her mouth set in a grim line.

Elaine crossed to the back stairs. "With any luck they're lost and going from room to room." She led the way up the narrow winding steps and Tessa followed, ready to do whatever it took to defend her home. She shoved away her fears and focused on Elaine's back as they climbed toward the second floor.

Chapter Twenty-Three

"WHAT NOW?" BENITA rested her chin on her hand. She played with the placket of Astrid's shirt.

Astrid stretched out on the mattress. "I don't know. I didn't get to debrief with Tessa because someone bolted." She tugged on Benita's curls. "Not that I minded the results of chasing you down. Why did you leave?"

Benita shifted her gaze, avoiding Astrid's eyes. "Guilt. Afraid of Tessa knowing I know. I knew she loved me. And I love her. Have loved her since forever. I've blown her off, so many times I thought she was about to tell me she loved me. I let her believe it was casual. Kept her at a distance. Pretended to not care. I hurt her. And now I have to figure out how to make it up to her. I don't even know if that's possible."

Astrid rubbed Benita's back in small circles. "I had to admit that I faked my own death. Surely you can admit to loving her. She forgave me. She'll forgive you. I wouldn't have pushed her in the scene if I hadn't been sure. Never doubt the power of love, Benita."

The door to the room slammed open.

"What the fuc—"

"Isn't this pretty? Get out of that bed now." A thin man stepped into the room and pointed a pistol at them.

Benita and Astrid scrambled off the bed. "Who the fuck are you?" Benita stepped in front of Astrid.

"The man who is going to splatter your brains all over this room if you don't do what I say. Out the door now."

Astrid gripped Benita's shoulder. "Stop. Don't antagonize him."

Benita wriggled out of Astrid's grip and turned to face her. "I'll do whatever the fucking fuck I want to." She shoved Astrid backward before she turned and stepped toward to the man.

"Shut the fuck up and let's go. They're waiting for us."

Astrid took a step toward Benita. "Do as he says."

"The fuck I will." Benita dropped down and spun and whipped a low kick, sweeping the man's legs from under him. Astrid stood transfixed to the spot, fear freezing her. Benita pounced on the man and swatted the gun from his hand.

"Get it." Benita smashed her elbow into the man's nose. He swore and swung wildly as blood spouted from his nose.

Astrid picked up the gun. Her palms were sweaty as she gripped it. Benita and the man struggled on the floor. Astrid set the gun aside and picked up the bedside lamp. Benita was on the bottom now. The man had her pinned and his arm in a bar across her throat. Rage flowed though Astrid. She brought the heavy brass lamp down on the back of the man's head. He screamed and collapsed on top of Benita. Astrid grabbed him by his shoulders and rolled him off Benita. He pushed up from the floor and struggled weakly to his feet.

"*Porra. Idiota de merda.*" Benita scrambled to her feet, squared up, and kicked the man full in the face. His head snapped back before he crumpled to the floor and lay still.

Astrid turned Benita to look at her. Her face was puffy and red where the man had struck her. "Are you okay?"

"Do I look okay?" Benita turned, spat on the man, and kicked him in the head. "That fucker was trying to kill me. Would have killed me. Us." Her eyes narrowed.

"How did he get in here?" Bile rose in Astrid's throat. "I thought the house was secure."

"Rats only need the tiniest of holes." Benita yanked her clothes in order. "Come on. Bring the gun. We need to find Elaine."

Astrid stooped and picked the weapon up.

"Give it to me." She took the gun from Astrid and pulled the slide back. "Idiot. He didn't even have a round chambered."

"Do we just leave him here?" Astrid eyed the man. His neck was bent at an unnatural angle. She nudged him with her foot.

Benita reached down and touched her fingers to his neck. "Porra." She shoved her hair back with her hand as she stood. "Unless you want to drag a dead man down the hall, yes." She turned from Astrid and strode away muttering to herself.

*

ELAINE PAUSED IN the hallway outside the library. She

held her finger to her lips. Tessa stilled, straining to hear sounds from the library. Her pulse sped up with the quiet. Elaine pressed her ear to the door. Her mouth drew down and her brows furrowed. She signaled to Tessa to follow her.

Tessa held the rolling pin across her chest like a bat. Elaine clasped the doorknob, turned it slowly before she shoved it wide. The silence and lack of response from anyone in the library hit Tessa like a punch to her gut.

Elaine stepped inside and Tessa followed. She took steady breaths, holding on to everything Millie had taught her about how to stay calm when all she wanted to do was run. The library was a shambles. The card catalog had been dumped and scattered. The couch and chairs were overturned.

She raked the room with her eyes. Fear grabbed her, dug its claws into her. Where were Martha, Lucia, and Myfanwy? Elaine stalked the room slowly. Tessa stood frozen to the spot. A groan came from the far corner of the library.

Tessa bolted toward the sound, realizing her error too late as a man wrenched the rolling pin from her hands and punched her in the face. The blow knocked her down. Pain exploded along her jaw. Her vision clouded, she scrabbled backward, kicking blindly. A hand on her collar dragged her to her feet and shoved her away. Her chest ached. Her throat burned. Tessa swallowed the bile that rose in her throat.

Elaine stepped in front of her. "Try someone your own size, asshole." She slapped the man across the face. He staggered and swung his fist. Elaine stepped inside his guard and punched him in the gut before she delivered an elbow to the back of his neck, dropping him. She gripped his hair with one hand and yanked his head up, grabbed his chin with the other, and twisted sharply. Tessa winced at the snap.

A slow clap made Tessa turn toward the sound. A petite woman flanked by two men stood in the doorway. "Well done. I see age hasn't slowed you down."

Elaine rested her fists on her hips. "I'm only going to ask you once, Widow. Where is my sister?"

"Widow? So formal. Come on, you used to call me Jacqueline."

Elaine took two steps toward the woman. The men on either side stepped in front of her. Despair settled over Tessa. Some help she had been. She scanned the room, trying to imagine how Millie would have reacted in the same situation.

Jacqueline shoved the men aside and strolled into the room followed by the men. She wagged her finger at Elaine. "Ah, ah, ah. You don't want to do anything that will make me do something you don't want me to do."

Elaine pinched her nose. "This is not a movie and I'm not in the mood for theatrics. Where. Is. Martha?"

Jacqueline held up her phone and turned it to face Elaine. A photo of Martha, Lucia, and Myfanwy, naked, bound, and lying on the floor, appeared. "She and her playmates are safe in her office. For now. Unless you do something that makes me send word to kill them."

Elaine lifted her chin. "What do you want?"

Tessa blinked at Elaine's calm tone, as if she were discussing the weather. She clenched her jaw to keep from screaming. Dead. They were all dead. Astrid had been right.

"What's mine. I'm here to collect a debt I've waited years to collect."

"I don't owe you anything."

"Oh no. Not you." She sniffed. "I gave up on getting my heart back from you many years ago."

Tessa stared, her gaze shifting from Elaine to Jacqueline. Lovers? They had been lovers?

Elaine rolled her eyes. "Not that again. I don't love you. For fuck's sake, is that why you're here? You think threatening to kill my sister is the way to win me back?"

"No. And I've moved on. Not that it's any of your business. I'm here for Roxanne, although she calls herself Astrid now. She stole from me. I want my money back, with interest."

Elaine rubbed her chin. "This is about money? How much do you want?"

"More than you have. And it's not just the money. She made a fool out of me. And I'm not in the habit of letting people do that."

"No need when you do such a good job on your own." Elaine rested one hand on her hip.

Jacqueline's face twisted into a snarl. "You are still a bitch. And I haven't forgotten about Oslo."

Though the open door, Tessa caught a glimpse of Benita, flanked by Astrid. Her heart squeezed hard. Would Elaine give up Astrid? In Benita's hand was a large pistol. Tessa chewed her lip, racking her brain for what to do.

Elaine stepped closer to Jacqueline. Her movement served as cover for Benita's entry to the library. Tessa held Benita's gaze briefly, before Benita shifted her eyes indicating Tessa should not draw attention to them.

Tessa forced her gaze from her. Jacqueline stepped back and away from Elaine. The two men edged forward and drew guns from the waistband of their pants. "You're good, Elaine, but even you won't be able to deal with them in time stop me from killing your sister. You cost me three good men and thousands for the cover-up in Oslo." She pushed her lip out in a pout. "And I loved that house, I hated having to sell it."

The hairs on Tessa's arms stood up as Benita crept up behind Jacqueline. In an instant she grabbed her upper arm and pressed the gun to the side of her head. "Tell those assholes to drop their guns or your brains will be all over this library. Astrid, get her phone."

The men turned toward Benita, bumping into each other. Taking advantage of the situation, Elaine launched herself at them and took them to the ground. Tessa stepped up and stomped on the hand of the man closest to her. The gun fell from his hand, and she kicked it away from them.

He grabbed her legs, sending her crashing to the floor. He rolled on top of her and straddled her waist. Her vision narrowed as rage welled up. She arched up, unseating him. She spun around and wrapped her legs around his shoulders and head. She gripped his wrist and wrenched down as she rocked her hips up. He screamed when his elbow snapped. Tessa rolled them over and delivered a sharp punch to the side of his head. The man went limp.

*

ASTRID WRETCHED THE phone from Jacqueline's grip.

As she did, Jacqueline jerked free of Benita's grasp, spun, and slapped the gun from Benita's hand. Astrid stuffed the phone into her front pocket.

At her feet, Benita and Jacqueline grappled for the gun. Terror gave way to rage. She swept her eyes over the room for a weapon. Among the scattered books, her gaze landed on the leather-bound copy of *Through the Looking-Glass*.

She snatched the copy off the floor.

Jacqueline slipped Benita's hold and rolled off her, quick as a cat. She snatched the pistol from the floor and scrambled to her feet. Panting, she looked out of the top of her eyes at Astrid. "I've dreamed of doing this." She straightened and lifted the pistol, her hand trembling.

"So have I." Astrid spun away from the barrel and brought the heavy book down on Jacqueline's hand, knocking the gun aside. She shoved the edge of the book into her throat as hard as she could.

Jacqueline staggered before she dropped to the floor. Astrid straddled her, pinning the smaller woman's arms to her sides with her knees.

"Get off me." Jacqueline struggled under her.

"Fuck you." Astrid wrapped both hands around her neck and squeezed hard. Every bit of rage poured through her body into her fingertips. Every moment she had ever looked over her shoulder, and every minute she had spent apart from the love of her life, fueled her fury. Jacqueline's face paled and grayed as she choked her.

A red haze clouded her vision. Fingers pulled at her arms and she shook them off. *End it. No more running. No more hiding. No more fear.*

A shout in her ear, then a sharp slap snapped against

her face. Astrid jerked her hands free and balled her hands into fists, ready to punch whoever slapped her. Jacqueline sputtered and coughed, gasping for air.

"Stop, Astrid. Stop. Don't." Benita's face was in front of her. She cupped Astrid's face. "Come on. Elaine will handle this."

As Astrid stood, her knees wobbled.

Jacqueline rolled to her side. She wheezed and coughed but made no move to run.

Benita wrapped her arm around her waist. "Let me help you."

Astrid shrugged out of her grasp. "I'm fine."

"The fuck you are but we can talk about that later." Benita frowned at her.

Astrid turned from her accusing stare to survey the chaotic scene. Elaine stood over the two men, quietly talking with Tessa. Tessa. In the melee she had lost track of Tessa. Tessa's chin was on her chest as she listened to Elaine. Astrid pulled Jacqueline's phone from her pocket and held it up. "Elaine."

Elaine held Astrid's gaze a long moment before she took the phone. "We need to get to the office." She reached down and clasped Jacqueline's upper arm. "Come on. You haven't outlived your usefulness. Yet." Benita held out Jacqueline's pistol to Elaine.

"No. One more thing to keep track of. How many men do you have left?"

Jacqueline quirked her mouth. "Like I'm going to tell you?"

"We left one in my room." Benita rubbed the back of her neck. "He won't be joining us unless there is life after death."

Jacqueline's mouth drew down. Elaine turned to her, clasped both arms, and shook her savagely. "I will not ask again. I will throttle you right here, right now, if you do not tell me how many more of these assholes are in my house. How very dare you, sneaking into my home. My home!" Elaine shouted in her face.

Jacqueline's haughty façade crumpled in the face of Elaine's fury. She shifted her eyes to the two men on the floor before she brought her gaze back to Elaine's face.

"Only these."

"No one in the office?"

Jacqueline shook her head in the negative. "No one else in the house."

"Where is the car?"

"Half a mile down the service road."

"What's it look like? How many with it?"

"Dark-green sedan. Only one. William."

"You brought your child to a kidnapping? Deliberately placed him in danger? What the hell is wrong with you?" Elaine's brows furrowed.

"He's over twenty-one. Family business is family business." A flash of fear crossed Jacqueline's face before she smoothed it.

Elaine leaned forward until her nose was an inch from Jacqueline's face. "If you have lied to me, I will kill you." She turned to Tessa. "Tessa, call Millie, use the code, give her an update, tell her what to look for, tell her to detain William and deliver the car here. Then call the kitchen and inform the others. Tell them to stay put until Millie gets here. We still need to sweep the house. I don't trust Jacqueline as far as I could throw her." Her voice was sharp as she swept her gaze over the men on the floor.

"Astrid, help Tessa and Benita collect their guns and any other weapons, empty their pockets of everything, strip off any personal effects, watches, etc., and leave everything on the desk." Elaine locked her hand around Jacqueline's upper arm and dragged the gasping woman along behind her as she strode to the back of the library.

"All right." Astrid chewed her lip as she stared at the bodies of the men, no threat to anyone now. Her gut roiled as she took in their blank stares and limp forms. She could do this. Would do this, to help Elaine. She glanced up at Tessa, whose gaze was fixed on Benita. Her shirt was ripped, her face already bruising from the fight. Her lip was split and bleeding. Astrid shoved her hands in her pockets, pressed her lips together. Now was not the time to discuss what had transpired between them in the dining room. Tessa glanced in Astrid's direction briefly before she crossed the room to Benita. They would talk, later. Or not.

They held each other a long moment. Tessa ran her hands over Benita's arms. "Are you hurt?"

"I'm fine, Bebê." She cupped Tessa's face gently and turned it to the side. "We need to get you some ice."

Tessa leaned her brow against Benita's forehead. "How come you don't even look like you've been in a fight?"

"Lots of real practice." Benita looped her arms around Tessa's neck. "You did good, Bebê. I would have fought a hundred to get to you."

Astrid turned from the tender scene as her adrenaline faded. Her job was done. Tessa and Benita knew now, even without the mind-fuck scene, how much they meant to each other.

And that was as it should be. Astrid chewed her lip. Would they ever forgive her for being the lightning rod of trouble she was? She spun in a slow circle, surveying the damage to the library. Dozens of books lay scattered over the floor. Others rested haphazardly on broken shelves. Her heart ached as she picked up a torn paperback of *The Price of Salt*.

Her gaze fell upon the dead men. A profane violation of this space. The memory of her first kiss with Benita rose in her mind. She turned from the ugliness before her and closed her eyes. The scattered books made her heart hurt. Surveying the destruction of the library had Astrid ready to resurrect the men and kill them herself for defiling Tessa's happy place. And after this what were the chances of her being hired now? She covered her mouth and wondered if even all her savings would cover the cost of the cleaners. One body was one thing. This was something entirely different. She would give them every bit of her savings to end this with Jacqueline. So long as Jacqueline drew breath would Astrid, or any of them, now ever be safe?

No matter. She plucked up her courage, held tight to her anger to bolster it. "I need to see how this ends."

Tessa glanced up from Benita's arms. "Elaine gave us directions."

"She did. But I'm not willing to let her shoulder all the responsibility for ending this. I've lost fifteen years of my life. She murdered Clarice. I don't care what happens. I will not stand by and let her take anything or anyone else from me. I need to know that Jacqueline will never threaten me or mine again." Astrid frowned at the wall of shelves at the rear of the room. "Where did she go with her?"

Tessa pointed to the far wall. "On the left. Third shelf up from the bottom. There's a copy of *The Stone Gate*. Pull it toward you. A section of the bookcase will slide back. There will be a panel of switches and two doors. Press the middle button twice. It will open the door that leads to the passage to the office."

"Bebê, we need to go with her." Benita clasped Tessa's hand.

"No, you don't." Astrid lifted her shoulders and let them fall. "No sense in all of us having to deal with Elaine's wrath."

Benita kicked the leg of the man closest to her. "These idiotas de merda are not going anywhere." She bent and opened the man's coat. She ran her hand over the inside pocket and pulled out a clear plastic case. Inside were three empty syringes. She tossed the case to the floor and continued to search the man. The handle of a small revolver protruded from his waistband. Benita pulled it free and placed it on the desk. "Let's go."

Astrid suppressed her shudder. "Should I bring one of their guns?"

"No. Unless, you have some skill you've been hiding. Elaine will handle it."

Astrid led the way to the back of the library, following Tessa's directions, ready to see the end of this nightmare. There would be time for sorting things with Tessa and Benita later. She had to finish this with Jacqueline, now and forever.

Chapter Twenty-Four

TESSA TRAILED BEHIND Astrid as they walked along the dimly lit passage to the office. Her body ached and the cut on her lip throbbed. Benita followed close behind them. Astrid stopped at the panel that would lead to the office.

"Wait—" Tessa stepped in front of Astrid and whispered. "Listen first. I don't want to surprise Elaine."

Astrid moved next to Tessa and they both pressed their ears against the panel. Tessa frowned. "We shouldn't be here. If we startle Elaine, it might give Jacqueline an opportunity to escape."

Astrid's shoulders slumped. "You're right. I shouldn't be here." She turned and squeezed past Benita. "We should do what Elaine said."

Tessa stared at the dejected set of Astrid's shoulders. Benita touched her arm. "Go to her, Bebê. She needs to know it's okay, that we're in this with her."

"We are?" Tessa touched Benita's cheek.

"We are. *Eu te amo muito.* Now go, I'm right behind

you."

Tessa followed Astrid's retreating form as she made her way back to the library.

She squinted against the bright light as they entered the room. Astrid moved woodenly. She righted the end table and stopped to collect the books lying near it. Tessa's heart squeezed hard. She loved her still. And understood now. Astrid had been trying to save her, had saved her from Jacqueline, saved her from death, or from the never-ending nightmare of being trafficked. She had risked everything to keep Tessa safe.

Astrid stood and lifted her gaze to Tessa. "I'm so sorry."

"For what?"

"This." She gestured to the room. "All of it. I should never have borrowed money from her. This is all my fault."

"The hell it is. She's a maniac. And she has had it in for Rowan House and Elaine for years. This was just an excuse."

Astrid turned away from Tessa. "I was so careful. How did she find me?"

"Remember the creeper from the ferry car park? The one who asked you for a light?"

Astrid turned back to her. "Yes."

"I've seen him before. Always the same thing. Asks for a light, fumbles with his phone a bit as he's asking. The last three pickups we've had he's been there. And who knows how many before. I think Jacqueline has been paying folks to watch for our traffic, to see who comes and goes. I don't think she's known where you have been, or you wouldn't be here now." Tessa lifted her chin toward

Jaqueline's accomplices. "Those guys don't play. They would have drugged you and had you back to her in record time if they had found you."

"They came because of me." Astrid stepped back and stumbled over a book. Her arms pinwheeled. Tessa bounded forward and caught her before she fell. "Hey. Stop running. Please."

"I'm okay. Release me."

"No." Tessa tightened her grip around Astrid's waist.

"What?" Astrid's brows drew down. She rested her hands on Tessa's shoulders.

"Not until you promise to not leave me. I can't—won't survive if you leave me again."

Astrid relaxed in Tessa's arms. "You have everything you need here. Benita. A found family who will do anything to keep you safe. Why do you need me?"

"Because, idiota, she is in love with you," Benita crossed the room. She stepped up behind Astrid and encircled her with her arms with her hands settled on Tessa's hips. "You belong here. Right here." She rested her cheek against Astrid's back.

Astrid looked away from Tessa's face. "You two belong together."

"Sim, and you belong with us." Benita met Tessa's eyes over Astrid's shoulder. "There is enough love for all of us."

Tessa held Benita's gaze. "For all of us."

Astrid lifted her chin, shifted in Tessa's arms so she could see both of them. "How will this be?"

"However the fuck we want it to." Benita shifted her gaze between each of them. "I want you to be with us, Astrid. If you want to be." She turned to Tessa. "Forgive me for not saying so sooner. I love you. I always have loved you, and I'm sorry I didn't say the words to you before.

Tessa inclined her head toward Astrid. "I'm sorry it took Astrid pushing for me to tell you. And I'm sorry we weren't alone."

Astrid stiffened in Tessa's arms. "I don't belong between you two."

Benita gripped Tessa's waist, locking Astrid between them. "No. You don't get to run unless it's really what you want. Say the words and I will let go, but you are going to have to tell us to our faces that you don't want to be with us." Benita's harsh whisper echoed in the room. "I didn't risk everything to save you to have you bail out for whatever reason you make up in your head. So tell us now before we waste one more moment wishing for what we can't have."

The moment drew out between them like spun glass. Tessa swallowed the ache in her throat.

"Please let me go."

Benita released Astrid and stepped closer to Tessa. Astrid shrugged loose from their arms. Benita shifted over and took Tessa's hand, her grip bruising.

Astrid's eyes shimmered. "I can't make any promises. I don't even know where I'll be in a year. Or if I will be in a year."

"What the hell are you talking about? If you will be." Tessa wrapped her hand in Benita's shirt to ground herself. "Are you considering ending your life?"

"No." Astrid's voice was quiet. "I'm no longer in that space. There was a time I considered it almost daily. This is not the first attempt on my life. Do you think Jacqueline will simply stop? I'm tired, Tessa. I'm tired of all of it. Running. Hiding. Pretending to be stronger than I am. Being alone."

"You're not alone."

A sad half smile crossed Astrid's face. "That is sweet of you to say, but unless I find refuge here, I am." She shifted her gaze to Benita. "You have everything you need here. Both of you. Don't ask me to complicate your life. You don't have the power to make the offer. My future is in the Mistresses' hands." She gestured to the chaos on the far side of the library and grimaced. "I've already cost them a huge amount of money with the cost of the repairs to the house and the cleaners. Don't ask me—please don't ask me again to commit to you two. I can't."

Benita's hand settled on Tessa's lower back. "I understand."

"Do you, Tessa?"

Tessa pressed her lips together. Not trusting herself to speak, she turned away from Astrid. The reality of their situations settled over her shoulders, weighed her heart down. Benita's hand on her back and her steady presence were the only things keeping her from flying apart. The uncertainty of their future together stung. Astrid was right of course. Tessa and Benita alone could not stand against Jacqueline, and her organization. A searing ache grew in her heart. She was going to lose Astrid again, and this time it would be so much worse, because as much as she loved her, she would not leave Benita, or her Rowan House family.

The door to the library opened. Elaine stepped through the opening alone. Tessa's gut twisted at Jacqueline's absence. "You have their weapons? Did you empty their pockets of everything?"

"I think. I want to check them again in case we missed anything." Tessa stepped away from Benita and returned to the bodies.

"Use the bin to hold them. When you check them this time, feel their clothes for trackers."

"What?"

"After a little encouragement, Jacqueline explained how they tracked Astrid here." She held up a small white square. "This is what you are looking for."

Benita crossed the room to help Tessa, mumbling a steady stream of swear words as she did.

Tessa watched Astrid and Elaine from under her lashes. Tessa strained her ears to hear what they discussed as she searched the man's coat and pants for the tag.

"Tessa, Benita, meet us in the kitchen when you are finished." Elaine turned away from them and left the library. Astrid followed her and matched Elaine's brisk stride, never looking back.

"Don't, Bebê."

"What?"

"Don't go where you just did. None of this is your fault. Whatever happens." Benita held up a square that was the match to the one Elaine showed. "It was in his watch pocket. Did you find his?" She tossed the plastic tag into the waste bin. It clattered as it fell and rattled when it hit the bottom of the can.

*

"WHERE IS JACQUELINE?" Astrid had managed to wait

until they were in the hall to ask.

"Having a discussion with my sister and Lucia." Elaine stopped outside the kitchen door. "Unless you want to be more involved in this than you already are, I wouldn't ask anything you don't want answered."

Despair-tinged rage Astrid had stifled bubbled up. "Involved? She has been stalking me, waiting to pounce, wanting to kill me or worse for the last fifteen years. I have not had one second of peace in my life. I could not be more involved. Tell me. Now. Where. Is. Jacqueline?"

Elaine shifted her gaze to the mantel clock. "I expect that by now, she is very ready to make a deal. Does that make you feel better?"

"A deal? My life for her leaving you alone." Astrid stepped back from Elaine.

"I'm going to pretend I did not hear you say that." Elaine's brows drew down and she squared her shoulders, leaned slightly over Astrid, asserting her height difference. "What kind of person barters another life? How can you think I'd trade the life of my wife's best friend, and someone I have come to think of as a friend?"

The hurt expression on Elaine's face pierced Astrid to her soul.

"If I were going to do that, I would have handed you over in the library and saved us a fuck ton of money."

Astrid rested her chin on her chest. "I am sorry I even suggested it. I apologize."

"Elaine?" Petra called from beyond the kitchen doors.

"Yes. Open the doors, love."

The scrape of metal on metal echoed in the dining room as Petra opened the doors to the kitchen. She rushed through the opening, Robin on her heels, and enveloped

Elaine in a hug. Astrid left them there. Her heart ached after observing the tender words and kisses between them. Visions of Tessa and Benita filled her mind and she wiped her eyes. Elaine was the image of all that a Mistress should be, willing and able to do anything to keep her submissives safe.

Astrid crossed to the counter. The light scent of lemon filled the well-ordered kitchen. The counters were uncluttered. Each area of the kitchen was tidy, every item in its place. Would Astrid ever have a place? Not here. Not when she had brought such chaos to the orderly world of Rowan House. Thank goodness there had been no guests. Astrid shuddered as the what-ifs piled up and spilled down her cheeks. She braced her arms on the counter and rested her forehead on her arms. A familiar raw ache settled in her chest. Alone. And by her choice. She could have said yes, should have said yes to Tessa and Benita. But how, how could she? What did she have to offer them?

A cool hand pushed under her hair and settled on the back of her neck. Another settled in the center of her back and rubbed in slow circles. The familiar scent of Tessa's cologne intertwined with Benita's perfume surrounded her. Unable to stifle her tears, Astrid gave in then, in that moment, surrendered to their care and their love.

Chapter Twenty-Five

BENITA TOUCHED TESSA'S chin and gently turned her head. "When I look at you, I want to kill them all over again."

Tessa winced as she shifted, her ribs reminding her of every punch that landed. "As satisfying as that might be, I'd rather use my energy for good."

Astrid frowned. "You both need a warm soak in a bath with Epsom salts." She looked away from them. "Do you want more ice?" She shook the ice bucket.

"No, my skin needs a break." Tessa shifted to her side and passed Astrid the washcloth.

Astrid replaced the bucket on the bedside table. "I wish I'd asked for some wine."

"We can order some." Benita reached for the room phone.

"No. You two shouldn't have any with the pain medications and I don't want to drink alone."

"It looks worse than it feels. I'll be fine tomorrow." Tessa reached for Astrid's hand and clasped it, interlacing their fingers. "Leave it, Nurse Ratched. Come lay down with us." Tessa tugged gently. The bedsprings squeaked as Tessa shifted closer to Benita, making room for Astrid.

Astrid lifted her chin. "We should do that one. If I get to stay. I would love to perform her character. She wore such delicious outfits in the show. Such repressed energy and tension between Mildred Ratched and Gwendolyn. Mildred finally acknowledging her feelings for Gwendolyn, after she risked her life to protect Mildred. Taking a bullet for her. Nearly dying to save her lover. The scenes between them are incredibly sensuous. Not to mention their costumes were divine. I've always wanted to play Gwendolyn, such contained power in her character."

Tessa patted the space she had made on the mattress. "Come on. After recent events we'd certainly have insight into their desperation and desires. Enough shop talk. Lie down."

"I don't want to crowd you." Astrid shifted her gaze to the bed and picked at the sheets.

"Where is my kick-ass Mistress? We aren't going to break, amor. Come here." Benita gripped Astrid's wrist above Tessa's hand. "We aren't letting go until you get in this bed."

"Do I need to remind you who is in charge here?" Astrid's eyes gleamed.

Tessa's pulse sped up as she watched the dance between Benita and Astrid.

"Maybe." Benita set her teeth on her lower lip.

Tessa swallowed hard. No matter how many times she had seen Benita bite her lower lip, use it deliberately on the most hard-ass mistresses, it always undid her. Witnessing the energy between Benita and Astrid drove home to her how much they would miss Astrid if she left. Tessa rubbed her thumb over the back of Astrid's hand. "I think we need a lesson, Ma'am."

"I see." Astrid glared at Benita. "You both survived attempts on your life, defeated men half again as large as you and have the bumps and bruises to prove it, and you want to scene?"

"What better way to celebrate we are alive?" Benita yanked hard, and Astrid collapsed on top of them. Tessa rolled to her side, making space between them. She slid her leg over Astrid's thighs, pinning her in place.

"What are you doing? You're going to hurt—"

Benita kissed Astrid. Her protest dissolved into a deep groan that rattled Astrid's chest under Tessa's fingers.

Benita pulled back, pushed Astrid's hair from her face, and tucked it behind her ear. "Do you want us to stop?"

Tessa paused, waiting for her consent to continue.

"No." Astrid slid her arms around Tessa's and Benita's shoulders. "Not ever."

Tessa leaned up to peer in Astrid's face. She kissed her, teasing the seam of her lips open. Astrid opened to her, gave in to her deep kiss. Benita's hum of appreciation sent a wave of want through Tessa. Every ache and pain receded as desire rose, sweeping away her fear. Astrid wanted them. Wanted to be with them. And no matter what happened going forward, that part of her world would be settled.

Benita tugged at Astrid's shirt. "I don't like this shirt."

Astrid frowned. "Are you insulting my sense of fashion?"

"No. It's just in my way." Benita yanked the bottom of Astrid's shirt free of her waistband. "And I'm not having good feelings about this skirt either."

Astrid rolled her eyes. "You are incorrigible."

"Sim." Benita unfastened Astrid's shirt. Tessa bent to place a kiss on each bit of Astrid's warm skin as Benita slowly exposed her.

"Bebê, is this not the most exquisite bra you have ever seen?" Benita ran her finger under the lace that bordered the sheer cups. Astrid's nipples tented the see-through fabric.

"It is." Tessa drew her fingers over the soft swell of Astrid's breasts. "And her breasts are sublime."

Astrid panted as her gaze flitted back and forth between the two of them. "What are you going to do to me?"

"Whatever we want to, unless you tell us to stop." Benita smoothed her hand over Astrid's stomach. "I like to play with my food before I eat it."

Tessa pushed Astrid's shirt off her shoulders, pausing to nibble along her collar bone, rewarded by her sharp inhale of breath and tight groan.

Tessa urged her up, took the shirt off completely, and tossed it aside. Benita had moved between Astrid's legs, shoved up her skirt, so that the matching panties were exposed, along with her suspender belt. The scent of desire rose between them. Benita glanced up at Tessa. "Should we leave the shoes off or on?"

"On." Tessa palmed Astrid's breasts. "Do we need to restrain you? Or will you be good?"

Astrid's eyes flashed. "Do you want to? Would you like that? See your Mistress bound? At your mercy?"

Tessa's heart squeezed hard. Her Mistress.

Benita rested her hand on Tessa's thigh. "What do you want to do, Bebê, with our Mistress? Show her what she's gotten into?"

She moved between Astrid's thighs and nuzzled the thin fabric of her panties, darker between her legs, evidence of her excitement.

Tessa slid her hand inside Astrid's bra, rolled her nipple between her thumb and forefinger. "Raise your hands, grip the lower rail, and don't move."

Astrid held her gaze as she lifted her hands and wrapped them around the lower rail of the headboard, her knuckles white where she gripped the low brass rail. "I thought you're the ones who needed a lesson?"

Tessa folded the cups of Astrid's bra down to expose her nipples. "This is what happens when you hesitate, Mistress."

Benita straddled Astrid. "Sim. You had your chance." She rolled her hips. "Now it's ours."

Astrid arched into Benita's movements, pleasure playing out across her face.

"Bebê, get my favorite thing." Benita bent and kissed Astrid.

Tessa left the bed. In the closet she pulled their toy box off the shelf. She flicked the latch and surveyed their private collection of toys. After locating Benita's favorite dildo, she took it and the harness it fit in from the chest and slid it back to its place. She leaned against the closet doorframe to watch Benita and Astrid.

Benita's hands were latched onto Astrid's nipples, and she plucked them in a rhythm, moving her hips in a steady motion. Tessa's clit grew thick and ached as she took in the scene. Astrid partially dressed, her skirt rucked up, with Benita teasing her nipples. Their tight groans and sensual whispers echoed in the quiet of the room.

Tessa paused long enough to slip into the harness and seat the toy. After snagging a bottle of lube from the nightstand she stood next to the bed. "Where do you want me?"

Both women turned to look at her. "In this bed," they said at the same time.

Tessa flushed. Benita and Astrid laughed.

"Bebê, I think you need to lay down, and let us take it from there." Benita inclined her head toward Astrid's hands which had remained on the bedrail.

Tessa tapped Astrid's hand. "You are released."

Astrid moved her hands from the headboard and settled them on Benita's hips. "Shall we?"

Tessa glanced between the women. Their expressions were feral. Tessa swallowed. The dynamic had shifted, she was no longer in charge, that much was clear. Benita moved off Astrid. She picked up a hair tie from the bedside table and pulled her hair back, using it to secure her mass of curls.

Astrid unzipped her skirt, arched her body, and slid out of it. She tossed it off the bed and added her underwear to the pile, followed by her bra.

"Get on the bed, lay flat on your back." Astrid's gaze was laser sharp.

Tessa placed the bottle of lube on the bedside table before she laid down. The toy stood rampant, the heavy weight of the base against her clit setting off ripples of pleasure. Benita wrapped her hand around the fat dildo and tugged. As she jacked it slowly the vibrations were delicious.

"So big. You can take all of that?" Astrid kneeled on the other side of her. She added her hand to Benita's and together they manipulated the toy.

"Sim. All of it. Would you like to watch?" Benita had the devil in her eyes and her voice.

Tessa rested one hand on Benita's thigh and the other on Astrid's hip. The women kissed as they continued their motions. The rhythmic press of the base on her needy flesh was exquisite. Her heart was full watching Astrid and Tessa kiss, take their time enjoying each other as they gave Tessa pleasure. She panted and arched into their touch, shifted until she could slide her hands along their slick thighs to touch their clits. Benita opened her legs, allowing Tessa access. She swept her fingers over her clit before she slid inside. She watched Benita's face as she fingered her.

"Don't forget Astrid, Bebê." Benita tilted her head toward her.

Tessa shifted her gaze to Astrid's face. She moved her hand from her hip, traced her fingers over her thigh before she rested them on the crease of her leg.

Astrid opened her legs and shifted closer on the bed, as she and Benita kept up their strokes. She lifted an eyebrow. "Waiting for permission?"

"Yes." Tessa panted. The sensation of having her fingers inside Benita drove her pleasure.

"Do it."

Tessa pushed her fingers into Astrid's wet heat. She closed her eyes to savor the sensation of being inside both women at once. Her nipples tightened. Her clit was rock hard as she fucked them both. Dizzy with desire, she panted and focused to stave off the orgasm building in her belly.

A hot hand landed on her breast and squeezed her nipple hard once before it settled in a familiar plucking patten. Benita. "Yes. So good. More." Tessa moaned as her body responded with waves of pleasure that spread out over her from her breast down. Fingers on her thigh pinched her before teasing under the harness strap.

She widened her legs. Barely-there touches on her labia had her spreading her legs wider in invitation. One finger entered her, followed by the achingly slow insertion of more. She surrendered to the sting and burn as it gave way to a sharp want for more and she arched up to meet Astrid's slow deep thrusts.

Tessa opened her eyes. Astrid's mouth was open, her breathing rough. She shifted her gaze to Benita. Benita's eyes were dark as she held Tessa's gaze. They were connected, the three of them, currents of desires spinning out between them.

"I'm close, so close." Astrid held her gaze, her hips rocking to meet Tessa's thrusts while she kept up her own rhythm, matching Tessa stroke for stroke.

Benita's body tightened around Tessa's fingers, signs that she was as close as Tessa. "Come with us, Bebê. Now."

Tessa's body jerked as waves of pleasure crashed over her. Astrid stroked her sweet spot. She bucked her hips into their hands, the combined sensation of the toy pressing against her clit and Astrid's strokes detonating her climax. Panting, she focused on the sensations as the women followed her, their bodies rippling around her fingers, their cries and moans of satisfaction melding into a cacophony of pleasure.

*

ASTRID PAUSED IN her strokes, unable to continue as her pleasure shook her body. She glanced at Benita, her face a mask of satisfaction. She met Astrid's eyes. "Move your hand. I have something to show you."

Astrid released the toy and shifted on the bed. Tessa withdrew her fingers. "Sit on my face, Ma'am. Please." Tessa trailed her slick fingers over Astrid's thigh.

"Face me." Benita had shifted and was straddling Tessa. "I want to watch you come while Tessa fucks me."

Tessa plumped the pillow under her head. Benita offered Astrid her hand. She turned on the mattress, lifted her leg over, and settled herself on her knees over Tessa's face. Her warm breath tickled her thigh before she placed a kiss on her clit.

Astrid held on to Benita's shoulders to steady herself. Benita clasped the head of the toy. "Watch me." She lowered herself slowly on the thick toy until she was flush. Astrid stared, openly shifting her gaze between the sinfully delicious sight of Benita sliding down the thick shaft, her blissful expression.

Benita's eyes were heavy lidded, her pupils blown wide. "Mmm. So good." She rose and fell at a slow pace, languid. Her heavy breasts moved with her actions, the effect mesmerizing.

Tessa's hands gripped Astrid's ass, urged her closer. The first touch of her tongue sent a rush of pleasure through her and she gasped. Tessa teased her tongue between her labia. She suckled her clit, rolled her tongue over it before thrusting her tongue deep. Astrid held tight to Benita's shoulders to steady herself.

"She's good at that, isn't she?" Benita rested her hands on Astrid's breasts, palmed and cupped them before she thumbed her nipples.

"Extremely good." Astrid trembled, closed her eyes against the pleasure.

Benita clucked her tongue before she squeezed Astrid's nipples in an iron grip. "No. Don't hide from me. I want to see when you come for us. Show me."

Astrid opened her eyes and fell into the dark pools of Benita's warm gaze. For them. They wanted her to be theirs. Both of them had risked their lives to protect her, had suffered for it, and asked nothing more than for Astrid to love them, to acknowledge she loved them. Her emotions caught her, and she faltered. Her orgasm eddied away from her, and she bit her lip to keep from crying out. She lifted clear of Tessa's mouth. Tessa locked her hands tight on Astrid's hips, preventing her from moving further. She nuzzled Astrid's thigh. "Stay. Please."

Benita stared into her eyes. She lifted her hand and cupped Astrid's face. "Don't do that, amor, don't think too much. Feel. Enjoy. We are alive, and here. Come for us." Benita's tender words filled up every hollow space in Astrid and flowed down her cheeks. Benita swiped a finger over her tears and licked them off her finger. "You belong to us, Astrid, no matter what you say. No one whose tears taste as sweet as yours could ever walk away from us. Come, amor, give us that gift too." She bent to Astrid's mouth and kissed her. A lazy, sensuous kiss. She sucked gently on Astrid's tongue and drove every thought from her mind but the sensation of Tessa's mouth on her clit and Benita's mouth on her own.

Astrid gripped Benita's shoulders, gave over, and

came, rocking her hips on Tessa's face, crying her pleasure into Benita's mouth, giving the women what they wanted, what they all wanted.

Chapter Twenty-Six

ASTRID STRAIGHTENED HER skirt and blouse as she stood before the dark wooden door leading to the office. Her stomach tightened and she inhaled deeply and exhaled slowly before she opened the door. The clock in the hall chimed nine. Astrid knocked on the door as the last note ebbed away.

"Enter," Lucia called from behind the door.

Astrid opened the door, stepped into the room, and closed the door firmly. Elaine, Martha, Lucia, and Petra sat in heavy armchairs arranged in a semi-circle in front of the desk. Their mistress masks firmly in place, their expressions revealed nothing. Astrid had spent the last evening practicing what she would say when they declined to hire her. She had perfected her response, rehearsed her speech so they would never know how devastated she was to be sent from Rowan House. A place that had become more like home than any other in the short twelve weeks she had lived there. After the events of the last two days, how could they offer her a position? Employing Astrid would be too risky, cause too much chaos, too much drama. Astrid stepped into the office.

"Sit down." Lucia gestured to the chair centered across from the women.

Astrid smoothed her skirt, sat, and crossed her legs. She met each woman's gaze in turn, gathering her strength. She firmed her chin. Whatever happened she was loved, had the love of not one but two amazing women. They could never take that from her. The logistics of their relationship could be worked out later.

"Astrid?" Petra's voice broke through her thoughts.

"I'm sorry, what?" Astrid swept her gaze over the group.

"I asked you if you were still willing to invest in Rowan House's enterprises, to become a full partner, or if recent events had put you off?" Lucia's tone was neutral.

"You're asking me to join you? As an invested partner?" Astrid shifted in her seat and leaned forward.

Lucia lifted her chin and pinned Astrid in place with her gaze. "Yes. As we discussed in our initial invitation to audition to join us." She placed her hands on the desk palm down. "Although some of us had reservations, your performance during the unpleasantness with Jacqueline convinced all of us you would be a valuable addition to our house."

"As a part owner?"

"Yes. If you are still willing to invest in our business. Martha will work out the details with you when you are ready to sign."

"I haven't accepted yet."

"Are you serious? You would say no? To us?" Elaine's brows drew down. "Really?"

"Give her a minute, love." Petra rested her hand on Elaine's forearm. "I didn't say yes right away, did I?"

"May I have a few hours to think about it?" Astrid smoothed her damp palms over her skirt.

"Any objections?" Lucia skewered Elaine with a hard glance. Elaine huffed out a breath and shook her head in the negative. "Please take your time, Astrid. This is much more than simply a financial arrangement. You will become part of us. Part of our family. And much like a family, after this, only death will take you from us. You will retain your freedom, but you will be expected to act in the best interests of Rowan House in all things." Lucia leaned back in her chair and crossed her legs. Petra reached over and clasped Elaine's hand. Astrid studied the fierce women before her, offering her a place in their kingdom, each a queen in her own right, who saw her as worthy of joining them.

Martha placed her hand on Lucia's thigh. "If you have any questions about the financial side of things, Astrid, I will be happy to answer them, including logistical questions about how our affiliate houses are run, and our plans for the future."

Astrid stood. "Thank you for your offer. I'll let you know of my decision."

She willed herself to walk from the room, only breaking stride after she turned down the hall leading to the dormitory.

*

TESSA LEANED INTO the strokes as Benita brushed her hair, the drag and pull on her scalp reassuring and soothing. "When do you think we'll know?"

"When we do. Mistresses run on their own time, you know that."

Tessa met Benita's gaze in the mirror. "No matter what happens, it's real between us, isn't it?" She searched Benita's expression.

"Our love?" Benita rested her hands on Tessa's shoulders. "Our love is the realest thing I know. And I'm going to spend the rest of my life showing you that." She turned Tessa and brushed a kiss over her lips.

Tessa pulled back. "But what about her? Was she acting? Just playing a part. Was she?"

"How can you ever know any of us mean anything? We are professionals. We make our living making people believe that for a little while, someone cares for them the way they want to be cared for." Benita held Tessa's gaze.

"I can feel you. Feel how much you love me." Tessa pulled Benita into her lap.

"Right. Same with you. I sense your love. Don't you sense that with Astrid? Trust yourself, trust what you feel."

"I did before and it didn't make any difference." Tessa hated how small her voice sounded.

"How can you say that? She gave up her life for you, Bebê."

Tessa scrubbed her hands over her face. "I want to believe that."

Benita placed her hand over Tessa's heart. "Your heart knows, listen to it."

A sharp rap at the door shattered the quiet.

Benita placed the hairbrush on the vanity. She pressed a quick kiss to Tessa's cheek. "We will be okay,

Bebê, whatever happens."

Tessa opened the door.

Astrid held her arms out wide. "Say hello to a new Mistress of Rowan House."

Benita rushed past Tessa, hugged Astrid. "They said yes?"

"And offered me a partnership." Astrid swept Benita into a hug. She kissed her and held her hand out to Tessa.

Tessa stared at them. "And just like that I'm supposed to be happy? You weren't willing to commit to us before. We're supposed to just act like everything is fine between us?"

Astrid stared at Tessa. "I haven't lied to you, Tessa. I was not, am not willing to risk anyone's life but my own. I can't go back and undo what I did before. I regret every second of pain and heartache I have ever caused you. But what would have happened to you and the others if I had surrendered to Jacqueline? I did what I did to save you, not because I didn't love you, or want you." Astrid released Benita and stepped back into the hall. "I understand if you can't forgive me. Some days I can't forgive myself. I won't stay if it will cause you pain."

Benita snatched Astrid's hand. "You are not going anywhere. We are not going to do this idiotic dance. Tessa, are you serious? What is going on?"

Tessa rested her chin on her chest. "I can't do this without a promise. Without a commitment from Astrid, she'll never leave me again."

"You want me to promise that right now? After all these years? What if you decide in six months you hate me?"

Tessa lifted her chin. "I could never hate you. Ever.

Even after you left me, I never hated you. I love you. And always will love you. As much as I love Benita."

"Bebê." Benita crossed to Tessa's side and slid her arm around her waist. She peered into her face. "You need this?"

"I do. Or I can't do this. I'm not going to waste my time on someone who's not all in."

Astrid rested her hands on her hips. "You want me to beg?"

"What if I do?" Tessa faced Astrid.

"That's not want you want really, is it?" Astrid strode into the room. She cupped the back of Tessa's neck in an iron grip. Tessa swallowed as Astrid's ice-blue gaze swallowed her whole.

"Kneel."

Tessa released Benita's hand and sank to her knees. She stared up at Astrid's face. Her heart hammered against her ribs as Astrid knotted her hand in her hair.

She tugged hard, pulling Tessa off balance, and her gaze pinned her in place. "Are you willing to serve me, Tessa Morgan, for the rest of your days, as my submissive?"

Benita's gasp pulled Tessa from the moment. She struggled in Astrid's grasp.

"No. This is between you and me." Astrid tightened her grip in Tessa's hair. "You said you wanted to know if I'm all in, I expect the same. I'll get to Benita in a moment. Now. Give me your answer."

"What about Rowan House?"

"What about it? You said you wanted to keep serving clients. So do I. What is the issue?"

Benita's hand on her shoulder steadied her. "Say yes,

Bebê.”

Tessa’s chest tightened. “What about Benita?”

*

ASTRID RELAXED HER grip. She flicked her gaze to Benita’s. Benita lifted her chin, then lowered her gaze. She sank to the floor next to Tessa. The moment strung out between them. Astrid studied the set of Benita and Tessa’s shoulders.

“Benita, are you willing to serve me and Tessa?”

“Yes, Mistress.” Benita clasped Tessa’s hand. “Yes, Bebê.”

“Eyes to me.”

Tessa and Benita lifted their gazes.

“I expect that you will honor your Rowan House commitments in all things as I will. I will cherish, keep, and protect you both above all others for as long as I draw breath.” Astrid leaned down. She cupped the back of Benita’s neck and kissed her. Benita leaned into her, surrendered to Astrid’s bruising kiss. Astrid released her. Benita lowered her head, wrapped her hands around Astrid’s ankle, and kissed the toe of her pump. “As long as I draw breath, I am yours.”

Astrid kissed Tessa’s forehead, her cheek, then her mouth. “No takebacks,” she whispered against Tessa’s lips.

“No takebacks, Mistress.”

“Stand for me.” Astrid released her grip on Tessa and stepped back.

Benita and Tessa stood side by side in front of Astrid.

Astrid opened her arms wide. “Come here.”

Tessa and Benita rushed forward and wrapped Astrid in their arms. She closed her eyes and savored the love and strength that surrounded her. Home. At last.

Epilogue

One year later

GIA'S BROAD SHOULDERS stretched the fabric of her crisp white shirt as she lifted the last of their suitcases into the limousine trunk. "Is that all, Ma'am?"

"Yes, Gia. Thank you." Astrid entered the car, followed by Tessa and Benita. Gia closed the door after them before sliding behind the wheel. Astrid removed her sunglasses and tucked them into her purse as Gia pulled away from the curb smoothly.

Traffic was thick as they exited from Malpensa airport. Horns blared, and the car stopped and started as Gia navigated the car toward Franciacorta. Across from her, Benita and Tessa peered out of the window.

"How much longer?" Benita turned to Astrid.

"At least two hours to the vineyard." Astrid swiped open her phone and pulled up the file Martha had sent for her to review. A sliver of anxiety wormed its way under her skin. As much as she appreciated the Mistresses of

Rowan House's faith in her, doubt bubbled up about her new role. What did she know about operating a house? Let alone a training house? Rowan House's latest acquisition, an estate house in the quiet Italian countryside surrounded by vineyards, promised to be an excellent location for women seeking to explore their sexual desires with the safety that a Rowan House subsidiary could offer.

"Are you working? You're working. You promised." Benita's pouty tone drew Astrid's gaze as she ran her tongue over her lower lip. "We'll have plenty of time to work when we get there. And we have dinner with Miss Vivian and her partners tonight. It's been ages since we had your attention."

Astrid glanced at the phone clock. "Twelve hours and fifteen minutes, give or take, hardly qualifies as ages. I'm spoiling you."

Benita lifted her chin and met Astrid's gaze. "I think you should punish me."

Astrid closed the file and tucked her phone into her bag. "For interrupting my work? What makes you think you've earned my attention?"

"Allow me to show you, Mistress." Tessa used the flat of her palm to ease Benita's short skirt back, revealing a lack of panties and her suspender belt.

Desire rose in Astrid's body. "Have you traveled the entirety of our trip from Rowan House without under-wear?"

"Sim." Benita toed off her pumps. She rubbed her stocking-covered foot over Astrid's shin. "I wanted to be ready to celebrate our new home." She eased forward until she knelt on the floor. She pressed her warm cheek against Astrid's calf. "You're so tense. Let us relax you." She slid her hands along the length of Astrid's leg and teased her fingers under the edge of her skirt. "Please, Mistress."

Tessa pressed the button to slide the partition separating them from Gia into place. "We'll be so busy when we get there, Mistress. Or should I say Head Mistress?" She loosened her tie and slid to the car's floor next to Benita.

Astrid studied her subs. Her subs. Both so committed they were willing to leave the safety of their home to start over with Astrid. Love. They loved her. And found ways to let her know every day. Now she would show them. "Strip. Both of you. Do you remember *The Stone Gate*? The novel I asked you to read?"

"Sim. Which scene?" Benita unbuttoned her blouse.

"Queen Anne's return to the Sorceress." Astrid leaned back and stretched her arms out along the back of the seat. "We'll have to improvise a bit. Tessa, you'll be the guard, Willa, and Benita, you will play Queen Anne. I will be the Sorceress."

Tessa and Benita stripped out of their clothes. After folding them neatly, they placed them on the bench seat behind them. Astrid raked her eyes over the two women who kneeled before her.

Astrid reached out and snatched Benita's wrist. She tugged hard until she lay over her lap. "Tessa, your belt."

Tessa pulled her belt from her pant loops. She folded it in half and presented it to Astrid. "Sit next to me. Hold her legs still."

Beneath her hands, Benita squirmed devilishly. "Oh no. Not that, Sorceress. Please, I'll do anything you want." She wiggled her hips and arched up, presenting her ass perfectly. Astrid held the belt in front of Benita's face. She kissed the smooth leather.

Astrid lifted her chin. "Open the partition, Tessa." She drew the belt over Benita's cheek before she lifted it and brought it down hard across her ass. Benita squealed and rolled her hips.

Tessa pressed the switch. The window rolled down.

"Gia. Take the long route to the vineyard."

"Si, Signora Lepler. Would you like some music?"

"No. Benita's sweet cries will be music enough, thank you."

"Signora Lepler, the side console is supplied with the equipment Tessa requested. If she presses the black button on the left side, the compartment will open."

"Tessa...requested?" Astrid turned to Tessa.

"Yes, Mistress. Just in case." Tessa lowered her gaze.

"In case of what?" Astrid reached out and lifted Tessa's chin with one finger.

"In case you wanted to remind us who we belong to."

Astrid turned her attention to Gia. "*Grazie*, Gia. That will be all."

"My pleasure, Signora."

Gia raised the partition between them.

Tessa pressed a wide black button, and the console panel slid back. Inside were black wrought iron cuffs connected by a short chain, a short flogger, and a harness with a thick dildo attached.

Astrid shifted her gaze to Tessa. "Perfect. Let's show her what happens to naughty girls who go without undergarments without permission." Astrid rubbed and squeezed Benita's luscious ass before she brought the belt down across her cheeks. "You may be queen, Anne, but you answer to me. Why were you bare under your gown?

Were you hoping someone would fuck you?" Astrid whipped the belt across Benita's ass.

"No, Sorceress. I was—I was hot. I couldn't sleep."

"I bet you were. I've got something to cool the fire between your legs. Willa is going to fuck you while I watch. If you're a good girl, I'll let you lick me afterward."

Benita moaned. "On no, not that." She moved her hips in a coital motion and opened her legs. "I've never… Oh, Sorceress, please, I want the belt, Sorceress, please."

"Willa, prepare yourself." Astrid slapped Benita's ass with the belt again. She reached under her and drew her fingers over Benita's wetness, drawing tight circles over her clit. Benita's chest vibrated against Astrid's leg with her deep groan.

Tessa strapped the fat toy in place.

"On your knees, Queen Anne. Willa, enter her so you're flush against her thighs. No movement until I command. If either of you comes without my permission, you'll regret it."

They moved into position silently. Astrid's nipples tightened against her lace bra as she watched them. Tessa held on to Benita's hips and pressed forward until the toy was buried deep inside her. She inhaled sharply as she listened to their soft moans. Astrid snapped the belt across Benita's smooth skin.

Benita cried out, and her hips wiggled in response. "Thank you, Sorceress."

Tessa panted, her knuckles white where she held on to Benita's hips as Benita bucked against her. "You may move, Willa, fuck her slowly. I want to see all of it." She brought the belt down again, laying another red strip next to the first.

"Yes, Sorceress," Tessa and Benita answered in unison. Each time Tessa pulled back, Astrid laid the belt over Benita's ass. They fell into a steady rhythm punctuated by soft sighs and tight groans.

Benita's cries and Tessa's groans surrounded her. Calm settled over Astrid. Her subs had known what she needed, what would soothe her, and whatever adventures and challenges awaited her, her subs would be there for her.

"Please, Sorceress. Please may I come for you?" Benita panted.

"Will you go without undergarments again without my permission?"

"No, Sorceress."

"Willa, fuck her. Until you both come."

She laid the belt on the seat and watched them, enthralled with their performance. Benita screamed her release, followed by Tessa's deep groan as she finished. Tessa eased the fat toy from Benita's body, eliciting a sharp cry, then a deep moan from her.

"End scene. Look at me, both of you."

Benita panted, her chest rising and falling as she looked up at Astrid. Tessa turned her head to gaze at Astrid. She shifted her gaze from one to the other in turn.

Astrid shifted forward on the seat and cupped their chins. "Thank you, thank you, my loves. For following me on this adventure." She bent to kiss first Benita and then Tessa.

"We're yours, Mistress. Where you go, we go." Tessa caught one of Astrid's hands and interlaced their fingers.

"Sim, you're ours, Mistress. No takebacks." Benita walked her fingers over Astrid's thigh. "May we rehearse the next part of the scene? The one where Queen Anne's hands are bound behind her back and she sucks the Sorceress's breasts until she comes while Willa fucks her? Please. Mistress, it's my favorite scene."

Astrid lifted her hand to the top button of her shirt. "You'd like that, would you?" She unbuttoned her shirt, exposing her bra. "What about you, Tessa? What is your favorite scene?"

"The scene where Queen Anne sucks Willa while the Sorceress flogs her."

"Can we do both, Mistress, please? Do we have time?" Benita bit her lower lip as she gazed into Astrid's eyes. A steady beat of desire pulsed in her belly as she considered both scenes. Astrid glanced at her watch and shed her blouse. "You've been thinking about this, haven't you? Brought exactly what we would need to work on the scenes, didn't you?"

Tessa and Benita joined hands. Tessa held her gaze. "Does it please you, Mistress?"

"You always please me. More than you know."

Astrid held her arms wide. Tessa and Benita leaned in and wrapped their arms around her. Home. Wherever they ended up in their travels, they would always be home.

Annotated Movie/TV series that inspired scenes in Follow Spot

The following is a list of sapphic movies and television series that I watched when I was creating the outline for *Follow Spot*. I have always been intrigued by actors and love it when they are so good at their craft, I become completely immersed in the story. Some of these shows, I watched simply to see how the writers and actors worked together to create their fictional world. It was hard to choose which of the many scenes that were ripe for Astrid and company to recreate in *Follow Spot*, but I settled on those that worked for Astrid, Tessa, and Benita's story. I have enjoyed watching these movies/shows many times and I hope you'll find a few you like from this list. I have included links at the IMdB website for more details about the movie/television series.

Movies

Carol (www.imdb.com/title/tt2402927)

Based on Patricia Highsmith's novel *The Price of Salt*, this is an age gap romance set in the 1950s with beautiful costumes. Rooney Mara and Cate Blanchett set the screen on fire with their desire.

Atomic Blonde (www.imdb.com/title/tt2406566)

Kickass Charlize Theron as British spy Lorraine Broughton. She and Sofia Boutella, who plays Delphine, are smoking hot together. Warning: not a happy ending.

The Old Guard (www.imdb.com/title/tt7556122)

Charlize Theron again, this time as a three-thousand-year-old warrior, who kicks ass and has some smoldering on-screen energy.

Professor Marston and the Women (www.imdb.com/title/tt6133130)

Biopic about the creator of Wonder Woman. Although this is supposed to be about the three of them, Professor Marsden really takes a back seat in the romance between Olive and Elizabeth. Warning: heart-rending at times, but they get a happy ending.

Below her Mouth (www.imdb.com/title/tt5073620)

A roofer woos a fashion director away from her fiancé. If cheating is a trigger, do not watch this, otherwise enjoy the hot scenes and excellent chemistry between Erika Linder and Natalie Krill and appreciate their happy ending.

Kyss Mig (Kiss Me) (https://www.imdb.com/title/tt1859522/)

Swedish with English subtitles. Another film that has a woman leaving her male partner for a woman. Plenty of humor, sexy times, and they get a happy ending.

Television

Tipping the Velvet (www.imdb.com/title/tt0324264)

Based on the book by Sarah Walters. A period drama about Nan Astley's long and winding road to finding her way to love. One of my favorite novels, well done for the small screen.

Gentleman Jack (www.imdb.com/title/tt7211618)

This period drama tells story of industrialist Anne Lister and her romance with Ann Walker. Suranne Jones and Sophie Rundel set the small screen on fire. If you can find the BBC unedited version, watch that as the HBO version deletes some scenes that are priceless. Humor, intrigue and yes, she gets the girl. My all-time favorite on-screen kiss between the leads.

Gap: The Series (www.imdb.com/title/tt23725386)

Thai, with English subtitles. Idol Factory, available

on YouTube. This is a newer series that features a romance between an ice queen and her new hire. Based on a Yuri Manga novel, the show deftly handles their romance and age gap as well as social class differences. The chemistry between Freen Sarocha and Rebecca Armstrong in the leading roles is off the charts and they get the happiest of endings.

Stupid Wife (www.imdb.com/title/tt21652514)

Portuguese, with English subtitles, available on YouTube. What would you do if after ten years of marriage your wife woke up one morning and didn't know you or the child you had together? Priscila Reis (as Luiza) and Priscila Builar (as Valentina) are the leads, and their chemistry is everything. Although I hate the title, this series follows the couple as they work their way back to their relationship. The drama is everything you would expect and more.

A note about novel *The Stone Gate*: *The Stone Gate* started out as a fictional novel that one of my characters from my novella *Shifting Flames* (part of the *Soul Burn* duology with Megan Hart) had written. The plot of her story revolves around her work with another writer to turn it into a screenplay. From that time on, whenever I needed a fantasy romance book for my characters to bond over, or to tuck an easter egg into a novel, I used *The Stone Gate*. My editor, Elizabeth Coldwell, has been after me to write it for real for years and I am happy to announce that I plan on doing that this next year. Stay tuned for updates.

About the Author

Brenda Murphy writes short stories and novels. She is a member of Romance Writers of America and the Golden Crown Literary Society. When she is not loitering at her local library and writing, she wrangles one dog and an unrepentant parrot. She writes about life, books, photography, and writing on her blog, writingwhiledistracted.com.

I hope you enjoyed reading this book as much as I enjoyed writing it. For information on book signings, appearances, work in progress snippets, previews and sneak-peeks, sign up for my email list at:

Website: www.brendalmurphy.com

Join my private readers group on Facebook: www.facebook.com/Writing-While-Distracted

Twitter: @bmurphysideshow

Other books by this author

The Rowan House series
Sum of the Whole
Both Ends of the Whip
Knotted Legacy
Complex Dimensions
Double Six

The University Square series
On The Square
Lockset
Bookends
Music from Stone

With Megan Hart
Soul Burn

With Megan Hart and Fiona Zedde:
Love Blood and Sanctuary

Connect with NineStar Press

www.ninestarpress.com

www.facebook.com/ninestarpress

www.facebook.com/groups/NineStarNiche

www.twitter.com/ninestarpress

www.tumblr.com/blog/ninestarpress